CONTENTS

In Memory of Ed Gorman, Harlan Ellison, and William Goldman

INTRODUCTION

The first convention I attended as a professional writer was the 2006 StokerCon. The toastmaster was Tom Monteleone—considered by many as a *don* of modern horror—who gave an insightful speech in which he claimed that horror was the most honest of all literary genres. For horror to work, it must make the hairs rise on the back of your arms and you have to stop reading to reassure yourself that the windows are closed, the doors locked. You can't fake a reaction like that. Monteleone explained that it was easier to make a reader laugh or cry than it was to have them question their safety at the gut level.

Years later, as an instructor with the Regis Mile High MFA Creative Writing program, I had the opportunity to mentor many aspiring writers. I found that most of my students, like other newbie writers, tended to hold back, either because they were still trying to learn how to best express themselves or they worried about taking their prose too far.

Brenda Tolian did not have either problem. From the first work of hers that I read, she thoroughly embraced the horror genre, taking every opportunity to mine its tropes to great effect. She depicted the San Luis Valley—to some, an overlooked backwater in Colorado—not simply as metaphor but as its own cauldron stewing with the problems that afflict our American society. Her stories unleashed monsters that disinterred themselves from myth and memory to bring vengeance on their transgressors. Victims and villains were dragged out and dissected without pity, reacting to the machinations of greed, infidelity, abortion, kidnapping, witchcraft, drugs, cults, homicidal psychosis, serial killers. Her titular protagonist, the Blood Mountain of la Sierra de la Sangre de Cristo, birthed and presided over the mayhem.

During my second semester with Brenda, when reviewing her revised manuscript at times I had to pause my reading as I was awestruck by her outrageousness. In her thesis preface, she explained why horror was the best medium to explore and discuss historical and contemporary issues such as hierarchical power struggles, violence against women, the breakdown of norms through vengeance and exploitation, and murder as a tool of political and sexual oppression. Heavy topics to be sure but Brenda was able to weave horror and its tropes into the narrative in a way that was organic and necessary to every story.

What I'm saying is that with *Blood Mountain*, you are about to be served by a master. Lock your windows, bar your doors, keep a loaded gun handy, because Brenda Tolian is going to creep you out and you'll love every minute of every gruesome spectacle.

Mario Acevedo

Denver, Colorado

[1]

Your eyes drag across the valley, rolling over the uncountable hunched forms of sage and rabbitbrush. Not for the first time, you wonder what it would have been like living anywhere else in America. Your sight travels from the rearview mirror then drops through the windshield resting on the hot mirage that wavers before the Great Sand Dunes. Each location carries a memory both good and bad for you. It's the bad that has your guts tied up. You sigh, your vision ripped across the rocky sides of the Sangre de Cristo mountains.

"Blood of Christ," were the last words of the first priest before he died here so long ago. Blood of Christ might just be your last recollection. The asphalt shimmers under the sun almost like it could be melting. You see a raven and a hawk sharing opposite ends of a telephone pole, just waiting for something to turn up dead.

Your coffee went cold hours ago, and the department radio is silent, only waking to sputter fuzz or clip a report of some speeder on Highway 17, twenty miles behind you. The AM radio crackles then rolls into Eddy Arnold yodeling the beginning of "Cattle Call." Your wife Sandy probably has supper laid out on the table, waiting for you to pull up in the drive. Even if you left now, it would be close to an hour before your headlights lit up the front step. Your fingers curl around the steering wheel, but the patrol car is not on, not moving.

Your Glock 19 lies across your lap, black and cold. You've been thinking about it for an hour. Not the first time, and if you don't pick it up and press the barrel to your head, it won't be the last—a game of Russian roulette, the cylinder spinning in your brain.

Every time you cut out of a crime scene, you drive here, wrestling with the demons of valley and mountain. You hear the voices of the dead. They call out in singsong from caves, old mine shafts, and under floorboards. They scream from the belly of the mountain herself. They push fingers from inside, scraping to get out in your daydreams and nightmares: the ones you found, and the ones still listed as missing.

Today they found a head and two hands minus a body, left on a Buddha shrine up on the holy highway. The head even had payment for the afterlife left under the tongue—a shiny 1979 Iraqi Dinar someone said. Didn't matter it was crazy, that made it almost normal to you; a U.S. quarter would have seemed strange. Normal here was strange.

The dead eat part of your soul. You never forget. It's like a movie reel of corpses that just got tattooed into your psyche. You can't run away because they only follow in dreams and flash up, glitching in the daylight. No one who knew could argue that you didn't follow every clue, every tip called in. The public destroy you on cable and pop-up internet podcasts, but they don't understand that you are left a hollow man.

Your grandfather warned you that the job takes something from you daily, but you didn't listen even after he told you the stories days before he blew his brains out. Your daddy obeyed and became a low-key government official straying far from enforcement. But you—you took that badge as a challenge, ignoring all the old man said.

"Blackwood?" a voice asks wrapped around static from the P25 radio.

You ignore it at first, moving your hand over the gun and then hanging it out the window.

"Dave, Sandy has called in twice."

Silence.

"She's worried about you."

You lift your hand, dropping it till it hovers over the gun before reaching for the radio. You click the button filling up radio space, air, speech. Your eyes still locked on the mountains that seem to transcend from blush into blood.

"Tell my wife I'll be there in a while."

You hold the radio to your lips, watching out the window. You want to say so much more, but you don't.

Your grandfather lived longer than most, and those stories, when he told them, made you wonder if he suffered from fragility of mind. They seemed impossible, dreamed up to scare you out of taking the badge. He told the first one directly from his father—cracking open the great hunger of the mountain. You enjoyed that first tale, but he didn't tell it with the usual humorous glint in his eye; in fact, he said it with dead seriousness. When you still didn't believe he pulled out an old yellow newsprint dated from the 1880s.

Cannibal escaped from Cottonwood Jail House…

BLOOD MOUNTAIN

Saul Eaton stumbled down the rocky trail, dried blood embedded between his yellowed teeth and nails, hands fastened to the lapels of a dead man's jacket. The gray wool smelled of sweat and rotting meat, but this did not bother him. He paused a moment taking in the full view of the dun-colored valley below and the rolling San Juans to the west. The scent of juniper and cedar perfumed the light wind that blew from the north. Purple-hued quartz crunched under his borrowed boots, running east, and west, forever marking the sacred place of metamorphosis.

The mountain sloped like the hips of a woman and a quartz bluff jutted out, exposing her bone-white skull. Massive jaws opened in hunger and three smaller caves marked eyes and nose. Above the curvature of the skull was a trepanation opening, drilled into the skull bone of the mountain through thousands of years of wind and water. The opaque entrance was covered in deadfall, a mask that would await revelation, the secret contained within Saul Eaton.

Saul flexed rough hands, holding them out as if inviting an embrace. Everything was new, from the sensations that fluctuated inside the body, to the eyes that looked out. The meat of men heavy in his stomach, and the dull pain of never-ending starvation scraped behind the smile of a newborn predator.

The mountain hid something raw, her angular exposed bones only hinting at the power that drove men to a strange dance that often ended in death. The greed men entered with was unequal to the hunger that churned in the bowels of the mountain. Only with the sun's rising and setting were the bloody teeth of the mountain revealed, each point prominent, shaded in blush, outlined in gold and crimson.

Saul knew what the mountain wanted, and reluctantly left her contrasting light and shadows in search of it. He could feel her inside, soft lips like the wings of bees, tickling inside his mouth, down his neck, and slipping into his crotch. His long trek down her rolling thighs filled with dreams and delirious quaking.

The mountain possessed him, pressing into the fibrous nerves of his body, her fingers slipping into bones and fusing between the muscles. She quivered within, dictating movement, pushing into every corner; her mouth fused to his, her sex conjoined. She laughed, and it shimmered down his spine like mountain water, cold and sharp.

Saul and a small prospecting party of seven searched the high elevations for gold and silver. Prospecting, though rarely worth the effort, was all he ever knew in adult life. More of his days were spent below the ground than above and it was within this darkness that he felt most at home. The men formed a motley crew of sorts, weathering the hot summer and dead of winter, where violence always whispered in the bitter wind.

When he first heard her voice, they were into their second year of working the cavern and their luck was waning. This prompted the men to go deeper into the tubes, sliding on their knees and bellies. On that day, pushing his pickaxe and lantern before him, he passed comrades, choosing one tunnel unexplored.

Saul did not hesitate, diving into the dark that warmed the farther he went. The slick walls tightened around his body until it abruptly yawned into a large chamber. The lantern light seemed to multiply, dancing off thin gold veins that raced up the chamber's ribs.

Though the gold was evident to the naked eye, it was dirty, hardly worth the effort it would take to get it back to the surface. Saul decided to try anyway, praying that it would fill in with better quality behind the surrounding rock.

He set the lantern down and took up the ax, throwing it hard against the wall. The metal sunk into the soft veins, pulling the gold outward. Saul reached down, picking up the ore and held it to the light. Still unhappy with the quality, he pocketed it, turning back to the wall. The pickax had opened a narrow space in the stone that was deeper than his fingers. Warm air hissed out of the opening and undulated like a strange whisper. Saul stepped back, puzzled, and pressed his face closer to the almost vocal sound seeping out of the negative space. He took up the ax again, never once considering that the sound might be the hiss of poisonous gas.

The metal hit the hard rock, resisting, vibrating up his arm. Saul swore and swung again, this time pulling a full revolution. The tip hit and slipped into the mouth of the opening.

Tongues of blue flame erupted from the darkness licking up the handle. He tried to release the ax, but the blue fire burned hot, engulfing his arms like kerosene. Saul danced backward, the air filling with the blue light. His skin melted and fused to the pickaxe before the handle split in the heat. He tumbled, consumed in flame. Skin blackened, disintegrating into sulfurous smoke. Body fat boiled and sputtered before cracking open like a potato over a fire. Saul screamed behind fused lips, unable to douse the flames.

The strange fire lit up the stone. The cavern wall was swirling with crazy movement. Saul twisted on the ground in agony, fastening his eyes to the gold veins' serpentine motion. The last vision before death.

An outline of a woman began to scintillate within the rock, the dark fissure fusing together. The gold veins pulsed with illumination, highlighting hips, breasts, and arms. The form solidified like a statue. The monstrous body sweating fire, stretched long legs, pulling out from the rock. The creature shook out its glowing limbs, sending blue fire outward and slowly moved, lifting a leg to straddle his hips.

Saul struggled below her; the pain was making him delirious. Gnashing his teeth, he attempted to open his mouth, the melted corners tearing.

She smiled down at him, razors showing between her lips. Her movements smooth in the dueling flames of their bodies. The creature threw out her arms, letting her body go limp and tumbled upon him. She dropped; the crushing weight of hot stone pressed into his body inch by inch. He felt his soul fleeing to the borderlands between organs and muscle.

The creature slipped into him like a meat suit. He closed his eyes in surrender, unable to move as the mountain surged into veins, nerves, and organs.

He lost consciousness.

Saul rose through the monochrome layers of dream; he found his body outwardly healed. There were no flames. His unburnt skin was white in the lantern light. He laughed, reaching to touch his skull that had surely been injured by rockfall, but his hands felt nothing out of the ordinary.

Inside, however, he felt squirming. Something like worms moving under his skin, looping around the bones. He remembered the woman and sat up. In his mind, he heard her for the first time, the golden laughter of the mountain. She wriggled deeper, stabbing into his limbs, pushing him to stand. Saul could not object, they were perfectly fused into one.

It was curious, but he felt no fear. Saul only felt her warmth as she passed through his body—switching the remaining pain into pleasure.

They crawled the cavern tube in tandem, the scent of the other prospectors filtering on the close cavern air. The coppery smell of blood awoke the first pangs of hunger in his guts. Saul gnashed his teeth, jaws popped, opening wider in anticipation.

Saul found the first man sleeping, lantern low, shovel clasped between calloused fingers. Names he should have known could not be recalled. Hunger built in his belly, erasing any memories of before. He leaned down and pressed his lips into the soft bow of the man's head and neck, licking upward, savoring the taste of salt, and sweat. She swam inside him, slipping into his face, melding into the bone, wearing him like a mask.

She pressed against organs, his guts rolled, and together they bit hard into the neck and shoulder. Blood filled their mouth, forcing Saul to swallow in big gulps. Teeth sunk deeper into the flesh, catching on the rubbery tendons of the neck. In unison, they pulled, ripping the tight bands with a satisfactory pop. She laughed, the sensation reverberating through him in a pleasing wave.

The man screamed himself awake, rough hands snapping to the neck that pumped out blood. He rolled, stumbling to his feet, the shovel clattering to the ground.

Saul pounced, digging fingers into the bleeding man's elbows, pulling him into an embrace. The man shrieked as teeth gouged into his flesh. The serrated edges of Saul's nails cut into the skin, ripping into the resisting muscle. Hot blood continued to fill his mouth. He chewed, mixing saliva with the meat. She encircled the inside of his mouth with her own and churned his tongue, savoring the flavor in combined pleasure.

When night fell and the moon crept the hard edges of the mountain with cold colorless light, Saul rubbed the last kill upon his body. Entrails looped around his knees in the damp soil like pale flattened snakes. Within, the mountain purred, content in his belly. He understood that the mountain was inside him. The hunt's sacredness and its following consumption sent Saul's body in a slow rotation under the constellations. The thoughtful mastication marking the moment, unlike any moment before. The mountain directed him from that secret place with all her terrible beauty.

In the morning, Saul slid down to the creek, dipping his hands into the frigid waters. He scrubbed the blood off, knowing that the townspeople down in the valley would not understand. Heightened senses made the world new; he smelled the soil and rock that held the creek on either side of its downward run. Tiny vibrations hundreds of yards away alerted him to the movement of animals. Popping sounds of cells regenerating in sun-ripened blackberry bushes and ferns were uncovered, frightening him at first. He was not himself. No—he was something new.

Sunlight cut beams in whirring sounds through the canopy of trees that bent above. The mountain whispered her vitality and expressed her devouring appetite, eventually obliging him to seek the sustenance she required in the valley below. He left her with an ache in his heart—a promise to return on his lips.

On April 12th, 1872, Saul passed through the Los Sabio Indian Agency and unloaded the wagon he had come in on. Onlookers later said he was ruggedly handsome with strange blue eyes, appearing neither young nor old. Some said he radiated a certain charisma and determination that was strange for one who had wintered so long in the mountains.

To his credit, Saul fabricated a somewhat plausible story of the demise of his prospecting party, knowing that not even the Utes would understand what the Goddess of the mountain had shown him. However, in his sky-blue eyes, something made the elders uneasy, and they were relieved when he continued his journey.

After he left the Ute's land, the elders recalled stories of the ancients who spoke of creatures that lived high in the mountains and fed off the flesh of men. Some of the oldest told stories of meeting such beasts describing them as giant hairy creatures that smelled of rotting meat. The younger ones nodded, not questioning the experience of such ancient hunters. They all knew the sharp difference between grizzly bears and the horror of the creatures described.

Saul, in his time there, exhibited a natural smile and a Christian disposition in their presence. Yet, the oldest among them felt the oscillations of spirit that hinted at darker things within, that must never be mentioned. They knew that the Anglo had disturbed something on the mountain. He was not the first white man to walk down touched in dark ways.

Three days later, he entered Cottonwood's only saloon, spilling gold dust and small nuggets upon the worn counter, ordering up whiskey for himself and the men present. The audience was captivated by Saul's tale and sat in awe of the grandiose story of survival during the winters of '71 and '72, the lone survivor of the seven men who had set out to dig their fortunes.

The old-timers nodded, agreeing that the hardship of prospecting was of great difficulty. The harshness of the previous winter with her raw bitter bones had been the worst in recent years. With sympathetic pats upon Saul's back, it was decided his story was accurate. They had no reason to doubt the rugged, almost childlike countenance of the man and granted him a blameless ledger of account.

Saul retired later that afternoon to the rooms above the saloon. His only requirement was an open line of sight to the mountain. Moving a chair over to the window, Saul rolled a cigarette as a stain of red dripped down her rocky thighs in the distance. At first, the hum started to build in the forehead, and she shivered within, sending vibrations rolling across his body. His skin flushed and prickled, limbs becoming heavy. His head bent back, the cigarette dropping from trembling fingers curling tight on the chair's arms.

They breathed together and exhaled from a place deep in the chest. She pressed herself into his thighs and groin, moving in swirling motion. He came and then came again in total surrender to her shadow that swirled within. No woman had ever elicited more profound arousal within him. She did not let up. She held him there, trembling until the edges caught fire, and then slowly like banked embers dulled into a thick blanket of blackness. She lifted from him, melting into the night sky pierced by the diadem of glittering stars that he imagined crowned her. Only then as her delirious hold lessened could he shuffle his feet and retire to his bed with hushed murmurs of speech that he hoped carried the distance over sage and mesquite to her ancient heart.

He dreamed that night of parted velvet. Slipping into tight womb-like spaces, Saul spiraled deep into the ground. His cumbersome feet sliding on the loose rock as he followed the musical laughter and soul-sweeping drone. The heat and damp sunk into joint and bone, clothing discarded, until Saul walked naked into the darkness. His body throbbed with desire. He called out to her, reaching out extended arms.

Grasping hands reached out of the darkness taking hold of his body, stroking, and then disappearing. The hot salty taste of seed and flesh in his mouth, and the thickness of blood like molten copper drew new waves of dangerous euphoria. Saul was swimming in honey, encased in the interior of her hive. There was no desire to ever seek air. In the darkness, he fell exhausted and slept as if in a cocoon.

In the glimmering morning light, he splashed cold water on his face, his body heavy in the civilized world. The distance from the mountain was more than visual, it was an ache, a vortex pulling. She would only be strong here in dream and sunset.

Some unusual summer weather had fallen on the higher peaks of the mountains, draping them in a white shawl. The sun rose to set the edges in gold foil until the mountain released her hold, allowing the sun to go aloft. He felt like the sun at that moment and secretly wished she would take it with her teeth, wrestling it back down into her hard belly.

Saul put on his boots and stood, stretching out the tightness of his muscles. He noticed with sadness that her voice whispered indecipherably now, a fraction of the power so far from her body. An overwhelming flush of disconnection washed over him.

He shook his head, pushing back on this feeling and exited his room, taking the stairs, two steps at a time in false optimism. His plans depended upon his selling of a story that would cause a rush of men to the mountain.

The owner behind the bar looked up and nodded. Another middle-aged man glanced his way, already mixing whiskey with his coffee. Warmth radiated from the fireplace across from the stairs chasing away the morning chill. Empty tables freshly scrubbed sat ready for early morning patrons. The roughshod counter bar wrapped most of the western wall with a crude mirror behind, that fractured Saul's reflection. He could see two images there, divided between the broken glass and opaque darkness that reached out gnarled fingers in either direction. In one, Saul appeared how he must look in the valley with a chiseled face, comfortable smile, and a freshly shaved face. On the darker side, his eyes were sinister, his mouth full of razor teeth almost beast-like.

Startled, he rubbed his eyes, noting the image changed as he walked past, merging the darkness into the light.

He took a seat beside a middle-aged man at the bar and ordered two drinks. The owner filled the order, and Saul pushed one to the man on the stool beside him.

"Why, thank you, Mr.?"

"Eaton, Saul Eaton." He replied as they clinked glasses.

"Why you're the fella I heard about that came in yesterday." The man said, his face flushing, red and bibulous from years of alcohol abuse.

He smiled in a way that looked like it pained him some, "Seems I missed the goings-on."

Saul nodded as he received a cup of steaming coffee from the owner who held a look of amusement on his face.

"I heard that you've been prospecting in the Dry Gulch area. Any luck?" The owner asked smiling.

This was the opening Saul had counted on.

"I thought you might never ask." Saul smiled, trying to hold eye contact with both men.

"It's been a long while since I spoke to others, long indeed."

Saul took a drink of coffee then proceeded to go through pockets of his coat. Both men watched him leaning forward. He shook arms out of his coat, revealing a canvas haversack slung across his chest hidden beneath.

"Indeed, I have the blessing of Christ himself," Saul said, secretly impressed with his ability to sound normal.

Saul hefted the weight of the bag in both hands. The two men were curious, leaning in to see. Saul borrowed a towel off the bar and wiped a place indicating that whatever came out of the bag might have value enough for a clean surface. Sweat dripped down as he untied the rawhide loop, dumping out the contents with a thud on the table. A large gold nugget glittered on the bar before them. The men seemed frozen in place, mouths agape and eyes wide. The buttery gold had no other deposits in it, declaring its pure form, most men would never see in their lifetime.

"That's a 27 troy ounce, pure as if it were handed to me from the gates of heaven," Saul said, sweeping his hands around the nugget.

"Dear God…" The man said, his eyes fastened on the gold. "This comes from the Dry Gulch?"

"Near there, but a man must have his secrets," Saul said with a wink that felt awkward. He continued, "I filed papers on the claim and aim to get supplies and men to work for me."

Saul waited a few moments, letting both the men bounce the implications in their heads.

"May I?" The owner asked, his hand reaching out for the gold. The man was tall and well dressed, suggesting he was from some eastern city.

Saul nodded. The bartender took it up, feeling the weight, and held it close to his face.

"Well, damn me, pure as a Sunday virgin." He said, handing it to the man on the stool, who took it trembling.

The man's face flushed as he licked his piggish lips. He turned the gold watching it sparkle.

"My name is Roger Belfort," he offered, "and if there is promise in those mountains, then I would like to be first to sign up," He said.

Roger held the ore close to his face smelling it, rubbing his thumbs on the surface.

Saul reached to take it back, and Mr. Belfort reluctantly let him. Saul placed the nugget back into the burlap.

Gold induced a paradox of madness that overtook men. Saul knew that the cavern only held surface gold, but the nugget, taken off one of the devoured men, said otherwise. The real value coiled hungry in his belly. Saul only needed volunteers to enter.

"I need workers before it starts pissing rain and snow upon the mountain." Saul said, tilting his head and forcing a sad smile to his lips, "I can't see how I can do it alone."

He sipped his coffee and then added, "I aim to be ready within the week."

Mr. Belfort nodded, wiping a sweaty palm across his face. "I'll find you those men," he said, standing too fast, nearly knocking the stool over.

"Give me an hour, and I'll have this place full of those who are willing to do the job, Mr. Eaton," Mr. Belfort said, and then bent in an awkward bow. A bit wobbly, he took up his hat, finished his drink then scooted out the door.

The owner laughed. With mirth, he took up the bottle from behind the counter and poured Saul another drink before offering a hand. Saul took it, shaking the man's hand before downing the second drink of the morning. The whiskey felt comforting and warm, numbing the diminished voice of the mountain.

"I'm John Lilian, the owner of this establishment," he said, pouring out a drink for himself. "I wasn't here yesterday morning when you came in."

Saul nodded, rolling tobacco, then licking the paper.

"Where are you from?" Mr. Lilian asked, tipping the drink before picking up a towel. He tried to keep the peculiar look of amusement off his face while cleaning the glass.

"I don't see that to be relevant out here in the territories. I could say from anywhere." Saul lit his cigarette and declared, "There, I will say from anywhere."

Mr. Lilian shrugged.

"Mr. Lilian, do forgive me. I'm not used to talking so much. I saw such things up there that have changed me." Saul said, exhaling smoke. "The gold, though bright, does not compare to the hardship that the elevation calls for."

"You care to tell the tale?" Mr. Lilian asked.

Saul inhaled smoke and then slowly let it out, his mind wandering.

Flashes of bloody faces and limbs bathed in moonlight arose. He recalled bare feet on the cold, damp earth running. Men screaming among the trees echoed, and the mountain rumbled below. A ghostly face looking up, begging, raving. Saul smiled to himself, remembering the feeling of his teeth sinking into the meat, swallowing the hot bloody chunks in great gulps.

He shivered, reaching for the shot glass. He swallowed, noting it was cold and sweet, the very opposite of blood.

He set the glass down and pulled from the cigarette, the smoke trailed lazy ribbons to the ceiling. Glancing around the room, Saul sized it up for what came next. He expected a crowd.

"No need, Mr. Eaton, to explain," Mr. Lilian said, holding up his hands and then leaning over the bar, eyes flashing." We all have our own tales after all, don't we?"

Mr. Lilian walked over to the window, "I may close up this place myself to follow you on up there." He gestured toward the door with his towel, "I suspect half the town will do the same."

A week passed before the men were ready. So many signed up that Saul shifted plans to accommodate. In some ways, it felt like the gathering of cattle before an extended drive. On the appointed day, Saul arose full of fitful anticipation for the coming Recogida de Ganado.

Mr. Belfort, already busy directing the loading of supplies on wagons, yelled for the men to finish. The clapboard wagons were hitched to quiet mules that were bred for the mountain's brutal terrain.

Saul looked on while eating breakfast with Mr. Lilian, who had been up early packing barrels and supplies, planning the liquid needs of working men.

"Great thing about the territories," Mr. Lilian said, chewing, "when a man has a mission, he can seemingly do the impossible."

He gestured at the men, his fork dripping egg yolk.

Saul grunted his agreement bending over his own plate.

"Looks like twenty men or more out there ready to go."

"Excellent news," Saul said, staring down at the unwanted food.

Mr. Lilian continued eating with the hunger of a man who knew that he was leaving town for tents and fire-cooked grub.

He paused and looked at Saul. A sudden shadow crossed his face, his eyes shimmering with something like blue sparks.

"I dreamt of insects last night, they were in a great cloud over the mountain. The horde hovered there then flew into my mouth. I tried to scream, but I couldn't. The whole bloody mass of them filled me and vibrated in my body."

He laid his fork on the table, his face confused, adding, "It was so strange—the feeling of something creeping inside of me."

Saul stared at him as if he heard a rattler under the table, his hands gripping the edge of his chair.

"I don't know about your dreaming, it sounds like the dream of a woman," Saul spat, standing up suddenly bumping the table.

Her voice quietly laughed, vibrating in his guts.

It took two days to cross the valley and three to climb the first stretches of the mountain's rocky sides. Saul rode in parallel most of the way, learning how each of the men handled the terrain and stressful situations.

The party reached the crystal skull outcropping and marveled at how the quartz dazzled in a deep mauve under the burning sun. The trail was an almost perfect path to the cliff face they would eventually climb to reach the cavern. Saul directed the men to make camp there.

The great height was stripped of oxygen, and the men were relieved to get to a stopping place. Some of the men were clearly fighting for air, falling to their knees, their mouths agape. Others were overcome with the sickness that the mountains could bring on, vomiting even the water that they drank.

As the camp was struck, Saul tethered his horse and walked further up the trail to the skull's crystalline face, placing his hands on the sun-warmed quartz, giving thanks. He swept his eyes beyond the outcropping that reached out like horns above him, knowing the cavern of her mouth awaited.

"Soon," she purred.

Saul shivered, feeling her body uncoiling inside of him, her fingers sweeping the inside of his skull.

"Soon," he answered back.

He headed back down to camp and rested beneath the sky after conferring with the men and Mr. Belfort to agree that they would all explore the cavern in the morning. While he drifted off to sleep, the sky took fire across the valley, turning the face of the mountain blood red, the teeth-like edges dripping down to the shadowed gulches. For a moment, the skull stood as the last vision of the night, glowing crimson—the mouth open, hungry.

With the first rays of morning light, Saul rolled out a map of the cavern's interior. The men crowded around him with sleepy eager eyes.

"The cavern is massive," he began. "The gold vein begins after 200 yards climb inward, after our descent of about 90 feet vertically. There is only this one way in until we dig another."

The men spoke among themselves, eventually concluding that the gold was worth the risk of both the climb and the single entrance.

Saul, satisfied, pointed to various spots on the map suggesting the men's multiple roles as they readied to embark upon the first survey. The men followed his finger, some looked worried at the prospect of a descent into the unknown interior that had only one way in or out. Mr. Belfort suggested that they immediately look for a place where they could breach for another exit and ventilation. This suggestion calmed them, and four men were assigned to the task.

None of this meant anything to Saul, who knew what their outcome would ultimately be. Saul being a patient man, agreed to their conclusions. He also assured them that he had erected a lever system that could safely transport men and supplies to the bottom. As some continued to question, he declared that he would be the first to go into the darkness, proving the system's safety. Reassured, the men loaded packs to carry on their backs up the mountain, leaving most of the camp supplies.

The climb was brutal, especially to those who had the mountain sickness. The men often paused to catch their breath. When they rounded the horn-like boulders, Saul went first through them and found the brush pile that hid the entrance of the cavern. He pulled bramble and thin tree limbs from the open mouth. One by one, the men peered into the opaque blackness of the hole.

Some balked, and he could tell they were attempting to reason out the worth of dropping into a space that seemed to have no end. He uncovered his lever system and, with the help of some of the men, erected it over the hole feeding the thick rope through the pulleys. He attached the wooden plank, wide enough for a man and tools to sit upon and let it swing over the opening.

Saul had no desire to stop the momentum of the men. From the canvas haversack, he produced the gold ore and held it up in the sun. The ore sparkled in his hands, and the men went silent, replacing their fears with the promise of becoming rich in one dazzling glance.

"This is what we are after," he shouted. "I assure you that there is wealth beyond measure deep in the mountain. And gentlemen, we will cut it out with such ease that you will all be rich men before winter!" he cried, his voice echoing off the cliff sides.

He directed two men to work the levers pushing the roughshod swing over the hole and climbed on himself, gently kicking out over the cavern's gaping mouth. He nodded as he was lowered into the familiar darkness.

Saul felt her fingers at work inside him, hunger licking the interior of his mouth. His lantern exposed the curved slick sides of the cave. The temperature plummeted with each yard he dropped, the rich smell of mold and water filled his nose. His boots touched the hard, slick surface of the cavern and, after a few moments, the darkness dissipated as his eyes adjusted. The hole above shone brightly with a multitude of curious faces looking down.

The lantern light seemed to be swallowed by the massive cavern system. The sound of water flowing soon joined with the miners' speech as one by one, they were lowered. The addition of their lanterns exposed various passages that disappeared into the gloom.

Within the hour, all men but the two left topside to operate the levers were gathered below. Saul noted that most still carried their revolvers, but this didn't worry him; it excited him more. It was not just the hunt that excited him but also their behavior under the pressure of the mountain and her darkness.

Saul looked around until he spotted Tommy, a young man of German descent. He motioned him over. Saul had not picked Tommy for his experience but had decided he would be the one most excitable by the meager amount of gold in the chamber farther on. The young man was also slight in build and could slip through the small opening.

"Have you ever been in a cavern before, boy?" Saul asked, putting his arm around the young man's shoulder.

"No, sir, never." he said, his face looking both excited and fearful.

"You're gonna be my point man in this. Be ready to be the first man in."

Tommy stiffened under Saul's arm.

"You're the thinnest one here, son. I will make it worth your time and effort."

Tommy shifted his weight as if the movement helped him think. Saul knew he was looking into the darkness, debating.

"Being my point man in this might mean being my well-paid point man further on."

Saul patted Tommy's back, turning his attention to the men.

He shouted orders and directed the men to drop the shovels, pickaxes, and buckets beside a large outcropping of a stalagmite that arose from the floor. The men explored the space in wonder, noting the vast speleothems that dropped from the interior of the first chamber like waterfalls frozen in time. The new lanterns exposed dazzling crystals that emerged from the rock. The light caught the crystals, refracting the beams in mind-numbing splendor. High columns stretched between the ceiling and the cavern floor, warping the blunted sensibilities of the men. Saul could see upon the men's faces a progression of questions and a fear that some creature might arise from the deviating chambers.

Saul, careful in his steps, started confident into the swallowing darkness. The men followed gaping at the walls that glistened with moisture. With the glimmering lights and the seeping water, the walls seemed to breathe like a whale's belly. The air became dense and fresh, filling with babbling sounds, suggestive of moving clean water.

"The mountain's blood," Saul said. "Drink if you like. It's as clean as the Virgin Mary's tears."

Saul swept his arms outward, his lantern exposing the underground river that cut its way through her body. She swirled like the river through his veins, his chest building in euphoria.

Some of the men stopped to drink from the water, and he wondered if perhaps they might be slowly unraveling in the dark as he had. The icy cold grasp of the water greeted him as he stepped into the dark swirl. Saul filled his cupped hands and sipped the nectar of her body. He filled his hands again, pouring it over his head and letting it fall down his face. Shivers rolled over him as water dripped down his neck and chest. He grinned into the murk. The water appeared crimson below the lantern light, and his mouth filled with saliva. He almost tasted the salty, penny flavor of blood.

"Soon," she whispered.

"Yes, soon," Saul agreed.

"Mr. Eaton, how much longer?" Mr. Belfort asked crouching down beside him by the river, gasping painfully.

Saul regarded Mr. Belfort, trying not to show annoyance. He cupped his hands, and this time drank deeply, his reflection playing strange on the water under the orange glow of the lamplight. Saul sat back and wiped his mouth on his sleeve.

Saul pointed into an eastern tunnel. "Not much farther, I reckon another hundred yards down that chamber. It gets skinny in that part, only one man at a time may pass." He stood up, stretching. "We'll blast it wider when we get the tools down here. Get Tommy ready. He will be first in as he has the most experience."

Saul urged the men on, struggling over the slippery surface, climbing rock, and descending until halting at what first seemed like a solid wall of stone. Saul called a man over, and together they heaved against the rock, each grunt echoing off the walls and into the dark. The air in this lower tunnel was warm and humid. Each breath became difficult and caused their hands to slip with each push. The rock began to roll, dislodging the debris above it, and the men covered their heads. Saul jumped away, narrowly avoiding being crushed before the rocks crashed into the cavern wall. Saul held his breath for a moment, allowing the dust to settle. Slowly and carefully, he approached the wall, holding up his lantern to reveal the hidden opening. The men followed his light and crowded around the small two-foot-wide hole; their eyes riddled with doubt.

Saul plunged his head and body into the hole, disappearing, then came out crouching. "Tommy will go in first. It's a tight fit, but I assure you it's safe enough. Give him a lantern, and he can report back."

No one moved, including Tommy.

"Come on, man! It's gold!" one of the men shouted.

They began to push forward, maneuvering Tommy to the opening. The young man, breathing heavily, looked at Saul and Mr. Belfort before getting down on all fours. It was tight, but slowly he got his body through. The men voiced encouragement as his feet disappeared into the dark. The other men, Saul knew, would not have as easy of a time getting through. As Saul recollected, it would be a mixture of crawling and crouching most of the ten yards.

A hush filled their side of the chamber, with only the eerie, faraway sound of the scraping of Tommy's boots and lantern as he made his way to the other side. The noise stopped, and they held their collective breath. Minutes passed that seemed to stretch to eternity.

"Did the kid fall in a chasm?" someone asked over Saul's shoulder.

"It's a straight shot, done it a hundred times," Saul assured them.

"Gold!" Tommy yelled. "Lord almighty, it doesn't end."

His voice sounded weird, distorted by the tunnel as it traveled the length of the opening. The men whooped and hollered, the sound ricocheting through the cavern. They lined up for the long process of entering one by one.

Saul was forgotten, with only an hour at best before he would be missed. He took a lantern and backtracked through the long slippery path. Every step brought him closer to her.

The light from the entrance beamed down in a circle. Wrapping fingers around the rough rope, Saul yelled at the two men left topside to man the lever and swing.

The men looked down in confusion as they hoisted Saul up on the swing.

Every muscle was taut with anticipation. His veins raced hot, dilating, pushing the blood faster. The teeth of the mountain began gnawing, seeking a way out of his belly. Desperate hunger awakened in its terrible need. Her humming populated in his head, filling his mouth with the movement of insects. Saul sunk his teeth into his lip to contain the howling.

The men pulled him up in long jolting draws of the rope. The crimson strangeness of the coming sunset hour was falling on the earth, framed within the cavern's mouth. Saul felt like an enormous creature sliding through the mountain's birth canal.

One of the men pulled the swing up and over from the opening, oblivious to the change. Saul placed his boots on the hard-packed earth. Head bent, and blood trailing down his chin, Saul sniffed the air. The sickly-sweet odor of sweat and dirt arose from the men, filling his nostrils.

They spoke to him, but only her humming was communicated within his brain. He looked up at them through blown pupils, his breathing quickening and devolving into grunting.

"Mister?" one said, reaching out a hand to steady Saul on his feet.

Saul grabbed hold of the man's arm and wrenched it, bones cracked and popped as the joint twisted and released. The man screamed, trying to pull away. Grasping hands clawed into Saul from behind. He slapped the other man away with superhuman strength, sending him sprawling into the dirt and rock.

Saul turned to tear into the first man. The man tried to fight back with his remaining arm. Saul clenched the useless limb, twisting until the skin pulled open, shredding vein and muscle.

The mountain pushed her arms into his own like a glove as she pressed herself inside, and together they yanked off the limb in a web of flesh, skin, and spurting blood.

The man looked at his limb in Saul's grasp, still screaming, futilely using his remaining hand to staunch the blood flow from the tattered shoulder. He fell to his knees, barely conscious. Saul lifted the arm to his mouth and began to suck the blood, letting it pump into their combined mouth before taking bites, tearing at the flesh.

The blood delivered sustenance. Saul could feel the mountain crying out for more with a need he could not hope to satisfy.

The man was crying, still holding his shoulder. Saul dropped the bloody limb into the cavern.

Saul took hold of the man's remaining arm, dragging him screaming to the lip of the cavern. The man's eyes opened full, bulging, and confused. Saul smiled before tossing him, screaming headfirst down the opening.

Behind, rocks tumbled down the mountain side. Saul turned. The second man struggled with shaking hands to pull his gun from the holster. Saul lunged, swinging bloody fists until he felt a bone-crunching connection with the man's jaw. The momentum sent both rolling.

Saul pulled his knife, slashing, catching the man on the arm and then slicing down to the wrist, feeling the blade sink between bone and joint. He jerked hard on the blade, twisting like one would cutting a chicken until the man's hand dangled by only a flap of skin.

The man screamed, pulling his body away from the knife until his hand lay severed in the dirt. He threw himself at Saul, kicking out with his feet until they both hit hard and slid down the gravel. The struggle inched closer to the brow of the crystal skull.

Saul pushed on the knife, burying the blade to the hilt over and over. Fingers clawed at his head as they somersaulted. Saul thrust his knife upward into the ribs, ripping sideways. He could feel the blade biting flesh and bone. The man screamed and then collapsed on the blade.

He lay beneath the corpse, enjoying the warm weight and thick blood that baptized his body and the press of the mountain below soaking up every drop. His hands still clasped around the knife, buried into warm guts.

After a time, the hunger returned. Saul started a fire as night began to take over the sky. Slicing off chunks from the body, he savored the flesh raw. The rest he stabbed onto long sticks, anchoring them in piled rocks over the fire, watching the fat drip and sputter into the flames. After eating his fill, he lay contented, sucking the marrow out of bone.

Hours into the night, he began to hear the frightened voices of the men as they called to him from the hole. They had found the body with the limb ripped off. They argued amongst themselves as to which mountain predator had killed the man. Some of the men fired their guns upward, sending bullets whistling into the crouching trees. Other bullets ricocheted within the cavern, followed by screaming. Saul smiled, moving closer when he recognized Mr. Belfort, yelling for them to stop. He listened for a while, crouched at the edge, dried blood crackling on his skin.

Mr. Belfort cursed him until his voice cracked and then fell into pitiful weeping. Saul heard them down in the dark scraping around, trying various methods of escape. It was hopeless, no shovel or bucket would give them an exit.

Saul would bring them up in time.

The mountain rumbled within, stretching the phantom limbs. Saul knew then that she had required this same bloodletting for eons and would continue till the end of time. The blessing or curse of the land firmly affixed above the protruding forehead of the crystal skull.

Over the coming days, the men became desperate as they sat trapped amongst the rock and substandard gold. At night she pulled him down into herself, detaching his soul from the body. He plunged into her at those times, falling through the layers of sand, soil, and rock.

The men, one by one, were brought to the surface. He stood naked to greet them, his hair gathered into horns of hardened blood, his body and face painted in a mixture of dried dirt and blood. His victims were sick and weak, but often hopeful, their fingers clutching their guns with maybe one bullet left. Only a time or two did they come up shooting. Those died quickly as he kicked them to fall back in the dark. The others were presented with only one option.

"Run," he told them.

For a time, the men below were allowed the brief comfort of being the hunter.

He allowed the hunger to build in his guts, as she slipped into him like a glove. The process of their merging built until climax. Together they ran, together they pounced upon the prey, teeth slicing into flesh careful not to kill in that first bite. He loved it best when they watched.

No words could dissuade Saul from his desire to eat them, still alive, sucking and chewing.

Some of the leftovers he tossed down in the dark. He listened as they fought over the scraps. Still, some died of unknown causes there in the dark. He hunted until the last living man remained, stubbornly refusing to be pulled up.

In those autumn chilled days Mr. Lilian screamed up at Saul from the darkness. His words were mostly gibberish. At night Saul listened to the man scraping around in the dark like a scavenging rat. Sometimes he called down testing the man's sanity and sometimes was afforded a conversation that seemed sane, until it descended into vocalizations of the visions that were now invading Mr. Lilian's mind.

At first, Mr. Lilian attempted to persuade him with the gold, reasoning that they were both the wealthiest men in the world. Other times he begged for whiskey. Mostly he raved there in the dark, whispering—always whispering.

The aspen turned gold the day Saul lay beside the hole, dropping an arm over the lip, his eyes tracing the line between light and dark ninety feet below. Mr. Lilian walked the line as if balancing on its edge.

"Do you see her yet?" Saul asked, his voice transmitting through the echo chamber of black.

Mr. Lilian did not answer at first, but Saul heard him, dragging his boot on the stone as he walked.

"I hear her so clearly, feel her with every sense," Saul said

"Who?" Mr. Lilian shouted up to him, his face small, eyes blinking.

"The mountain," Saul answered, leaning over the gaping opening.

"Oh, her…Why, of course. She is here," he said in a weak, breathy voice.

Saul shifted his weight, suddenly excited. "She is everywhere," he said, the buzz in his head growing like a plague of locusts. "Allow me to pull you up to see," he offered as he did every day and night.

The figure walked the circle a foot or two then stopped. Mr. Lilian looked up again, "Mr. Eaton, you should come down." He paused then said, "I think I understand the game after all."

Saul shook his head and then considered that perhaps it was what she might want. His first, after all, had been down there. He waited, hoping she would pour herself into his brain, giving direction, but the mountain was suddenly so quiet.

Saul waited watching the man from above.

He watched until the sun dipped from its noon crest and Mr. Lilian curled up on the edge of the circle in sleep. His hunger was growing absent of her own. Without her voice in that moment Saul felt confused, almost greedy. His hunger felt wrong but overwhelming.

Saul tied the rope and steadied the lever, lowering himself down. Mr. Lilian did not stir as Saul approached from above. Hand over hand he worked the rope. The smell of sour meat wafted upwards, made thick and pungent by the humidity.

A pile of rotting meat and corpses lay in a tangled mess of limbs, shit, and blood to the left of the sleeping man. Mr. Lilian slept like a newborn, his head only a few feet from the pile crawling with maggots, twitching as if alive. Human waste polluted the cavern floor and the pristine waters at the bottom, turning them into stagnant inky pools.

Saul touched the ground, untying the knot around his waist. The man did not stir as Saul placed a hand on his chest, feeling for the rise and fall of breathing. His face was covered in crusts of blood and dirt. He looked almost childlike, his features softened and peaceful. Saul was rewarded with the tiniest motion, an indication that Mr. Lilian was still alive.

Saul walked over to the tangle of bodies, one was that of Mr. Belfort, who did not last a month. The body twitched slightly from maggots feasting. He dropped down, reaching out his fingers. In the limited light, he discerned that the shape of the man was not whole. Much of the leg was deeply gnawed, the skin rolled back like parchment. The long bone had deep gouges and was cracked at the bottom. Saul lifted the leg and followed the bone down with fingers and eyes to its cracked nub. The marrow had been sucked out, leaving a hollow tube. He put the bone to his mouth, letting his tongue fit into the opening, tasting the leftover slime.

Behind him, the sound of rocks rolling out of place echoed off the cavern walls. Crouched with the bone on his lips, Saul's muscles tensed. He listened.

He knew that the man had risen.

Saul dropped the leg. He shifted side to side on his haunches, turning, listening—suddenly overwhelmed with hunger. The movement continued behind him, gravel crunching, something dragging in slow motion. Saul arched his head up, sniffing the air and only smelling the thick syrupy scent of rotting flesh. He stood up, slowly turning.

The sound stopped.

The figure of Mr. Lilian stood on the dark side of the circle of light. The man's body was weaving. He shuffled forward, the light illuminating his face. Something was different in his face. Saul shook with the impossibility.

The mountain was staring at him from the orbs of Mr. Lilian's eyes.

He was grunting low, a smile that was hers forming on those lips.

A shrieking sound bubbled out of Saul. Tears sprung to his eyes. It rescinded upwards then fell into the recognizable hum between his ears. The hum trickled down, becoming less of a sound and more of a vibration in his mouth, making his nose and gums itch.

Saul locked wet eyes on Mr. Lilian, who moved as if something else was animating his body. A low moan gurgled up from the cave's bowels, hot and fast as if the mountain were exhaling. Both men turned and peered into the darkness.

The vibrations changed into clawed fingers. The mountain began howling, jamming those claws into the bones of his skull. He reached up, covering his ears, but it was no use. He could not shut out her shrieking.

Mr. Lilian came closer. His skeletal face twisted, mouth gaping with reddened teeth. He snapped up a bone from the cavern floor.

Saul moved in a delirium of pain.

The hum went deathly quiet as if the mountain were retreating from his body, snapping away from bone and organ.

Spinning Saul fell, gravity pulling him into the rotting corpses, dead arms and legs suddenly moving to hold him.

Mr. Lilian stopped, looking into the dark as if hearing something. He closed his eyes, smiling, whispering into the air.

"Wait…You can hear it?" Saul shouted, trying to be heard over the oscillations of raw sound, hands clawing into flesh.

Mr. Lilian's eyes snapped open, clutching, and unclutching the bone. It was not Mr. Lilian who looked down at him—it was her.

"Oh, I hear her sweet voice now, Mr. Eaton. Indeed, I do." Mr. Lilian said with a strange serpentine lisp.

Saul only felt the first blow as the serrated edges of the bone entered his chest. For a fleeting moment, her face morphed with that of Mr. Lilian in crazy colors and crawling insects, and after that, a heavy sinking into various levels of darkness that offered no escape. She was at his neck biting, ripping, her lips hard with suction. Behind his eyelids, blue flames danced.

He heard her laughing with the silvery shimmer of her body hard on his own. Saul tried to reach out to grasp her, but instead, it was curved nails that latched on, pulling downward. The blue flame danced until dimming into nothingness.

Saul's last thought was of how lonely and cold he felt.

A new man, born from the darkness of the mountain's embryonic womb, pulled himself up out of the cavern. He screamed; the sound bounced off the cliffsides and tumbled into the valley. He walked down from the crystal skull and crossed over the eastern Spanish trail, headed west across the sunbaked valley, his mind full of the hum of madness. His mouth dry with an unquenchable thirst.

[2]

No other mountain range drips blood as the sun sinks in the west. Some days it's only a dull pink, but most days, it's crimson, so impossible that your mind can barely handle it. All those mountains wear Anglo names now, but you remember when some of the old-timers used to call them different names.

Your grandfather remembered the stories of the first military posts that were new here when the Spanish trail was a trade route. Those stories were told to him when he was young. When you were a boy, he took you places and showed you the old bones of Fort Massachusetts, the petroglyphs, and the haunted places where nothing grew. He told you that the valley had once been a lake more like an ocean, and you tried to imagine it but couldn't.

The old man told you another story that fascinated you as a kid, but now when you think about it, you shiver. The dead place still is marked by a twisted cottonwood, and as you turn your head, you can see it framed by the dunes as clear as you ever could. You wonder how that tree still stands and how deep the roots must be to drink from the aquifer.

You went there once after the old man was put in the ground. A part of you wanted to catch a glance of her, the ancient goddess who changed in that place into something else. In the tangled roots, you heard the rattle of snakes and had to back off. If she was there, she had turned into something else entirely, something you were acquainted with—death.

A week later, you took up the badge and became a deputy. Death has followed you since.

You find yourself laughing at that, reaching for the cold coffee, and swallowing it down, the gun still in your lap, the blood dripping down the range outside the dusty windshield. The AM radio goes silent before Marty Robbins starts belting out "A Hundred and Sixty Acres."

You tell yourself to go home. You know when you stay out, Sandy worries, and she has endured thirty-five years of worry. You tell yourself so many things—your hand circles around the gun in your lap. You tell yourself it's all okay, that it's all under control. And in a way, it is—the cool metal, destiny, choice. You want to tell yourself that it wasn't always this way, but that is the lie of old men.

You wonder if in that last moment you will see her walk out of that tree. It was never a white man's story to tell—yet you still try.

ESTSANATLEHI

Jake first noticed the high gliding ravens as he came around the monolith dunes. About one hundred yards west of the trail, the birds were dancing in the turquoise sky on obsidian wings. He watched as their feathers splayed like fingers, catching the unseen breaths of the valley wind. They were not worked up just yet, in a frenzy, nor swooping down like black arrows from the sky to eat their fill. They watched something in the distance with the patience of God.

Jake tipped his hat back, slowing the horse, he spat through cracked lips and peered into the distance. He figured it could well have been anything out there: man or animal, injured or dead. He squinted, almost sunblind, and wiped his sweat-soaked brow with the back of a gloved hand. Jake watched for long moments contemplating the lost time and the danger in investigating. He thought about the possibility of it being a man down who needed saving and then thought about the problems and responsibilities that come along with being a Good Samaritan. He had lived a long time minding his own business.

He looked eastward down the trail that was only two dusty ruts, wondering who thought such a thing needed a name as grand as The Spanish Trail. The path was a long, unforgiving highway of mediocre profit, and there was no profit in being dead. There were small sections of the trail that draped over the mountain foothills connecting oases of aspen, pinyon, and raging alpine creeks. Then there were parts such as where Jake found himself now, with the lonely emptiness of a graveyard only visually touched by the flight of birds and cloud. Nothing moved in either direction except the death vigil that circled overhead. To the east, the dunes rose hundreds of feet high, the color of human skin shifting like the body of a sidewinder.

Jake pulled his hat over his eyes to cut down on the glare that bounced from the sandy earth. Everything in sight had the remarkable aspect of being both living and dead out here in the vast open valley. The sagebrush looked

34

like crouching men in the distance, and he couldn't shake the heavy feeling of eyes following him. The lonely land had the appearance of emptiness and the feel of being crowded by ghosts, making him uneasy. Many before him traveling from the east had failed to recognize this, and often, he found their sun-bleached bones cradled within the grasping hands of the rabbitbrush.

He waited patiently, and soon enough, the shapes that seemed to have no movement began to flick tails or stomp a hoof, kicking up small plumes of dust. With those small actions, the vision was somehow augmented, and vast herds of elk separated from the sparse vegetation as if they had suddenly grown up out of the earth. Mystery lay upon this land and opened as it desired, using various lenses and playing tricks. The tricks often ended with deadly results to those who did not tread with respect.

Jake investigated the sky, watching the slow circular dance of black. He decided to follow the windswept path of the ravens and see what they were waiting for, checking signs as he went. The air felt thin and charged, exciting his skin, standing his hair on end. He noted the feeling of heavy dread and waited for the cause to reveal itself. At first, he saw nothing other than the occasional serpentine trail of a snake and the packed prints of elk. He studied them with practiced patience, able to read the tiniest impressions like a language.

Here an elk bedded down, and here a mouse skittered before a hawk swooped down for a meal. Nothing unnatural, he thought.

Jake could smell moisture on the wind and turned his head westward. The sky above the mountains began to build with late afternoon storms; sometimes, he saw lightning sparking across the San Juans' rounded peaks. The once-blue sky melted into golden lace and muted purple, and a wall of stacked cumulus clouds pushed upwards fat and angry. Thunder rolled within the belly of the clouds with a promise. It wouldn't be long before he and his horse would be caught in a deluge of cold, hard rain.

The storms here gave little warning, quickly racing over the parallel ranges, funneling down gorges, picking up the earth, and pushing it up into a solid wall of brown that swallowed everything in its path. Behind the wall would be another of ice, fire, and water so terrible that men were often never seen again. Sometimes they were found, their charred bodies still smoking from a direct hit by a thunderbolt, faces burned charcoal black, branded in expressions of agony.

He was about a hundred yards off from the place where the ravens circled. Jake dismounted, boots sinking a bit in the sandy dirt. He hunched down, pulling on his gloves, all the while trying to find meaning, a story of what was ahead. Jake saw blood dark and thick floating atop the sand. He ran a gloved finger through it, bringing it to his face. The metallic smell hinted at its freshness, and the taste affirmed it. Jake spat, looking up, still not seeing what had the ravens so patiently revolving in the sky. He took a few more careful low steps, finding more blood sitting jewel-like upon the rounded green cladodes of the humble prickly pear. Something like fear crept up his spine; nothing small would bleed this much.

His boots made no sound, and what noise there might have been, was drowned out by the quickening wind. Jake glanced up towards the Sangre de Cristo mountains as they started to turn red with the muted sun and coming storm out of the San Juans. Everything in the valley seemed to be awakening in motion and color. Jake couldn't shake the feeling that some sort of dark magic enveloped this valley.

He walked carefully, noting that the plant life was getting taller than expected for the time of year. He looked up to the mountains, still white with spring snow, and wondered if the rains were feeding the life here. The Navajo and Ute held this valley sacred and rarely encamped here, and it took some getting used to traveling alone in such a desolate place. Mostly he didn't waste time here, preferring the action in the Fort or the small community of Saguache. His travels weren't about sight-seeing but about finding a wife and settling down.

As he got closer to the ravens circling above, he heard something moaning that even the wind couldn't muffle. The mournful sound was human, causing Jake to hesitate. Memories of the war bubbled up of twisted bodies in blue and gray, soaking the ground in blood. Clenching his eyes closed, he pushed those troublesome thoughts away.

After a few deep gulps of the heavy air, he opened his eyes again. Dark shapes were darting downward, breaking the boundary of the circle. They landed, watching him with their soulless black eyes. The ravens squawked, flapping their wings, pecking at the earth with their thick black beaks. Jake approached, still following the blood that covered the trail. He walked the few remaining steps and skirted unusually giant yucca and cactus, all of which had glittering drops of blood upon their spiny leaves and thorns.

The wind shifted, and upon its wispy breath, the moaning changed into the keening language of a woman. The incomprehensible words rose and fell in a crescendo pulling from his mind memories of the tribes that sang outside the fort. The songs so haunting, setting his and every other soldier's teeth on edge. He supposed if it had been in understandable English, they wouldn't have worried so much, but the rattles and drums felt so exotic to the easterners that they couldn't sleep those nights.

Ahead of him, the voice lifted in high notes and then dropped into guttural moaning. He twisted away from the voice as thunder cracked behind him like the horrible sound of cannon fire during the battle of Chickamauga. His knees went weak with the sudden intrusion of memory.

A wall of wind approached, pushing rolling balls of tumbleweed before it. Jake watched the movement before feeling the spit of sand hit his face. The wind picked up, moving anything that was not rooted—like the valley mouth was exhaling. He pulled his hat down, holding it with one hand and covering his nose and lips with the other. Narrowing his eyelids into slits, he noted that the ravens did not move but stood their ground with their heads buried into their wings.

All around, the air filled with orange and brown particles, Jake focused on the disappearing and reappearing black forms. He could still hear the anguished cry beyond mixing with the howling of the wind. Each step forward was difficult with the shifting sand below and the wind pressing into his body as he made his way towards the birds.

Patches of blue pierced the blanket of sand as the wind raced past him. As suddenly as the wall had come, it dissipated, leaving a deafening quiet in its wake. Jake brushed sand from his face as he walked bewildered at what the trail revealed in front of him.

The vegetation was miraculously taller, tangled overhead like a long entryway. A raven bounced on clawed feet just ahead as if wanting him to follow. All around, he sensed the valley held its breath.

Hesitantly he took a step and then another. The piercing vocalizations flowed up and down, beckoning forward. The deeper he went, the more the tangle of thorny plants pressed inward. Jake fought his way forward, ignoring the sharp spines that pricked his legs. The enclosure of brush and cactus thickened, scratching his face and arms. He tried to fight the claustrophobic feeling of entering a labyrinth that he could not find his way out of. Again, the intrusive thoughts of corpses rooting in the trenches invaded his mind.

For a moment, he thought better of going forward, but when he tried to backtrack, Jake found the branches woven together impenetrable. Though the plants were green and desert dun, they looked like tentacles growing together, thickening, and sprouting fearsome teeth-like barbs that sunk into the dirt.

Hot bile rose in his throat; his legs felt weak. The plants grew under his hands, their surface warm. None of the plants should have been higher than his knee in the early part of June, and this freakish growth was beyond his explanation.

The woman's moaning pierced his ears, he pressed onward, thankful that the thick coat sleeves protected his arms. The damage continued, his clothing ripped, his body punished as if he were walking to Golgotha. The little bit of sky he could see churned. The pods of the yucca unnatural in spring began swelling, pushing open with audible pops all around. The yellow flowers flitting through seasons in a single moment. He prayed in a desperate whisper, but only the thunder and the keening voice ahead answered him.

He still couldn't see what it was, but the sound made his bowels feel like jelly. Sweat ran down his back despite the teeth-rattling shivers that shook his body. The moaning was punctured with agonizing screams as if the holder was being sawed in half. The blood trail at his feet was darker and pooling in places. Nothing bleeding that much could be alive.

The wall thinned suddenly like clasped hands releasing. Jake tumbled from its grasp, falling face forward, hitting the ground hard. Eyes closed, he drew in a deep breath inhaling sand and dirt. He felt the damp of blood soaking through his clothing. Drawing his knees up, Jake curled into a ball and coughed hard, lungs burning.

When the fit had passed, Jake slowly lifted his head. He wiped his gloved fists across his eyes, trying to clear the sand and blood. He was in an encirclement of writhing plant limbs. Two feet away was a human form whose mouth opened wide before emitting an ear-splitting scream. A dank odor of decay lay heavy in the enclosure, presumably from the dying woman whose chest rose and fell in jarring movement. The cry rose and fell into laborious breathing followed by chanting.

The words sounded ancient, almost like a prayer, and Jake felt sure that she did not cry out to the God he had been begging for salvation.

The old woman lay on a raised bed of rock and dirt. Her wrinkled body was draped in turquoise beads woven together into a great shroud. Her brittle body shook to keep up the song.

Jake struggled to sit up, his legs and arms rubbery. He reached out, then thought better of it crossing his arms across his chest feeling blood oozing from the scratches and puncture wounds. He pulled off the tattered gloves, ripped along the seams from the strange vegetation. The woman's eyes were closed yet moved quickly underneath the lids as if in a dream. The yellow yucca petals continued to harvest from their pods, exploding then floating in the air, settling upon her body and the sandy ground.

Above, the tangle of weeds did not cover the sky. The black circle of raven still rotated above. He flicked his eyes to the woman and then up again, watching as one bird broke from the loop. It spiraled, a floating body of black. The bird extended its wings out wide, capturing the wind, and then darted downward, landing beside the woman's struggling body. The bird lowered its triangular beak to the woman's gray hair and then raised its head, cawing loudly, almost as if it were beckoning her to get up.

Jake turned and threw himself against the wall, desperately shoving his arms into the morphing branches. The wall bit at him but did not part to offer an escape. A long sigh and then more words arose, pressing into his back as language never should. Jake crumbled, defeated, letting his eyes fall upon the incredible sight of bird and woman.

Her thin lips moved to shape words, her language a barrier that he couldn't hope to overcome. But he understood with sharp clarity that he was a trespasser in a sacred place. A place he did not belong.

The chanting seemed to fill his body and press into his bones, pulling him into the ground. Roots pushed up through the valley floor, snagging his feet and wrapping around his legs. He struggled as they inched higher, sprouting needle-like thorns that cut into his legs. Jake flopped onto his chest, digging fingers into the dirt, trying to pull himself closer to the woman. He kicked his legs hard, rolling onto his back, gripping at the roots to pull them away. The barbs tore through his pants and scraped a trail of red before releasing and sliding around his boots.

Closer now, he saw the woman making small imperceptible movements. Slowly her hands twitched and positioned themselves at her sides. Jake was sure he could hear the creaking of her bones. She pushed upon the stone with her gnarled hands, her upper body ratcheting into a sitting position.

Jake flicked his eyes to the biting thorns wrapped around his feet and back to the impossible corpse-like woman. The woman's long gray hair fell forward wiry and tangled, covering her face. Her head bent, and her neck cracked with a sickening sound as if she were forcing her face forward for his appraisal. Jake looked on in sickening dread.

She raised a long skeletal arm, pointing a shaking claw-like finger in his direction. Hair fell away, revealing a leathery emaciated face. The chant continued even as the finger was drawn forward to her lips. The song ceased for a moment and a hissing, "Shhhh," followed.

Jake swallowed spit as hot bile rose in his throat.

Her eyelids clicked open, revealing eyes milky white. Her hand dropped, revealing an eerie, crooked smile on her face.

"You came," she hissed.

Jake's mouth opened in astonishment. "Look, lady," he gulped. "I heard you screaming."

Jake could barely believe either of them was speaking.

Thunder rumbled in the distance. She turned then as if hearing the noise for the first time, angling her terrible face upwards. As she did so, Jake saw that the back of her head was cut away as if dashed upon rocks. Only jagged edges of the skull, meat, and blood remained. His stomach retched. The animation of her body seemed impossible; everything was impossible.

He tried to fight the invisible hands that held his feet, reaching out his shaking hands. He didn't know why he did so but found himself straining to take hold of her. He reached out a tremoring bleeding hand, lacing his fingers around her fragile wrist. Her pulse was weak, her heart barely beating, but she was real with blood still pumping impossibly through the vein.

"I can help you," he said though he did not believe his words.Her head fell forward. She smiled, then opened her mouth as if it hurt.

"Help me?" she said. " I have been changing since the beginning," she whispered, causing Jake to flinch with surprise.

He was sure the words were not in English, but somehow, he had understood.

Her jaw quivered for a moment like she was choking on her voice. Jake clung to her wrist. With an effort, she resumed the strange chant, her white eyes looking out blindly. Nothing else seemed to matter except the magical white of her eyes.

Below his hands, the skin of her wrist began writhing as if trying to slide off like a glove. He looked up and saw this fantastic undulating movement was overtaking the skin from the neck downward.

A violent seizure wracked her body, her head flung back, and her free arm thrown wide and stiff. Jake clutched at her hands, not knowing what to do. Her mouth opened and closed; her head twisted to the side violently. Blood gushed from between her lips, dripping down from the corners of her mouth and down her neck. The startled raven at her head took to the air, cawing loudly, almost like a scream.

The old sagging flesh of her body began to be clutched by unseen hands. Jake jerked his hand from her body, stupidly watching as her skin pulled like wet leather from her neck, fingers, and toes. It slipped downward glove-like, leaving exposed muscle and veins gleaming in wet pink meat. Jake could see the white of bone and cartilage.

Her head whipped back eyes flung open.

Everything around them was suddenly vividly alive, from the birds above in the churning clouds to the wall of grasping growth. The beads upon her body began to animate and glow in luminescence, glitching into iridescent June bugs that ran across her flesh as it slipped down her body. The bugs raced like shimmering ink spots to the ground and up his legs. He screamed, swatting and twisting, his feet still anchored in the roots. The fall of the yellow yucca flowers increased like snow mixing yellow into the blue of the beetles like a terrible living painting.

Jake dug the heels of his boots into the dirt, trying to put space between himself and the morphing bloody woman. The roots held fast, allowing only a few unrelenting inches, demanding that he witness the transformation. The skin continued to strip away from the woman as she was skinned alive by the terrible unseen hands.

The wind churned the air within the encirclement of cactus, pulling sand, yucca, and insects into a cyclone that went up to the sky. Angry clouds boiled around the edges in pale orange like a smoldering fire. Thunder boomed, sounding like giant boulders crashing down the mountains. Jake tried to be smaller, rocking back and forth like a child, arms clasped over his ears.

The woman's skin peeled away, pulling apart exposing even more fat and muscle with a sickening pop. Her jaw tensed; her lips pressed together, denying any sounds of anguish. Jake was helpless to do anything but watch the sickening process. The sensation of madness crept up his spine and rested behind his eyes, clawing into his skull. He still tried to push away from the woman, but the wall only held him in place, sending long daggers into his back. The woman regarded him with lifeless white eyes. Jake tried but could not break the hideous connection. Tears fell freely from his eyes as she drew him forward in a vortex of endless pain.

Images began to fill his head that he did not understand, human figures and racing animals that he had never seen before. They morphed into human-looking animals that were not human at all running on all fours through valley sand. Suddenly the valley was filled with a deep ocean and strange, enormous fish that swam until a gigantic exploding meteor swallowed the water with its hot breath. The visions continued culminating in a honey-skinned woman of unspeakable beauty walking naked through rain and snow. For a second, he walked beside her like a ghost through the mountains and the sand of the dunes. The heat of summer burnt his skin, then the icy-cold breath of winter froze him.

Now he hovered near her, his body thin like fog, breathing in her sweet musk. The vision filled with shadows, he watched her walking to this place in the bosom of the valley where she lay down to sleep upon a bed of sand and rock. Her sleep lasted years, and her beautiful body weathered, twisting like the ancient cottonwood.

Jake's eyes snapped open, the storm raging now with enormous dust devils taking shape around the external periphery, spiraling up into the sky like the pillars of smoke that had summoned Moses. The whole world was breaking up around them.

Most of her body was rendered down to the meat; only muscle, bone, and vein remained. The wet skin lay upon the ground, twitching as if alive. Jake stared stupidly as the skin curled in on itself. The surface still twitched and triangular scales formed, raised, and then locked into place. What had been skin was now twin serpents newly formed that wound their bodies together before slithering away to the edges of the enclosure, easily sliding beyond the warped wall.

Jake looked to the mutilated woman still impossibly alive. He bent over, vomiting until he was left with painful dry heaves. He was sure that he was dying. The woman raised her tremoring skeletal hand a few inches gesturing to her now lain open chest where the organ of her heart beat unencumbered, fully exposed—the gesture's meaning laying terrible across his fractured mind.

Her hand lowered to the ground beside her, and her finger bones dug into the sandy soil. As she did this, all the colors in his vision seemed to augment, growing more vivid. He tried to move but found he lacked any strength.

He saw her breath and heart slowing along with the movement of her fingers. Jake lowered his head to the ground listening to the heartbeat of the mother.

The terrible beat slowed with each breath pushed in and out of her peeled chest. It seemed in that moment that if she died, he and everything that existed would also blink out of existence. In this way, he kept watch, counting out those last moments, choking on tears that melted into the dirt.

He wondered if he would be found like those he buried during Chickamauga, bodies as far as the eye could see, bloating in the heat, limbs popping up suddenly to frighten the living. Those alive he'd killed, unsure if they were indeed dead. His soul shivered with the sudden memory. The valley floor began to thunder with the hooves of running herds. He closed his eyes, suddenly caught in the memories of battle and burial. The past and this present tangled in the vortex of this woman.

Insects gathered overhead in clouds rivaling that of the storm racing over the San Juans' eastern side. Her mouth opened again, and she whispered unknown words that seemed to cut the order of the earth. Her body contorted, and her last heartbeat passed through the valley of her chest, the veins releasing their tenuous hold of the organ as it fell, rolling inches from his face.

An ear-splitting crack rent the sky.

Behind it, a shockwave rolled over the valley, pushing Jake hard into the dirt. The tangle of thorns was pressed flat over his body and then ripped away, swallowed by the wind. Jake struggled to throw his arms over his head, feeling his body lift and then crack hard to the ground.

An oppressive silence filled the vacuum. Jake wondered if his senses had left him or whether the real world had blinked out of existence, leaving him in a strange version of purgatory, gray and silent. Jake spit sand, lifting his head. The desert floor was swept clean; only rock remained.

Jake moved his limbs and pushed himself up on all fours. Her corpse lay before him. Jake felt around until his hand located the charred heart. In his hand, it was brittle, tiny, almost nothing. He crawled, pulling himself to her side. The skin of her face had been spared, and she looked peaceful, almost beautiful.

Jake sat for a long time, his eyes flicking from her face to the heart in his hand. Above the dark circle of raven returned. He lifted his hand, smelling the organ, then stuck out the tip of his tongue and tasted it; the flavor was smoke and Earth. An intense compulsion-like hunger filled him, his stomach growling. He took a bite, chewed, then swallowed and continued until her heart rolled in his belly.

[3]

You twist the key and put the patrol car in the drive. The road stretches before you in yellow lines and potholes that spit up the half-ass job of asphalt filler. Instead of heading home, you sketch closer to the mountains. Eddy Arnold comes on the AM station, his lyrical voice singing, "It's a Sin."

You smile to yourself. Jeff Clinger, the old D.J. on the valley's AM station, must be on some reminisce trip of 1950's country music. He's an antique like you and sometimes throws on a tune for you special. His taste is old school country, the kind of music you imagine sung from a horse. You don't mind; the songs coming in succession seem to fit your mood playing in parallel to your thoughts. The sky in the rearview mirror, striped in purple and orange, slowly swallows the melting orb of the sun.

You know there are strange governing bodies on the mountain. You have bumped into them more often than you care to admit. They stand on the edges of crowds always watching. Members arrive to a crime scene before you do, whispering into ears until confessions or witness statements sound like badly written sit-com scripts. You're not sure if they have those magical powers they claim, but they do have communal power and that scares you more. Folks who they consider a problem just disappear or commit suicide. The statistics, if they ever got studied are off the chart for the size and location. The land is too rugged, the county so vast and your office of ten too small to do any victims justice.

You peer through the shimmering mirage that sometimes looks like a wall to some magical city. It's not though, you know that. But the caves and hidden gulches hide other things some natural and others man made.

You can't see them, but you know that the caverns and old mine shafts that gape like open mouths are up there going dark. You wonder how many became tombs, and then you naturally think about the feeling of crawling inside, pushing a flashlight, searching the mountains for the missing, mostly finding nothing or finding something you can't write up in a report. Either way, it always ended up changing you.

Last night Sandy tugged you awake, a half scream in your chest scraping like a slurry of gravel. The nightmares have increased in recent years.

Your wife suggests retirement more and more these days. You always smile and reassure her that you're okay, but inside, the nightmares remain; a young girl, mouth wide in a scream that never ends. Sometimes the nightmare girl begs you to come into the dark with her. She whispers not to leave her alone. You know this is partly why you continue, even pushing sixty-five, to do the job. Maybe, just maybe, you will find her.

THE STONE MOTHER

My body felt like it had lost a boxing match as the bus rattled on the broken pavement. My stop, a bare corner at the Family Dollar in Solis, was coming up, and I dreaded the last part of the journey. Hitchhiking another thirty miles to Spanish Creek felt impossible with a wrenching ache that started in my belly and throbbed between my legs.

The bus dropped me off in the empty parking lot as the sun began to rise. I shouldered my pack and started walking, breathing through contractions centered over my pelvis and racing up my spine. Warm wetness trickled down my thighs. Blood trailed in shiny drops onto the asphalt and my shoes. Worried, I lowered my pack, fishing out an old shirt, and looked around to see if anyone was on the road. In both directions, the road shimmered with a liquid mirage. Two vultures sat on top of the electric poles that lined the side of the road, wings outstretched, drying in the sun.

I crouched and pulled up my skirt, shoving the shirt into my underwear to staunch the flow. With effort, I stood and mustered enough strength to continue walking. With my underwear padded and hitching up my crotch, my worry increased. I never bled this much last time. I looked to the mountain, pinpointing the ridge of rock where Sister Yama's house sat somewhere in the blurred browns and greens. I knew that I had to get to Sister Yama's place fast, hoping she would know what to do.

Many days before, I prayed, and mountain didn't answer—at least not yet. I awoke with the dry heaves so bad that I purchased and pissed on a stick that definitively showed the pink plus sign. I walked out of the store bathroom, different than I had been only three minutes before, looking around at smiling friendly faces realizing that I had no clue who the daddy was.

If the Red Women found out, I would be matched with some random man looking to have a woman and family. Sister Yama, who I worked for, had me on her matchmaking radar. We maintained the community greenhouse together, harvesting the herbs that would become her remedies as part of her role as healer and midwife. I sometimes assisted in births, and after, she always smiled at me with a mysterious gleam in her eye, taking my hand expounding on the beauty of motherhood. I loved Yama like my own mother and would say what was expected, but never the truth. Individual truth here was dangerous. It was always better to fall into bliss.

Not telling the community I was pregnant was an unspoken crime; they still acknowledged that we were a part of America, but there would be consequences if I did not fall in line. All I had to do was walk by the bulletin board in the cafe's foyer to see the missing person posters. They were hung up not to find but to remind us who ran the place beyond the mock mayor and town board. I didn't want to be a mother, wife, or missing, so decisions had to be made.

That's how I found myself cramping hard and bleeding, bumping along Highway 285 on the bus that ran between Denver and home. I wondered if anyone realized I was gone, hoping they just figured I had taken off to camp alone in the woods.

It was believable, mostly.

We were free-spirited people who found our way in and out of the woods on our terms. I could not share that below the calm exterior I shivered inside, wrestling once again with the choices made without the wisdom of the mountain.

I used abortion as birth control when the stone seed root failed. It's not that I didn't want to be a mother someday; I just couldn't see myself as one yet. I lived in a tent just above town next to the creek that ran down the mountain, loud and furious. I wasn't quite homeless, but near enough; it suited me in a way that four walls never did.

The town of Spanish Creek was seventy miles from any other town, isolated and therefore different. In a way, I sought out a place to belong and feel loved. I never knew a sense of belonging in my life of deadbeat parents and foster homes of abuse and neglect. The community gave me this, and Yama, with her gentle way, made it feel like home. Sometimes you thirst enough for something, and then you end up drunk, far too entrapped to walk away.

Family groups were muted and almost sponge-like, changing and merging. If you were a young female and reasonably attractive, you were revered, almost like a goddess. This made womanhood confusing, as you became fair game to all the men; young, old, married, and unmarried. The women accepted and even joined in the intricate mating patterns with the men and with the women. The word harem was not a joke but signaled something deeply spiritual. The town was full to bursting, with babies and swollen-bellied women. I had never experienced anything like it.

In my first weeks in Spanish Creek, I wondered if perhaps pregnancy was a sign of boredom and then considered, having become more familiar with the place, that it might be the spiritual refraction of the mountain itself. No matter how society moved in the town, I still had not developed a calling to be a Blood Mother, as they called them. The Red Women were kind and enveloped me within the sisterhood, anxious to make me fully one of their own. I resisted, though, internally, wanting to remain the free spirit unencumbered by a husband and children.

I ended up on the bus, making my way to and from the Denver clinic rather than going to Yama. I made a choice about my body and life that might not be accepted or understood, but it was my secret to hold.

Nothing happens fast in the valley. It was an hour before a truck pulled over, and thankfully I climbed in. The driver was an old homesteader who, like me, had no interest in conversation. I watched out the window as the sun rose higher over the mountain range. We drove in silence as the scrub gave way to an aspen that crowded the entrance to town with clawed limbs, only hinting at the buds of spring leaves.

The old man pulled over at the Y in the road, one heading into town and the other climbing upwards before it descended into the valley floor. I clutched my abdomen with one hand and shouldered my pack with the other, carefully climbing out. I turned to thank him, noticing blood smeared on the seat. Embarrassed, I tried to wipe at the stain. The old man trailed his hand through the blood then reached out, grasping my wrist.

"Don't you be worried about that," he said nodding at the blood.

"Go on and see the sisters," he added releasing his hold.

He raised his hand to his nose, sniffing and then licking his fingers. My stomach lurched, but I kept my face neutral. The men here did not surprise me anymore.

He smiled and then drove off, his old truck rattling up the road away from town.

Fat lazy clouds sat heavy as if hiding something, their underbellies dark and gray. Sometimes I could feel the ground purring below my feet and other times like it undulated to meet my steps. I was not the only one; many reported this same feeling. I felt happy despite the bleeding and exhaustion as I settled my pack on my shoulders.

Dew gripped prickly pear, cholla, and rabbitbrush, creating a glitter effect that added to the promise of the coming summer. I never stopped feeling wonder or magic the closer I got to the mountain. There was something here that overpowered the mind. Some described it as a vortex, while others simply pointed up and said, "Grandmother mountain." I believed the mountain a living thing; watchful, waiting, drawing me in. I wasn't sure if I should fear it or let the mountain have its way. Mostly I felt like I waited for it to direct me somehow, like a god.

Yama stood outside her adobe house that blended into the pinyon. The woman was old with wrinkles and smile lines that suggested a life lived in relative happiness. Her eyes were a faded blue, almost white, tricking the observer into thinking she was blind. She seemed to be looking through me with the long gray braids framing her face. Sister Yama reached out gnarled fingers, permanently stained green from gathering plants, waving me in. She came closer, shrouded in her long hemp dress that was earthy in color with a deep blue shawl draped across her shoulder.

Yama took my pack and set it on the ground before wrapping me in her shawl, directing me into the house. The inviting scent of hanging herbs and the familiar warmth of her wood-burning stove greeted me. Dried flowers and roots that I had harvested with her hung in witchy bouquets amongst the iron and copper pots. Pale blue walls calmed the room while rose gold light filtered through stained glass windows.

I sighed as I dropped my pack by the door.

The older woman lit candles and incense, indicating that I should sit on the rug strewn with cushions in front of the fireplace. Palo Alto incense hung in the air in wispy smoke that was sharp and spicy. I sat, and after fetching tea, Yama followed, passing a steaming cup. The tea smelled of licorice and turmeric; it burned going down.

"Thank you, Yama," I said, feeling the warmth fill my body.

Yama leaned forward with an expectant look on her face and touched a hand to my belly as if she could sense the non-existent heartbeat.

"Sister Yama, it's not that."

"What, then, is it? Moon troubles?"

Thinking quickly, I nodded in agreement.

"I'm bleeding a lot, cramping bad…"

Yama laughed, "Well, that happens from time to time. I will get you a tincture."

Yama made to get up, but I reached and took her hand.

I swallowed, feeling the hesitation in my body, not knowing if I could trust this woman, knowing that I needed to.

"Something is wrong with me."

"Not just your moon, huh?" She said, then looked closer, the wrinkles of her brow bunching into a V. "A child then?" Yama asked, her eyes cutting into me.

I did not answer, but she seemed to read some of the truth in my face.

Yama finally nodded with a sigh. She pointed at a nest of cushions on the floor, indicating I should lie down. She walked over to a large wooden cupboard etched with Celtic symbols. From it, she pulled a wooden box that held her midwifery tools. She signaled that I should recline and hitch up my skirt. She cast off the blood-soaked shirt I had used to stanch the bleeding.

Yama crouched down between my knees, prodding with her hands. The pain was bearable but constant; I could feel the blood flowing from me, pooling around my hips. She made little noises as if talking to herself, lifting her head from time to time, her face unreadable. The copper penny scent of my blood filled the room.

When Yama finished, she folded thick towels between my legs. Lightly, she patted the inside of my calf and helped to put my cramping legs down. Reaching over to a large wicker basket, she pulled a thick blanket out and covered me. The loomed fabric was warm and heavy, smelling of cedar.

Sister Yama looked at me, the crow's feet at the corners of her eyes showing concern. She caressed my face and hair while hot tears fell down my cheeks.

"Oh, my sweet girl," she crooned as she took up the cup of tea.

Yama handed me the steaming cup and urged me to drink. I swallowed the hot liquid and felt safe swaddled in the blanket. I wondered if the tea contained a tonic with its woodsy flavor and the slow drop of ensuing sleepiness.

"Sarah, I see that something was done here that cannot be undone."

I felt like I was in ceremony, dizzy in the sweat lodge. Yama's voice sounded strange, sad, and far away. My name on her lips seemed hollow. I reeled, becoming thin and insubstantial, and my body felt light, not weighed down by flesh.

I slurred the words, "I'm sorry, Yama."

Yama nodded as if she knew. I laughed at the warped movement and swirling colors.

Yama patted my head, but I couldn't feel her touch.

"I will call the women; the council will decide what is to be done. Sleep, Sarah, sleep."

My eyes opened to hovering faces and forms around my body. After a few moments, I could make out the shapes of the women. Some pregnant; others were old; all had born children or were pregnant. I knew most of them as they pressed into me, naked or in simple flimsy shifts that did little to cover their bodies. The women were sitting on their knees, with their arms and hands interlocked. Their voices were raised in indistinguishable droning words, moving back and forth, hot, rhythmic.

My mouth still did not work. Sometimes I could breathe. Other times I was below the earth, sandy soil filling my nose and mouth. I tried to scream, but it was like choking on stones stuck in my neck, hands pulled at my skin, claws ripping under as if trying to grip bones.

Yama came closer, her hands shaking with an overfilled cup. I shook my head as some of the women reached out, forcing my mouth open. I choked on hot liquid as Yama tilted the cup to my mouth. I fought them, shaking my head, and spitting.

Yama frowned and tried again, this time gripping my jaw. The hot liquid went down my throat and spilled down my neck and chest. I coughed, but Yama placed a hand over my mouth and nose to prevent it from coming back up. The taste was bitter, and I could not tell if it was ayahuasca, mushroom, or some other crazy mix.

With the help of other women, Yama pulled me into a sitting position. The removal of my clothing revealed my belly strangely painted with red henna in indiscernible symbols. My foggy head wobbled, trying to take in the movements around me.

The sun in the windows showed the passing of lost hours. The Red Women chanted and rocked on their knees in slow revolutions.

I begged with my eyes up at Yama, heart racing. The room radiated heat and smelled of sweat, scented oils, and smoke.

"The Blood Mothers are calling up the mountain sweetheart," she said, answering my thoughts and continued in a strange singsong. Her hand caressed my face. "They are asking the blessed Mountain Mother for guidance. She will hear us—she always hears us."

Yama dipped a cloth into a bowl and pressed it to my forehead.

"I... I want to leave, Yama," I desperately whispered.

"Oh, child, the mountain will tell us what to do," she said, smiling.

"Yama, please," I begged, eyes darting across the writhing bodies, trying to remember where the door was.

I recalled a similar ritual for a Blood Mother a year before. Diagnosed with incurable cancer, the Red Women had used movement and chanting to build energy. They had sacrificed a kitten; its soft mews cut short with the tip of a blade. I had run that night into the woods, vomiting. I had stayed away from town for weeks.

I had almost left.

But the ritual worked—she was cured.

One could dismiss it as empty voodoo, but I knew better; it was the same energy that drove herds of elk off cliffs in an advancing storm. The magic here flowed dangerous and potent, always requiring sacrifice. I learned to respect it and even learned to work with it under Yama's wise teaching.

One of the women stopped chanting, her eyes wild as if she were downloading messages from the mountain. Yama silenced the others. The silence that followed, thick and deafening. The woman crawled forward on hands and knees, naked with long, tangled hair. Her swollen belly moved from the stretching of the child within. She smelled of sweat, and something tainted—a pulsing force between us.

"The mountain has told me," the woman began, "The mountain has told me that we must fill her."

She looked at me, then swept her eyes to the women that surrounded her. Yama nodded in agreement. I heard the words, "Fill her," like a crescendo all around me. It became a mantra on their lips.

Fill her—

The woman raised her arms, pulling the crowd closer. They nodded as if they had all silently communicated the same message and began to stand. The tangled-haired woman reached over, taking one of my hands while Yama took the other. Together they jerked me to my feet, helping to steady my legs. The crowd of women spilled out the door, waiting on the other side for the three of us to join them. I stumbled on my weak legs, a lamb being led, a trail of blood behind.

Outside, the full moon bathed everything in silver light, the air wet and pungent with the smell of clinging winter on the higher elevations of the mountain. Yama lived just in the tree line, and a well-worn trail up the mountains spine started in her yard. I shivered with cold under their claw-like grip on my arms. I tried to pull away, but my drugged body lacked conviction in action. The women seemed zombie-like as their heads all clicked up, like they all heard something at once, sniffing the air. I tried to speak, wanting to plead with them to let me go, but the only thing that came out of my numb mouth was spit.

The women joined in groups of two, wrapping arms around each other. Yama and the tangled-haired one hefted my weight between them, taking a position in the back. The moon, bright enough at this hour for there to be no need for extra light. Their strange chanting calmed, and with the solemnity of a gathering following a coffin, they began the upward hike.

The trees curled like gnarled fingers pulling our bodies up the steep path. I struggled to walk, a humming crackle taking up space in my head. The moonlight and path strobed in flashing patterns from the filtering light through the curvature of the trees.

I tried to ask Yama what their purpose was, but she ignored or did not hear me. On my side, the tangled-haired woman pressed close. Muted kicks of her fetus rippled below the woman's skin, reminding me of my empty womb.

They pulled me along to a bonfire that sparked beyond the trees, the beating of drums growing louder, thundering beneath my feet.

The drums grew louder. Everything dangerous and electric, like a storm was approaching the mountain. The women moved around the fire, their bodies throwing monstrous shadows on the ground and forest wall. They pulled me to a circle of stones, a medicine wheel configuration. I tried to utter a simple no, but my mouth only produced sounds of cotton-like moaning.

One of the Red Women came forward, passing Yama four lengths of rope that the two of them tied to my wrists and ankles. Yama pushed me down, and they worked together to secure me spread-eagled to the ground tying my limbs to rocks within the circle.

I concentrated, silently willing my arms to twist and move, the rope cutting and burning my skin, hopelessly growing tighter. Blood still flowed from my body, and tears stung my eyes. I looked up, trying to focus on the stars instead, and at this altitude, they felt close, almost touchable. I could see blinking satellites moving through the sky, running from this place on the mountain.

I tried to tell myself that this was a healing ritual of the Blood Mothers. The memory of the kitten with its neck slit and dead eyes raced forward, causing my guts to lurch.

My hands and fingers moved with tiny twitches. Sometimes it felt as if I watched my trussed form from above, looking down through a telescope. I wept for her, the one tied to the ground.

The drums penetrated the soil below, communicating through the rocks and rope. The dancers, frantic in their movement as the flames grew higher. Bright colors scintillated on naked skin as the firelight touched the dancers, flashing like tracers that wove into the trees.

Yama entered the circle, her bare feet near my face. Looking up, I saw her naked and painted form, revealing the low droops of wrinkles. Her hair hung tangled to her hips. She smiled at me with open lips showing broken teeth. I sucked in my breath and closed my eyes, trying to see only the blackness behind the lids.

The drums and chanting faded, settling into the eerie silence of the mountain. The wind whispered through the pinyon and cottonwood that clung warped to the high jagged cliffs of the mountain. The creek's violent rumbling and its rushing water escaped down and away from this place in the distance.

Yama raised her arms, walking around the circle. The chanting and moving bodies slowed and stopped in their revolutions. Her body looked like a stone in the firelight, ancient and weathered.

"We are here to honor the Sacred Mother of the mountain and ask for her blessing upon the seed and the womb!" she shouted.

Cries of agreement came from the crowd. I opened my eyes, peering up at Yama as she extended her hands to receive a burning wand of sage from one of the women, the smoke thick and earthy as I breathed it deep into my lungs. Yama bowed her head, silently praying, and then moved around the circle calling on the sacred directions. The ritual, a mosaic of beliefs, all centered into one for the desired outcome.

Yama's arms lowered; she spun on her heels, blowing on the wand, sending embers floating in glowing zigzags across my body. She continued smudging, intoning the goddess to accept my imperfect body. I blinked tears away as she invited one of the women into the circle with me. She was tall and had a tangle of red hair that fell in dreads to her breasts. She nodded to Yama, holding out her arms to accept the sage smoke on her body. Yama kissed the woman on the forehead. The Red Women moved forward, slathering her with green paint and setting a crown of rosemary on her head.

Yama turned, stepping on my wrist with her full weight behind her foot. She pointed down at me, and the woman walked over, hunching down between my legs, standing in the blood that soaked the ground there.

Her eyes were blue ice; no emotion moved there. The drums throbbed again, and the assembled crowd began a side-to-side sway, groaning.

The woman put her hands on my legs, forcing my thighs apart until I felt like I would crack open. She let her weight fall on me as I tried to repulse her actions. She moved with a heavy serpentine undulating. Her hands reached down, and fingers shoved their way into me until I screamed. Her hips moved faster, turned on by my pain.

The chanting around us wove into the panting above. The woman sounded like a screeching mountain lion, her high, keening voice joining the others. My body vacated through my screaming mouth.

Time fractured and folded. I fixed my eyes on the stars floating in dark spaces between. Sometimes I could feel someone bathing my belly with cold water. Liquid was forced between my lips, burning into my stomach. My legs cramped as though they were breaking.

Someone sat me up briefly, but my eyes did not open. I felt a sharp pain in my spine like a needle, and then everything went numb and black.

My eyelids opened to the dancing flames of the fire and the tangled slope down to the creek. I had an unobstructed view of the women fanned out down the mountainside, some standing in the rushing water to their thighs.

One woman lifted something heavy out of the water, but I could not see in the moonlight. She passed it onto the next, who then did the same. They were moving the heavy object to each other, hand over hand, in a long line of Red Women. The object's weight was such that some smaller women struggled to hold it in their arms. It traveled through the line until I could see that it was a stone.

Yama knelt beside me. She bit her lip in concentration, bent at her work, arms sawing in a cutting motion. Another woman stood just behind, handing her knives that shone in the firelight. I tried to hold up my head to see more clearly what Yama was doing.

She cut and parted the skin of my belly open. I stared at the bleeding slit that ran from below my breasts to midway between my hips. I could not feel anything from the neck down, not the pain, not the rape, only tugging. I commanded my body that was no longer tied up to move, but whatever they had done rendered my body useless.

I screamed.

"Ah, so the young mother has awakened," she said.

"Yama, please, I am not a mother."

Yama smiled and paused at her work. She pointed the bloody knife at my head, "Things change, don't they, in nature. The Goddess of the mountain, she speaks, and she will undo what you have done."

Yama laughed, stuffing cloth in my mouth and then secured another, tying it tight behind my head. My screams bounced off the barrier of fabric.

The last woman in the line approached Yama smiling down on the stone before handing it gently to her. The stone contained deep crimson and bluish-purple coloring, resembling a curled- up newborn fresh plucked from a womb.

With help, Yama stood, cradling the stone.

I watched in horror as the crowd turned their gaze, mesmerized by the stone, believing it a sacred child taken from the mountain. My body's electric pulse hummed, trying to save itself, but I could not move anything below my collarbone. I tried to scream, but the sound only gurgled beneath the gag in a desperate murmur no one could hear.

I labored to raise my head, and when I did, I saw my belly rent open and gaping wide with some sort of medical instruments that gleamed in the firelight. The world tilted and I was swept into the black of unconsciousness.

Before my eyes opened, I felt my body jerked back and forth sometimes gently and other times with violent pulls. I blinked a few times trying to focus on the play of firelight. Slowly I twisted my head, my body still unresponsive, draped in the strange blanket of numbness.

Shadows moved over me, voices filtered around mixing with the droning of the chant. Yama's face hovered over mine. My sight cleared and I could see the shuffling naked bodies looping around us.

With detached amazement, I watched as Yama jammed cotton packing between my organs and skin, staunching some of the blood. Another woman approached me, kneeling down with warm hands. She loosened the gag, pulling it from my mouth.

In silence I watched my autopsy.

"No. Baby." I whispered like my soul was escaping through my mouth, my head falling back. "Yama, no baby."

"Shhhh, sister. I know what you did." Yama said, whispering near my ear, cradling the stone as I bled out. " The Goddess returns to you sweet child".

She held the stone, calling out to the circle of Red Women. The stars above her seemed to swirl even as the trees' grasping claws reached out.

"Here, Sisters of the Blood is the seed, the babe of the mountain of female parentage," Yama called out, holding the stone at face level.

"No man required."

Yama approached the circle, allowing each person to pray and touch the smooth stone. They fussed over it in voices reserved for children. She then handed it back to her helper, who, in turn, rocked it and chanting in whispers.

After a few moments the woman returned the stone gently back to Yama's arms, who went to her knees beside me.

"Sarah, the goddess has her way of making things right that were made so very wrong. Women are always the healers, the creators, the birthers."

She leaned over and kissed my forehead.

"No, please, no," I murmured, choking.

She smiled at the stone and then began singing a lullaby as she lowered it over me. I wept gazing in horrible fascination as she pressed it into my uterus, stretching the organ around like a sock.

I heard the squishing sound of my body, its meat and organs rearranging around the thing. I only felt a deep tugging as Yama dipped a needle in and out.

I opened my eyes, and the stars were above.

I opened them later, and there were none.

The ammonia scat of animals assaulted my nose. I heard things in the dark, whispers echoing, and then firelight illuminating brightly. Above, bats moved, climbing over each other, disturbed by the intrusion of light. Old thick timbers of an age I could not guess were braced into the walls. I perceived that I was in an old mine, one of many that dotted the mountain.

Whispering voices bent and folded throughout the cavernous space. Yama stood over me, her face unreadable in the strange light. The whispering stopped; only the scratching sound of bats filled the space.

"Sarah is not empty but full of the seed of the mountain," Yama declared her voice stabbing through the flickering light and shadow.

Yama swept her arms over me like an incantation.

"She contains the stone, and the stone contains her. She is the mountain now."

"I'm sorry, Yama," I weakly begged over and over.

Yama smiled down, looking deep into my eyes.

"And now," she said, speaking to the women as much as she uttered the syllables for me, "my Children of the Blood, Priestess of the Red, we will leave Sarah here in the womb of the mountain."

Yama walked out through the women and men, who followed behind. They took the light as they retreated out of the space, taking their whispers with them. I begged through numb lips not to be left alone in this place. I was still alive, I thought. The monsters had gone and taken the light with them. I didn't get away, and below me, the mountain moved. I peered into the dark and saw strange shapes taking form. An icy cold began to bite my feet and hands, swallowing me inch by fleshy inch until I was feeling nothing at all— nothing except for the stone that rested on my spine.

Above, the bodies of bats rolled like thick black oil.

Below my hands, I felt the hard rounded edges of stone within my belly; it was the only thing that seemed real in the darkness. Sometimes I thought it lurched below my unmoving fingers. I couldn't fathom the passing of time in the inky blackness, no matter how I tried.

[4]

In the 1970s, the valley was quiet. Mostly farmers and ranchers, the hippies hadn't come yet, nor the gurus and gangs that followed the influx of drugs. The vices back then just marijuana and booze. In the 1980s, that started to change, and in the nineties, the department began to see crimes more on par with science fiction strange.

You started to dig into the microfilm in your free time, spending countless hours at the library. The machine was old, so you became adept at sliding out the glass plate and feeding the film spindle. You tried to look at the years your grandfather mentioned, after a while finding a thread of blood that flowed like the mountain tributaries.

Stories of mines that collapsed around miners, heroic rescue attempts but no survivors found. One article described the phenomenon as the mountain swallowing the men whole, a metaphor, a personification that sent your bones shaking. Other stories seemed more folkloric of brujas and witches dancing under the moon, only the ritual fire circles found. There were many names of those who disappeared in the past. The list grows as your department adds to it even when you find a body or the killer, justice that tastes good escapes you.

You continue to drive, the Glock in your lap. The valley stretches in a flat carpet of rock, prickly pear, and chollas. You try to envision it as it once was, a land-locked sea teeming with life. Did the mountain swallow the prehistoric monsters when she slurped up the waters? Does she still consume the missing now? Or do they percolate from the underground springs, their flesh and bones feeding the mountain's living skin?

The feeling you live with is dread. When a call comes in and you are once again digging your boot into the ground looking for the dead. You can't get a grip on this heavy feeling, and you wonder if this is how your grandfather felt before he pulled the trigger. He warned you this place was a hungry country.

SLAUGHTER LODGE

It started long ago when Jane whispered, "Shannon."

Her voice folded like an accordion there in the darkness under the corner of the bed. It started as a sound but then continued to grow, a tiny spot, a stain of shadow. The thing percolated days and weeks, sprouting spores that at first only darkened the walls. In the mornings, I scrubbed at the stain, but not even bleach killed it.

The spot began to move, spreading out fingers across the floor until it resembled a dark chalk outline, shadowlike as if a body decomposed there. At night it pulsed, glowing bioluminescence in crowded caps and open gills. I watched it, holding my breath, mindful of its breathing. As the night ended, the glow dimmed, leaving only large colorless eyes blinking. I knew the eyes as I knew my own body and logically dismissed it all as a dream.

With my eyes closed, I could imagine her body in slow decomposition like a time-lapse photo, documenting just how she left the world, leaving a stain and meat that fungi would attach to.

My beautiful Jane was buried far away in the mountains below the place I called the slaughter lodge, only her finger found, presented, and dismissed. The case was closed, the white plastic Jesus who had killed her walked. That was a lifetime ago. Fifteen years I hunted him, seeking the silence of the ghosts within and without.

I prepared. My focus developed into an obsession of a bloodhound. Jason, his name back then, got off with time served and probation, disappearing into the desert. He avoided prison, where it would have been easier to track him. Kill him.

Jane's finger bone, the only traceable connection, was deemed not usable for a conviction. I never touched it, just viewing it as a broken piano key at the bottom of a plastic bag waved around by the defense attorney—my mouth full of small animal noises that I choked on like hot rocks.

The scratching started again in the corner, faint at first. The fungi swirled there on the floor, taking on the shape of a toad and then stretched into the slope of Jane's hips, her breasts, long glowing arms raising, the fingers curling, her muted voice whispering.

I pulled myself to the end of the bed, still clutching her pillow. Peering into the inky dark, my eyes trying to focus, believing, and not believing.

"Shannon?" she said her voice like a question.

"Jane?" I asked, choking, afraid of the answer.

"Hurt—ripped," she whispered.

Then she screamed, the volume building until I hid my head under the pillow, both hands holding it firm over my ears.

I had no doubt that she was gone, though the officials could not say for sure. Someone even suggested that she just wandered off, absent her finger.

Her bones, white and brittle, called out to me from then on. She would push out from some lonely place in transmitted communication, a growth of blackness. I only got two years with my love before she left for a week, a year, forever. Jane's ghost settled like an embryo, curled up, snake-like in the dark corners, sometimes slithering outward. She grew there, sucking on the memories and rage. I understood Jane was not the same, taking shape in the room's dark corners glowing like a heartbeat. Her iridescent form leaning like an old woman, hair-like fibers over her face. A face I could no longer see, or she would not let me see. Things moved, plates and objects broken, windows smashed in the night. She was mindless in those early days, an infant poltergeist, an echo.

I would wake up hearing nails on the walls, scratching for my attention.

Jane would whisper, "This is how it was," followed by deep gouges ripping down the walls with invisible hands. Sometimes she simply pulled at the wallpaper in long thin strips, the sound of it driving me crazy. Restless, her spirit caught in a vacuum between the worlds.

I remembered Jason sitting with his defense team, the line of his back unmoving, his head not even turning. The defense attorney suggesting the bone found on Jason's property in a deep pit had no substance. He suggested that an animal had dropped it there.

Called to the stand, I was forced to admit that we had fought the week before she left for Jason's spiritual retreat. The Defense did not have to prove Jason did not murder her; they only had to prove that the State lacked evidence to convict. The defense attorney suggested that no one, including myself, truly knew where she had gone, that perhaps she was even then hiding out, healing from our break-up. Jason had motioned for the attorney at that moment, who leaned down to receive whispered words. The defense attorney turned then to me and suggested that perhaps I had taken the finger and sliced it clean off in a fit of rage.

I ran out of that courtroom, down the stairs into the subterranean bathroom, and screamed until I was physically removed.

Jason never betrayed the location of her body, holding on to his secrets. He never admitted nor revealed how he ended her life but pled guilty to a lesser charge of sexual misconduct of another—living—victim. A crime bred into men; after all, boys will be boys, will be boys, will be monsters.

But I knew; as shadow Jane whispered it to me in verbal symbols, "tree-door, lodge, rip, cut-hurts."

If I didn't listen enough, her illumined phantasm carved it in triangles, and x's on my walls, then stabbing over and over into the drywall until they were obliterated.

I knew what Jason had done.

Jason smiled that day, walking out of the courthouse.

I buried her ghost for as long as I could, traveling the country, leaving the mountains, the despair clung like a mourning veil. It was years before I heard a word of him again.

I finished college and attended medical school on the east coast, emerging as a surgeon and practicing in a small town. The hospital was tiny, but I was kept busy working the shit hours, my hands made strong from the ER. Years went by, and the surgery filled my otherwise empty life. I was content as one could expect between my bed and a scalpel.

At first, the ghost could not find me; there were no stains upon the carpet of my home. A sense of normalcy prevailed until I received the first letter written by a victim who survived. It was more of a testament of trauma that read as strange fiction.

"…raped me over and over for days. I was kept in a hole below the lodge where the light was shut out by a door. I am sure that Jane was down there too. Everything was fuzzy from the drugs…"

Her ghost began to grow in fuzzy black patches, her tubular glowing hyphae branching out. The same lengthy process of her projection and the bubbling agony pulled at my repressed memory threads. She writhed in the shadows, an angry spirit that begged for blood. Each word of the horrific testimony played upon my nerves. Though her ghostly voice was weak so far from the mountains, she began to sing like an out-of-tune piano key, night after night glowing.

After all the lonely years of blocking her and anyone else out, I suddenly could feel my hands floating down her skin, our bodies melting breast into breast, hips moving in time. Her poltergeist cried out in my dreaming an absent orgasm, a mindless desire, churning her broken teeth in my ear.

Of course, my sleep suffered, and it became apparent that I needed to do something when she began to invade the dark corners of the operating room. Jane's poltergeist crouching under chairs or the operating table by my feet as I cut into a patient's flesh. When I finally went home, I drank myself into oblivion, using spirits to calm the ghost that haunted the corners.

I discovered that Jason launched a rare mineral business appealing to Sedona, Arizona's spiritual-minded. Later he was arrested on charges of stealing artifacts from the Montezuma Castel National Monument. It was during this time that women began to go missing within the boundaries of Sedona and Scottsdale. I kept count of the women, but the authorities never connected them to him. His charges were strangely dropped, and he disappeared.

I stubbornly refused to untangle myself from the east even though my bedroom became a cocoon of the thick fungi caps. In some ways, I grew more used to her poltergeist than I ever did the weight of fear.

I kept hunting, my fingers flicking through records until an old ranch deed came up with his name. Jason had returned to Colorado. He was wise not to return to Spanish Creek but close, just north along the mountain's rugged hips. Around the same time, I found he had changed his name to Raven Del Rio and even got married.

I waited for Jason to reopen his sweat lodge. I imagined him crawling around on all fours, like an arachnid, spinning a web within the curved enclosure. I imagined Jane crawling into a similar darkness, stepping into the hot, humid air, not knowing what was below.

What was below? The urgency to return fell like a suffocating blanket.

I saw the future dead women in my dreams, and they pointed at me with Jane's ghost throwing her lichen over them, pulling them closer and closer until they all glowed.

I returned to Colorado, unable to ignore her ghost any longer.

Her spirit amplified, even in the tight space of the airplane. She crouched below the seat near my feet, her form more fungi than resembling anything human. Only her pale dead hands and face were visible, her skin peeling like old scabs. When I reached down, she snapped with tiny teeth, her phantasm passing through my fingers then pulling back into the shadow. There was no love remaining in that creature.

I rented a truck and traveled to the long-abandoned place on the mountainside where he had once lived, and she died. The long drive south on Highway 285 had memories attached to every significant turn. The summit of Kenosha Pass possessed a special memory that made my chest ache. I pulled the truck over, standing alone, the leaves green now with summer instead of the gold of fall.

I remembered how our bodies had fused just under the curve of aspen trees so long ago, my hands in Jane's hair trailing down between breasts, over her flat stomach until my fingers plunged into the warmth of her. Jane's breath coming hard at my neck as she gently bit my ear.

The memories kept at bay for so long hit my chest like a stone sending me to my knees. Primal cries echoed across the valley as I crumbled in the dirt. I felt her wraith watching from underneath the truck seat. I wiped my face glancing back, noticing the dark spores testing the light and retreating into the shadow. She was here in a way, but not really.

Tangled in all of this was her leaving me. She had met Jason at the hot springs, and they spoke in the spiritual mumbo-jumbo of the high valley. She went to a women's sweat ceremony and returned drug-fried, convinced she had seen God. I suppose then I was jealous, but something felt wrong, something I couldn't communicate with the right words. It was the words that came out that sent her running headlong into death.

I crouched on the ridge of Kenosha Pass until half the day was gone. I returned to the truck empty from the reckoning, eager to kill the pain. Jane uncoiled herself from under the seat and slowly wrapped herself around my feet.

I wasn't sure why I had come and was even more unsure of my intentions.

By the time the sun was encroaching upon the San Juans, I stood within the bare circle, now open to the sky, the trapdoor caved in with only a bit of brittle wood still clinging to a rusted hinge. The retreating light lit up a small square below; somehow, I knew her bones were there.

I squinted, peering into the dark, wishing to see her glowing arms reaching out so I could pull her back up. The sun sank into the San Juan mountains, turning the pinyon trees blood red. I waited for her to stir in that dark place, but she was silent in her grave.

I imagined how it happened—her lips on the cup, swallowing the hot, bitter ayahuasca, then bending to the deer hide flap of the lodge. The soil cool and then warm under her knees as she crawls further into the disorienting womb-like dark. The smell of Jason's sweat and the almost evangelical strangeness of his gibberish song as the grandmother tea takes hold. He is speaking, his voice traveling up and down until it is silent.

It is then that I look up, sensing her among the trees. Jane dances, separating into a thousand drops, like fireflies. She passes through me, filling up the spaces of my imagination. Jason's powerful body forcing her down, crawling over her—in her. Jane's hair shorn from the skull, her skin cut, pulled away from the bone, ripping. Her eyes widen as he cuts off thin slices of her flesh with a knife flicking them into his mouth like pieces of an apple.

He smiles as he chews. Jane's eyes start to dim.

"I give you new life within me," he whispers, reaching out a bloodied hand to close her eyes.

The rug pulled back, the door on the floor opening, his hands pushing and shoving her folded form into a space that seems too small to fit into. A heavy door closing, and the crowd of spirits howling a welcome.

I force my face upward, eyes to the trees, away from the dirt.

Jane screeches there, like the mountain bats communicating with piercing sonar.

His website, cluttered with Native American pop flash, advertised a ceremonial sweat with or without the Dreamweaver drugs. A nice way to say you could sweat, or you could get fucked up and see your god or whatever. Usually, this attracted a type; the recreational drug tourist, the sometimes spiritual, or those genuinely attempting to find God who didn't know better.

God or monster, he didn't much really care how he was seen until he decided to show his true face.

His quick smile and black-dyed long hair drew them in, his hands reaching out to the broken. A pricy invitation to sweat one's demons away in long ceremonies utilizing grandmother tea. He claimed non-profit status, but it was unclear where the money went. What the consumer did not know in making reservations was that they might, in fact, be consumed.

The sweat lodge was new, built to accommodate, inviting women to go deeper into the divine feminine. This was his advertisement, not even pretending to pander to straight couples or men anymore. He had teepees and yurts to rent for short-term and extended spiritual quests.

He was unusually successful.

The turn off to his place was marked with a statue of a bear carved in wood; rough and angular, it seemed as if the artist lost interest halfway through or was unsure what a bear really looked like. The long gravel road lined in large rocks and the weathered skulls of animals posted hip-high on scavenged poles grimaced down at me as I drove. Tattered prayer flags fluttered in sheared ribbons like ripped-up hopes. Fat Buddhas sat on rock cairns, smiling dumbly next to cement Jesus and Mary statues missing hands and noses. In the distance, dust devils churned up into the clouds in orange plumes, making the whole landscape a Dali painting.

I stopped the truck for a minute, pulled my hair up in an elastic band, and fished out my notes. I knew the address was correct, even though the decor was gaudy compared to Jason's first place. I never went with Jane to the site, but I did during the trial when it was on the market and empty. I'm not sure why I went except for a goodbye of sorts, hoping to find the rest of her under the moonlight.

Jason's ranch lay ten miles off ZZ road, far from anything, especially the Sheriff's prying eyes. Raven Del Rio, the new name still so bitter in my mouth. I would always think of him as Jason Johnson, my lover's murderer. I had to practice his new name and even now said it out loud as I drove.

The gravel and sand road meandered through big rocks and mesquite. The rabbitbrush was still green, not the yellow that made the weed beautiful in early August. A storm was building over the San Juans, and I wished it would sweep down, cutting the ninety-degree temperature. The smell of rain mixed with the wind created the cotton candy aroma that Jane had loved. I held the memory of her dancing in the warm mountain rain, her long sun-browned legs, her arms pulling me in as she laughed into my dripping hair.

My hands clenched the wheel until my knuckles were white. I blinked back tears, gripping the threads of cold hatred as I pulled into his roughshod parking lot. Slamming the truck door, I leaned against it, watching the storm cover the sun as it approached the mountain top, waiting. No one came out of the house as my eyes swept the land.

Rock cairns were stacked everywhere, and I wondered if bodies might lay blow, their skeletal fingers poking up through the ground. A broken carousel horse leaned on its nose in the sandy dirt still impaled on its tarnished brass pole, the colors faded, its teeth brown. To the south was a giant rock labyrinth under construction, at its center a slab altar of obsidian, and I wondered where he found such a thing. Everything seemed half-finished, not so much in progress, as if forgotten.

A woman came out, the door creaking and then slamming behind her. She was dressed in a long green dress, her hair piled back into a messy bun on her head. She looked worn and tired the wrinkles around her mouth indicating years of unhappiness.

She raised her hand to shield her eyes, looking me up and down with a frown.

"Dr. Shannon Brown?" she asked.

"Just Shannon, please," I said, walking toward her, my hand out.

"Mrs. Del Rio," she clipped hard on the title.

She pulled her arms inward, "Raven will be out in a few. If you leave your bags, I will get them into the yurt for you."

"I requested a tent."

"Oh, that's right. Are you sure? Snakes get inside, no floor, and all."

"Which one is mine?" I asked, ignoring her remark about snakes. "I can hike my stuff over since Raven is not ready yet anyway."

She pointed with annoyance to a large canvas teepee about fifty yards from the smaller sweat lodge. I nodded and pulled open the door of my truck, popping the seat forward. I glanced down at the floor, looking for Jane's darkness, but she was gone for the moment. I got my rucksack out of the truck and kicked the door shut behind me.

"Thanks, you can tell Raven I'm settling in," I said over my shoulder, heading to the tent.

She stood on the porch, and I could feel her eyes following me. I turned and waved at her as I pulled the door flap open. Mrs. Del Rio ignored me and went back into the house. I shrugged and went inside. The floor was bare except for a pile of furs, mostly cow and elk. I dropped my rucksack and looked around.

It was primarily empty except for the blankets and hangings made from cowhide. Above suspended from the poles were Celtic fetishes and elk skulls that clinked when bone hit bone.

"This guy needs to get his religions straight," I muttered, an abrupt try at humor even as my nerves rattled my body.

I pulled my sleeping bag out and unrolled it, kicking the blankets to the side. I sat and glanced around the tent. Shadows at this hour did not play at the edges. The skulls chimed above my head, wind tunneling through the door and up through the smoke hole. I reached out, hands checking that my medical bag was accessible. I then rolled up my pants legs, adjusting the Damascus knives, stowed down the outside of my tall boots. Outside, I heard voices and pulled on the tattered leg warmers worn to cover the blades. The real work began tonight.

"Shannon?" Jason called from outside the tent.

I grabbed my bag, slinging it over my shoulder, exiting the teepee, and stood up to meet him. I had changed a lot in fifteen years and only took the stand in court once.

Del Rio was flanked by two other white women. I could tell they were city dwellers who were trying to look the part. They both had crazy yoga gear, moccasins, and netted scarves tied around their waists with little gold bells.

Jason, aka Del Rio, looked older, his long hair now gray, flowing freely to his waist. He was fifty-five but still carried himself like a man who knew he was handsome. I knew the type.

He stared at me like he was trying to take a psychic temperature and tilted his head smiling.

"Shannon?" he said, again in a slow mock Navajo accent.

"Yes," I said, walking to him, my arms crossed, and a smile pasted to my face.

His eyes blinked as if caught in déjà-vu offering his hand.

He tilted his head, "Do I know you?"

"Nope, this is my first time in Colorado."

He smiled back, his eyes, still questioning, still trying to remember. I could see the struggle, and I loved the feeling of it. He took his hand back and crossed his arms.

"I hit the hot springs on my way in. Super relaxing," I quickly added, another lie.

"Yes, the hot springs appeal to many," he said, looking at the women who had moved in closer but still didn't speak. Something was off about the women like they were dazed—or plastic.

My Jane had met him at the springs, and with that memory, I recalled with pain our fight. It was the last time I saw her alive.

His eyes pressed into me, skimming across my body.

"So, I will guide you in the ceremony tonight?"

I nodded, "I need to clear myself of the negatives. You see, my lover died, and…"

"I see," he quickly said, cutting me off. "What was his name?"

"She," I said.

"What was her name?" he asked, not missing a beat.

"I'd rather not say." I patted the place over my heart, "It's hard to talk about."

He nodded gesturing at the women. "These women are here for similar cleansing."

The women nodded, even smiled, but the smile did not reach their dull eyes. He continued talking about the coming ritual, eventually introducing the women. I was sure the names given were not real and it didn't matter anyway. As he spoke Del Rio drew closer to me, his hand brushing mine. The song, "Can't Take My Eyes Off of You," started singing from my bag. Startled, I jerked it off my shoulder, dropping it in the sand at my feet. I dove for it plunging my hands deep inside, fishing for the small red Razor phone. The song kept on playing until I got my hands on it, clicking the silence button. The women seemed unbothered when I looked up, but Del Rio grinned down at me like a coyote.

"Phones are not permitted," he said, dropping the accent along with the smile.

"Alright," I stuttered, "Uh, one minute."

I stumbled back to the tent—the phone in my shaking hand. As soon as I cleared the door flap, I flipped it open—missed call from Jane.

"Shit!" I threw the phone across the tent.

I thrust my fingers into my hair, pulling, commanding my breathing to slow. Jane had haunted the physical world but never through technology.

"Not now!" I begged.

I paced the tent a couple of times before forcing a smile to my lips and ducking back out the tent flap.

I joined the waiting group outside, Del Rio's face serene again. The storm to the west was kicking cumulus clouds higher, lightning looping through them like a sewing needle, making the air smell metallic.

"You have fasted and are not on your moon?"

"Why is that important? I'm just curious as a doctor."

"Your moon is the unique way a woman is sanctified; it would cancel out the sweat."

I nodded, barely able to swallow a retort.

"Shall I give you a tour? Show you what I'm building here?" he asked.

"Yes, I would like that."

The desert floor was blanketed by rabbitbrush, yucca and cactus in yellow, brown, and green dots against the sand's dun color. Further to the east was the short pinyon line that crawled up the mountains first thousand feet. Some antelope ran on the horizon wavering in a liquid mirage. A storm skirted the valley north of where we stood in a slow blue wall and that turned dark brown as it sucked up the desert floor. Its thunder still audible though many miles away.

I walked beside him, the women a few steps back as if they had been told to do so. I glanced about, feeling their eyes on me, they still smiled, but it felt wrong.

We stopped at the entrance of the labyrinth, Del Rio sweeping his hands outward.

"My wife and I built this with the help of guests over the last few months. There's a magic that opens when you embrace the unknown. This is something that is being proven to me time and time again in the most astonishing ways," he said.

I placed a look of awe upon my face.

"The labyrinth represents the journey to your center and back again out into the world both literally and metaphorically."

The exit that Del Rio claimed existed seemed to be missing. The only way out was breaking the rules and climbing over the rocks that stood three feet high.

"There appears to be no way out, only a path to the altar in the center," I said pointedly.

Del Rio showed his toothy grin, looking back at the women who laughed as if on cue.

"You are still blind, but we will work on that."

He stepped closer to me, placing his hands on my shoulders, "We do this important work, channeling, meditating, spiritually clearing, anchoring the crystalline light and divine love wherever we go, whoever we serve."

His eyes closed for a moment.

"I am here to serve you as a pillar of light," he continued turning, dropping his hands down my arms, entwining his fingers into my own, pulling me along.

I commanded my body to relax, to not think of the knives in my boots. We walked farther on the property, Del Rio, talking about whatever cultish mumbo jumbo seemed to churn up in his mouth. He pointed to things commenting on the auras' vibrations while I got the lay of the land.

The boiling storm encroached closer. The lightning, no longer content to race in the clouds, reached out skeletal fingers to the ground. The tour was cut short by the sky ripping open, drenching the land.

Allowed to return to my tent, I prepared for the evening sweat. I smoked cigarettes and organized my scalpels, wondering how I would get them into the sweat lodge.

Dark came early, the rain slowing to a stop, and the gray holding on like a canvas staked to the ground. I punched Jane's number into my phone and got the, "This number is no longer in the service," message that I expected.

I waited, laying my head on my pack until the edge of the canvas started to ripple in the inching shadow. Her ghost, even senseless, was the only comfort in this place. Slowly she began to take shape, her body curled, knees up to her chin, transparent and pulsating in muted greens and blue fire along the edges.

I sighed.

We lay there, looking to one another, neither moving, our eyes locked. Jane's dead eyes were colorless and prominent in her emaciated face, lips dry, pulled back from yellowed teeth. She shifted in the shadows twisting the glowing threads until her chin rested on her hands. A sound like a cooing baby came out of her mouth.

I crawled closer, as close as I dared, not wanting her to go away. My hand crept, my fingers moving towards her spider-like, as I used to do. She snarled—her canines sharp—then hissed. Her body moved back as if the shadows were inhaling her.

Jane's asthmatic breath rattled from the shadow. The gravel sound smoothed then and flowed into the sweetest sigh. The glowing fuzzy hand reached, hovering, and then gently lowering, sinking into my flesh like butterfly kisses. My hand lit up with hers inside, and we pulsed like a heartbeat. Tears streamed down my face, the only thing that moved in the circular space.

"Shannon?" Del Rio called from the other side of the tent flap.

Jane's eyes clicked wide, and her form arched up dog-like, crawling back into the dark, the emptiness rushing back in. I rolled over, springing to my feet, a scalpel in my hand. I took a few steps towards his voice, my hand behind my back.

Jason didn't wait, opening the tent flap, ducking as he entered. The wind followed him, setting the fetishes and skulls above into chaotic clacking and swinging.

He smiled, and I smiled back.

"We are almost ready. The stones are heating."

Inclining my head, I rubbed the edge of the cased scalpel along my thumb. Del Rio took two steps closer, hands going to my hair, wrapping a long brown lock around his finger. His other hand reached for the elastic that held my hair in place.

I stood very still. Raising my eyes to meet Jason's. He pulled slowly on the elastic easing it down its length.

"Shannon, the spirits have been whispering to me."

"Really?" I said, tilting my head, so my hair fell over my shoulder to my hips.

"Yes," he said, trailing the "s" sound. He stepped back suddenly, his hands dropping to his side.

He smiled. "The spirits say that you are ripe like a peach, oozing the juices of the universal life energy."

Turning, he called out to his wife. She entered; her face lit up with a pained smile. In her hands was a folded blue dress, long and strangely modest. She shook it out, holding it up to my shoulders.

"Tonight, you will wear this," she said. "No underthings, your hair down."

Mrs. Del Rio stepped behind her husband. I held the dress in my free hand. They both clasped their hands and bowed, leaving the tent.

I let out a strangled breath, the scalpel falling from my shaking fingers.

Jane did not stir in the corners. She did not spill out of the dark in reassurance, her hand enveloping mine. I hated the man more now for stealing yet another lost moment with Jane. I hated his hands in my hair. I hated it, and it rolled in my chest, dark and dangerous.

Mrs. Del Rio came an hour later, leading me to the ritual place. The curve of the lodge blotted out the abyss of stars. The door flap glowed in a frown as if it had more knowledge than I in what was to happen next. Jane did not stir in the dark; I was alone.

We were made to line up just outside the entrance, a fire dancing a few yards away, stones glowing in flames. Del Rio appeared dressed in a much too abbreviated loincloth. His face was unreadable under a massive amount of oil paint in red and white. I glanced at the two women who still wore the glazed look of junkies.

Del Rio started talking, and one of the women took my hand, squeezing it. Her flesh felt cold and rubbery.

"I feel so honored to be here," she whispered.

I just nodded.

He spoke on transformation, the vortex, and the movement of power between humankind and the mountain.

Next, he made a movement with his hands, and the women both knelt on the ground, leaving me standing. His eyes flicked to mine, piercing black that reflected the firelight like a demon as I went down on my knees.

Mrs. Del Rio pulled a razor from a pocket in her skirt and went to each woman slathering their heads in olive oil. One after the other was shorn of hair. The moon glowed down on wet shiny heads white as knobs of plaster. I watched as the women seemed to transform: less human, skull like. Del Rio followed beside his wife, painting their faces in strange symbols, the same white and red that he had adorned himself with. When the act was finished, they bowed into the gaping mouth of the lodge.

I could feel the scalpel taped to my thigh. I felt the absence of my boots and knives. I prayed for Jane, but she did not come. I was trapped regardless of whether I ran or stayed.

I bowed my head, letting the woman take my hair, my skin tensing under the blade as it slid across my scalp. I felt the sting as blood dripped down my face from small cuts. I wondered when he took Jane's hair if she had knelt the same way. A tear mixed with the blood as I knelt docile as a lamb.

Del Rio awoke me from these thoughts, his hands on my face almost tenderly painting and tracing paint and blood. I closed my eyes, leaning into it, thinking of Jane. Was I thinking like Jane? My eyes flashed open, revolving, looking for her, acutely aware of her continued absence. A tendril of thought eased itself into my mind. I wondered if this was what she wanted? My knees suffering the stations of her cross.

Sweet, sweet Jane…

Del Rio ripped me from these thoughts pulling me to my feet. My hair in long loops all around, looking like wilted wheat. I could smell the juniper on his skin and patchouli mixed with his male odor.

"Sister, you are ready."

I nodded.

He took my hands, pulling me towards the glowing maw of the lodge.

I crawled through the door and sat down in the sweltering heat. The embers glowed, the light illuminated off the rocks that surrounded. The women hummed in low tones that made my joints itch as they swayed side to side.

Del Rio joined, carving in words of gibberish to the chant. I searched the floor for doors downward, but the earth was hard-packed and normal.

Mrs. Del Rio passed in a bucket of water and a large kettle full, I assumed of the ayahuasca. Soon both were passed around—hand to mouth. When the cup came into my hands, I pretended to drink deeply. I avoided the water as well, not fully trusting it was not drugged. It was dark in the heated womb of nothing, a perfect place to kill—a perfect place to die.

The heat built as stones were passed in and added to the center. The women began to vomit, and a new bucket was produced and passed for this expected result. The smell of juniper and cedar could not cover the sick smell of their stomach contents. After retching, the women lay back, giving in to the steam and dreaming.

Del Rio did not sicken; instead, he reached into a low cauldron dipping his hands inside. He next raised them cupped and dripping and whispered something before pouring the liquid on the fire sizzling.

"For Jane," he said. "For Jane and Shannon…"

My eyes shot to his. He smiled.

Space rippled between us. I could feel my own mouth open empty of words, tasting death. Around me, the women started to deflate, their faces melting inwards. Air and flesh just rushed out of their bodies like air escaping a balloon. The dirt below them was like a sponge as the fleshy bits, bone, and blood were absorbed.

Stiff with fear, I backed away, kicking dirt in his direction. He came at me like a predator, teeth flashing. I reached for my knives, forgetting that I didn't have them or my boots.

Del Rio crouched, still wearing the grin of a coyote. His eyes caught and held the firelight; the red paint dripped down his white skin, demonic, bloody.

Panicked, I reached my hands between my thighs, jerking desperately on the tape hidden there. I fumbled with the narrow handle of the scalpel, accidentally pushing the uncovered blade deep into my thigh. I bit my lip to keep from screaming. Hot blood spurted with my heartbeat between my thighs. I was sure I had hit the femoral artery and had five minutes max before I bled out.

Dizzy, I launched my body around the steaming stones. Del Rio moved like something otherworldly, quickly overtaking me in the small space. His mouth was at my neck, biting. His cock's swell pushed hard into my leg, letting his total weight fall upon me. My arms pinned below, I plunged the blade into his soft belly, pulling as the skin ripped like a zipper.

I kicked out with no effect. I yanked on the blade as Del Rio pummeled my face with his fists; I felt my teeth sliding down my throat in a gush of blood.

He pinned my arms down, smashing my hands until the blade fell useless somewhere in the dark. I saw madness in his eyes, a creature that always existed by consuming women's bodies. I screamed through broken lips. He grinned down at me, digging his knee between my legs, laying his weight heavy across me.

He pressed his lips into my scream, laughing into my mouth. The contrast of darkness and the glow of embers was smoothing into a gauzy mush. Darkness swallowed everything.

A sound I could not describe filled the lodge, something pressed into my thigh, something else wrapped around my arms. I felt strength rush into my limbs; the terrible howling was thick.

In the corner of my eye, an emaciated face glowed, dead pale but brighter than the embers. Jane fought to become more substantial, her mouth already wide and toad-like.

Spores poured out of her mouth. The tiny black fungi spread in the air then dropped like a wave, covering Jason's body in fast-growing replication. Jane's form snaked heavy in the dirt. Her eyes crazy as she bubbled towards his feet. Her mouth opened, a vast, terrible O. The orbs of her eyes disappeared inside her head. She inhaled, sucking in his feet. She exhaled and then inhaled again drawing even more of him inward.

Del Rio's eyes went wide as Jane's teeth sunk into his legs. He released me, turning, reaching back to stop the pain. I rolled away, watching spores dance faster in the small space—the spores attached to his face, chest, and arms filling the severe gash in his belly.

Jane stretched her impossible body, morphing into a tubular creature, a fantastic serpent. Inch by inch, she swallowed him gasping and growling—the smooth stretching membrane of her lips like a birth canal in a horrific reversal.

Del Rio screamed, writhing, flailing his arms.

Her lips slipped up his trunk, shoulders, and neck as his body twisted under the devouring teeth and the undulation of her smooth surface. The teeth scraped across his cheeks, clenching his head until he disappeared into her mass inch by inch.

I watched stupidly, wincing with the terrible crunching of his bones. Jane's form shuddered, Del Rio's hands pushing from inside her, pressing on the membrane of her swollen form. She contorted like a giant snake moving his encased body down, digested it seemed, into the dirt.

I faded as her body bubbled and shrank, morphing back into the familiar bioluminescence, shimmering like the glimmering embers of the fire. She lay there awhile, her chest rising and falling. I wanted to crawl to her, but I couldn't move my body, growing numb.

Jane's colorless eyes regarded me slowly. I reached out my trembling fingers, the blood loss making me dizzy as my vision glitched. Gracefully her hand swept upward to her mouth, pressing two fingers to her lips as if in a kiss.

I awoke in the hospital. Undersheriff Blackwood sat beside my bed explaining after a few awkward minutes that Mrs. Del Rio had been slain; ripped wide open on the obsidian altar, her entrails stretched over the labyrinth stone walls.

Del Rio, he said, was on the run and couldn't be found.

He shared that Del Rio had been a suspect in a few murders and sexual assaults years prior. I looked up at him from the hospital bed, mute.

"Strangest thing," he mused, leaning over my bed. "You should be dead."

I tried to sit up, jerking the tubes in my arm, "Excuse me?" I said weakly.

"Someone called it in. A woman, I think. The connection was terrible with static."

[5]

The sun sinks lower, inviting the strange transition to night. Ray Price starts in with, "Heartache by the Number," as the light fades. Twilight here felt otherworldly as if the valley and mountains invented the colors that only existed in this place and hour. You scan the land around you, knowing for a few moments it will come alive with elk and other creatures who also seemed to sense the power of the change. Antelope materialize from the landscape as if dreamed up, racing in your direction.

Some in the valley pick up the remains of the creatures unsettled by the sun's dropping and the brightness of headlights. The animals run headlong into cars and then collapse, mewling their agony on the side. Sometimes humans join in tandem screaming from the wreckage of vehicles that traveled too fast for the odd-lit hour. You have been there, red, and blue lights strobing in the eyes of the dying. The humans are picked up by an ambulance, the poor creatures you put down yourself with the knife you keep sheathed at your belt.

Sometimes someone comes along with a truck and takes away the meat. The valley is a place of consumption; nothing goes to waste, even potatoes that roll off the backs of loaded semis are gathered, bagged, and resold on the corners in Alamosa. Other times you drive away from the dead animals, and the next day the carcass is gone, probably sitting in some strange studio to become something else. Taxidermy is rarely employed here to preserve a hunting trophy—instead, the corpses are used in the creation of chimeras.

You equate this with control.

The radio bleeps static, then goes silent again like the dispatcher was going to add to your thoughts but decided against it.

Your grandfather told you that men lost control here, sometimes women did too. Like civilization was thrown to the wind even if the few towns had laws and order to a certain degree. The boundaries were mutable, and the rules ceased when you went off-road—everything you believed in, swore to uphold warped beyond the imaginary lines.

Control is just a simulacrum, a lie you tell yourself. You look out the window watching the antelope run and hop fences. They have freedom, and you have nothing but the lies you tell yourself over and over. The lies and terrible truths cage you in. For some it is worse than hell.

DARLING VALENTINE

The figure's epidermis was cracking, the parchment surface peeling back in places. Gretchen Ubel carefully extended the knotwork, trying to avoid picking up splinters from the skin. Though gloves would've been preferred, she could not accomplish the delicate task of tying the necessary knots with her hands covered. The oil she had applied weeks ago didn't achieve the job of smoothing the skin, the puckered seams still curling back with a pronounced shimmer along the hard edges.

She decided that the effect could be utilized in the more significant work. It added to the mysterious allure of her project. Months in the planning, the vessel was coming along nicely, each detail carried out with precision.

Gretchen whispered into the shriveled ear.

"Valentine, my love, open your eyes."

It was an absurd command to a static object, but she liked to think she captured a soul in the delicate vessel.

The eyes remained open, glassy, and black. Gretchen had injected indigo ink in small, calculated bursts into the shrunken filmy green orbs a few hours before. The circular shriveled blobs swirled, swelling with the darkest blue. The ink and chemicals injected solidified the blob-like spheres into an opaque black. Every injection after that of the tiny hypodermic needle added to the shine eliminating the dull milkiness.

The preservation of the orbs was the most delicate step requiring tweezers and scissors. The most challenging action required a sharpened hook to grab and slice the muscle tissue. It was her first attempt at the process of enucleation. The vessel had twitched a bit when she removed each of the globes. This step made her nervous, working with a vessel that still pumped air through the lungs, but the eyes would preserve best if taken fresh.

It was such a delicate thing, cutting the six extraocular muscles without a slip of the scalpel. Even one mistake would have rendered the spheres useless as egg yolk. Gretchen could have used glass like any taxidermist, but the art was married to the challenge.

She had carried out each step patiently over the last year, after first acquiring the vessel. For months she slept and tended the low fire, building thick smoke that enveloped the artifact drying out the flesh until it was its present form. Her new husband, Michael Ubel, worked long hours and never questioned her work as an artist.

She bent over the empty sockets wielding a glue gun that dripped slightly. Carefully she lifted the spheres, placing them into the sockets before drizzling warm ribbons of fixative around the edges. She squeezed a silver dye into the glue before it hardened, adding a mystical highlight to the black spheres.

The thing stared up at the ceiling through useless crafted eyes. She stood back entranced by her artistry.

"The eyes of a Goddess, the eyes of Isis," she whispered to herself.

Gretchen continued with the work, holding up the fragile wrists, wrapping them in a soft cloth before placing rope, and continuing her knots. The vessel now taking a workable form seemed more doll-like, and the new eyes gave it life. Gretchen stretched her thinking, trading the word "vessel" for the Valentine doll's more appealing name.

She used paint to cover the bruises and thick silicone to fill the cuts and holes. She had been rough in the early days and regretted it. The pungent smell of mesquite smoke still permeated the doll, but this was preferable to the dry cheese smell of rot.

Fingertips rubbed across etched lines that ran down from the shiny eyes, frowning at the imperfections. She brushed at them, but they remained, and there was no time to fill them in.

"You remember, Clara—erm Valentine, don't you? That's where we met out in the valley."

Gretchen cycled the memories through her mind, then shook her head.

"No, that's not right. We met that night with the calypso band."

She smiled, "When I met our Mr. Ubel."

When she saw them that first time, they were entwined like one body dancing, everyone in the room watched, wishing they had something so beautiful. Mrs. Ubel, only plain Gretchen then, a mouse watching from the corner. The terrible pain of desire growing in her chest.

Later, one of the Red Women advised that the mountain gives you what you want if you give it the blood.

Gretchen gave the mountain what it craved.

In the beginning, it was a demanding challenge of the mind, her sanity nearly broke early in the process. The vessel's beginning stages almost drove her to madness during the curing process. The thing cried out and moaned incessantly in the smoking shed. Only when she applied a mix of wormwood and barbiturates did it grow gentle. Finally, the heart of the thing gave out, and Gretchen could relax into the more creative work.

Her new husband never questioned the ongoing process. He mostly ignored her work in artistic taxidermy, wordlessly scraping up dead things he found on his way to work and delivering the dried-up animal corpses to her studio. He preferred not to watch her work, only appreciating the money she brought into the marriage with her macabre art. But no matter the sacrifices, she was rebuffed in her efforts to replace his previous lover. In his heart, she knew he hoped that perhaps someday the lost one would return home. He never understood that, in a way, his lover already had.

She looked down upon the face of the doll with a quiet sense of pride. The lips were still nicely sealed shut, resewn with delicate stitches of silver thread complementing the shimmering eyes.

"Yes, love," Gretchen said with reverence for the grotesque abstraction of sensual beauty that lay upon the table.

Today was the seventh anniversary of the first town masquerade, its conception born out of the boredom of deep winter on the mountain. The Red Women supported her vision and new self-confidence, her marriage allowed for a quick rise within the ranks and a certain measure of new power within the community. She was no longer the mouse in the shadows—she was Mrs. Ubel, a wife, and Red Woman of respect.

The workers completed the setup the day before, cleaning and preparing the house, draping the place in scarlet and aqua blue. The doll's perfect placement: the last step would be to act as a figurehead of a theater ship overlooking the crowd. Gretchen only needed to finish the doll.

She slipped the doll's stiff limbs into the white dress she had found in their trash. She asked her husband where the dress came from, but he remained silent about its origin. Of course, she knew to whom the dress belonged, and symbolically it was perfect for the artifact. The arms outstretched reinforced with wire were small in diameter, allowing her to tack the fabric on with straight needles.

Michael heard his wife in the studio above and switched music on to drown out the noise of her work. He never went up there; the creations with glass eyes disturbed him. The effects he desired in marrying her were fading, and the heavy sorrow still gnawed at his guts. At first, the feeling of being pursued by a woman a decade younger eased his loneliness. Gretchen's wildness and ability to command him had ensured that he didn't have to think in those early days. Few questioned their marriage, and when Clara left him, a replacement was expected.

Gretchen pulled pins from the corner of her mouth, draping the fabric carefully over the curling hard skin. The doll had been horizontal so long in preparation that it was with great enthusiasm that she planned the ornate wings. Tonight, the Valentine doll would fly above everyone like an angel. Gretchen began affixing the ropes with the dress pinned in place, with knots tied firmly at the joints. Finished, she slowly pulls on the ropes, raising the doll on a pulley system until the toes were inches off the ground.

Gretchen tooled the rope through the arms, weaving wings through the extended wire and a slip knot on the lower back. With a practiced motion, she snapped the rib bones and bent them outward. She pulled them wrapping them in wire, extending the wings by a foot.

She had taken great care in the curing of the neck and head, positioning it with scaffolding that, when removed, left it jagged and obtuse, the jaw more primitive and savage, especially with the silver-rimmed eyes and sewn mouth.

As the sun sinks into the rounded San Juan mountains, she pushed the fragile work by a wheeled platform to the top of the steps. The hesitant body resists the locomotion of movement and takes all her strength to maneuver through the long, open balcony encircling the house's upper floor. Though he offers, Gretchen refuses help from her husband, wanting the artifact to remain a surprise.

At first, she places the doll at the top of the stairs, but the blue and white lights don't glimmer off the flesh with the desired effect. She shifts her creation to the right, above where the crowds would gather below. Looking down, she imagines the faces looking up in amazement.

Gretchen touches her fingertips to the dry face of the Valentine doll and smiles. The beauty is beyond anything she imagined.

"He will love you," she whispers.

The following two hours spent weaving and knotting the ropes to various ceiling points require extreme care. The doll rises higher with each pull, filling the vaulted ceiling with glittering lace. The wings flutter in sheer voile with ribbons streaming downward, catching on the drafts of winter wind that press in from the celing to floor windows. She adjusts Valentine's long black hair, letting it fall forward from the emaciated head. The mouth glimmers stern, almost sad in macabre splendor.

Michael swirled the whisky in his glass, drained it, and filled it again. Outside his door, guests are already being welcomed by the Community Arts Collective. The guests received invitations that read like an instruction manual supplied with explicit directions on attire and behavior. It was an invite-only event, and guests were to adhere to the absolute secrecy of the CAC and the revered Red Women. As his wife prepares herself in her room, the guests filter into the vast house, adding colored layers to the flashing lights and droning music. Polite laughter and conversation intertwine with carefully picked professional tribal dancers, swinging hips with added bells and beads. The house, transformed from the mundane to the exotic, is unrecognizable.

Safely hidden behind eyeliner and a mask with black feathers, Michael watches the growing crowd. His beard falling to his chest in blues and greens glittering with silver beads. The welcoming warmth of whiskey sinks into his chest as he takes another drink, careful to resist raising his eyes. He doesn't want to see whatever it is that she has made. She insisted it was made with all her love for him alone, though everyone in attendance would share in it as well.

Hovering above, he can feel his wife's creation, but for a year, she has refused to show him; even now, a curtain of velvet hung over its massive center. All he could see were the ropes, ribbons, and lace hanging down.

He closes the door with a skeleton key that disappears into his pocket, reluctantly diving into the increasingly massive crowd as he seeks to remain invisible. He was always surprised at how many lived on the mountain, only coming out from their well-guarded lands for events like this. Most of the people he did not know and those he did, he despised. Of course, he would never say this out loud.

His wife made her entrance dressed as a corpse bride, smiling in his direction. She was in her element, proud and pointing up at the hanging curtain. He struggled not to follow the tip of her finger with his eyes. He simply was not drunk enough to look yet.

Her art was only part of her deranged interests, and the work seemed to be getting darker. He avoided her manic periods using work as an excuse, keeping up with a dutiful husband's expectations, detached—dead.

The masquerade grew more raucous as the night progressed, with patrons enjoying the various drinks and food provided by expensive caterers. Many were dancing in celebration of an event that could cut up the dreariness of the long winter months endured on the side of the mountain.

Gretchen slipped in beside him; he could smell perfume and woodsmoke upon her skin.

"Come with me; it's time," she whispered into his ear.

She pulled him onto a small platform erected for the occasion.

She gripped his arm, holding him tight in waiting silence. The guests' anticipation proved feverish as they moved in, a wall of garish color surrounding their hosts. Someone lowered the music, and all eyes turned to them.

Gretchen gripped her husband tighter, digging her nails into his arm, her face shining in the light, her skin dewy with sweat. She smiled, cracking the white paint in places.

"Hello," she began blinking into the bright light, raising a hand to shield her eyes.

"We want to thank you all for coming to the annual winter masquerade," she said breathlessly. "Tonight is special—the first since we were married last summer."

The crowd all called out congratulations, some applauded. Gretchen leaned over and kissed his cheek.

Michael perspired under the attention of the guests and the suffocating unknown above him. The thing felt like a poltergeist hovering in the room. If he didn't look, it would not exist. He didn't know where the overwhelming fear was coming from, but it pulsated in his chest.

"For my husband, I have done my finest work. I hope it shows the gratitude I have for his love." She laughed, her eyes glittering with tears, "You made an honest woman of me."

He was unmoved, but it didn't show. He felt discomfort growing in the pit of his stomach. His feet felt frozen in place as warmth raced up his neck.

She swept her arms upward, "My love, friends, I give you Valentine."

"Mariners Apartment," the Tamino version of the song, began to play on cue as the curtain fell to the floor. He watched as faces turned and angled upward to look upon the thing called Valentine. Gasps, praise, and applause filled the room. Michael concentrated on his wife's face as long as he could before letting his eyes follow. The gathered guests' applause swelled in claustrophobic sound. His eyes slowly crept upward in calculated measures to the installation above.

The Valentine doll was lifelike, pale, the size of a human, realistic bones protruded in sharp contrast to the fleshy bodies surrounding him. It was tied in kinbaku fashion, tight lines, and sophisticated design, its bones spread wide like wings. What looked like ribs continued outward splayed in a broad fan of lace. He felt sick as he realized that the thing was delicately pinned into Clara's dress, hung like a weeping angel.

He looked at his wife with confusion, hoping this was a sick joke. She still smiled, her face wet, oblivious to his growing horror. She turned to him, clasping her hands bouncing on her heels like a child proud of her work.

He sucked in his breath as his eyes traced the outline of knots that extended outward, suspending the thing above. Its hair fell forward like black feathers, brushed and silky, odd, and magical in its grim surroundings. The skin was dried and peeling as one would find on an antique doll from the 1870s, and he wondered how his wife had attained this effect.

His feet moved of their own accord as he walked across the hall and slowly took the steps gripping the railing until his knuckles were white. He stopped halfway up when he could see the face of the thing more clearly, the crowd behind him falling away.

He could sense his wife behind him but could not shape words, creating a membrane between them in his building distress. The smell of mesquite and decaying flesh was overpowering, making him feel nauseous.

The face was almost recognizable.

No, the face was recognizable. Clara!

Michael's heart thudded hard in his chest as his body went cold. The hairs on his skin stood erect; he dropped his hands from the railing, curling them into fists. His mouth opened and closed as he sucked in great gasps of air.

He knew this face as well as he knew his own. The eyes were dead, dark pools rimmed in silver, but the mouth he could almost remember the softness of kissing. The lips glittered with a silver thread, warring with his memory of living lips hot under his own.

He took the steps now two at a time, nearly falling.

Her leaving was a nightmare he dreamed so many times, so much so that he often walked the long halls of the house trying to shrug it off. He imagined in those moments that she had never left, that she was nearby. He swore he could feel her in the house.

He dreamed of this face every night and practiced what he would say, the questions he would ask if Clara came home.

His heart thundered dangerously hard in his chest as he approached closer. He moved along the railing, noticing her face etched with trails of tears. Her bones were exposed and porous, her eyes a dead black.

It never was a doll. It was Clara.

He thought she had left intentionally, leaving him for something, someone else. He had spoken to the Sheriff's department, begging Undersheriff Blackwood to help. But nothing ever came of it, no tips, no clues, no trail.

A wall of sounds like crashing cars and screaming filled his head. He put his hands over his ears, shaking on the brink of collapse. He choked on an urge to vomit and then did, wracked over until his ribs felt fractured.

Clara had never left—not really.

Digging nails into his palms, he decoded the story of her torture and death. His mind painted pictures of her mouth sewn, screaming behind the thread.

Gretchen had killed her.

He sensed his wife behind but still tried to ignore her. Her warm hands reached out, touching. His breath pounding hard and fast, the killer pressing into him from behind.

He looked up at Clara's gaunt face. Flashes of her smile and voice thundered across his mind reaching icy accusatory fingers into his heart. The orbs of her eyes began to ooze out the black dye which trailed down the brittle cheeks. He stumbled, the hands of his new wife catching him hard around the waist. He felt her breath on his back, the pressure of her hands like a serpent-like coil.

Taking a ragged mouthful of air, he turned. The crowd below smiled behind masks and makeup, unaware. Some moved off to get drinks or dance again. Michael bent forward, clasping his arms over his stomach. He looked to his wife, shaking his head mouthing the word "no" over and over.

His wife smiled down at him, the topography of her face peaceful.

The work changed her, rendering her more vivid; her chin proudly extended with the narcissism he had in some ways appreciated until this moment. Michael grasped the rail, trying to hold on to reality.

His mouth opened, but the words didn't come; they jammed up in his neck, building in a flood of madness.

"I think we're alone now." She paused, the music swelling with the laughter of the guests.

"You, me and our darling Valentine," she whispers.

[6]

You can't help but think about Deputy Larson. Sure, he annoyed you with his youth, good looks, and weak stomach. You reach for the cross at your neck, pinching the metal between your fingers. You and Sandy never had kids. You took to thinking about the green deputies as your own through the years; even Sandy did. You didn't just work with them but had them over for dinner and went to church with some of them. Their kids became your grandchildren and seemed to fill up that empty void you and Sandy shared.

You and Sandy tried once and watched over those magical five months as Sandy's belly swelled. You recall feeling the tiny feet kicking through the skin of her stomach. A tear escapes your eye, and you wipe it away. You almost lost Sandy then, all the blood, her lips going blue. She didn't see the fetus, but you insisted on being there in the surgery. You look down at your hands, remembering those precious few moments of the tiny form moving until it lay still like it was sleeping cupped in your palms.

It was a girl, your daughter dead in your hands.

Yet even now, looking out the window, your Glock 19 in your lap, you still don't feel her death or the magnitude of what you lost. You have seen what this place does to young women, children. You have seen the bodies in the woods, brains on the carpet, headless women hidden below floorboards. You have seen things you dare not speak of. And you realize in a way you are not sorry she died. You tell yourself that you and Sandy were spared in the simplest way possible.

The AM radio moves into Colter Wall crooning, "Sleeping on the Blacktop," and you start to weep; you can't stop. You can't tell if you're crying for your tiny lost daughter or Larson. You shudder—no one should ever have to hold their dying child. No one should ever see—

You push your palms into your eyelids, only a little ashamed. You hate those times when you felt helpless. You hated it more when you searched but never found a plausible explanation.

BLACK GOLD

The figure hung from the telephone pole in a macabre crucifix posture. Above the fresh-cut neck, several heads revolved sewn like an oversized crown, held together by galvanized wire. The gruesome thing was angled as if to catch the sun as it crested over the mountains. The heads rotated slowly like bottles in an ice cooler. They were meant to be seen, displayed with the artistic flair of a demented taxidermist. The wind howled around the unnatural thing; the figure's hands gripped the pole as it moved it backward and sideways in a coordinated rhythm. At the end of a series of such motions, the wind would slam the body and heads against the pole. I felt like the heads were screaming. I wanted to scream in unison.

I felt rigid. My heart pounded so fast it seemed to suck my breath down into my chest, cramping. I continued to watch in wild terror as the wind slowly pushed the grim spectacle. The crown dipped slightly forward, whipping back with an audible slap, sending the heads in another slow revolution like an old, rusted windmill.

I looked up stone-faced, trying to be professional, swallowing hard to keep from vomiting. I chewed my lip, turning my face from the corpse to Undersheriff Blackwood, his old face lined in perpetual angst and disappointment in the world. Dave never seemed shaken, and after thirty years on the job, he acted like he had seen everything a man could do to another, twice. He just kept looking up.

"Where are the other bodies?" I asked, still leaning over with my hands on my knees, fighting waves of nausea. I looked towards the mountains; their outline was sharp on the horizon, bare, the color of iron.

"Well, I reckon not around here," Dave said, spitting tobacco. "This here person is a new kind of fucked up."

I felt an inappropriate laugh born of nervousness choke in my throat. I clenched my jaw and coughed. Dave tried to hide it, but he hated being stuck with a green deputy. It was just a reminder that he had lost the election.

"Going to need a bucket truck to get that down," he said, pointing as if I wasn't aware of the thing hanging above our heads.

"I'll call it in," I said, kicking my boot in the dirt.

"That would be useful," he said, spitting before turning to the car parked across the road to block both lanes.

The red and blue lights flashed, making me feel nauseous all over again. I got in the driver's side and called it in, having to explain more than once before Dave took the CB impatiently in hand and told Shirley, the dispatcher, to send a bucket truck and two more patrols our way. I don't think she believed him or me for that matter on the particulars we were trying to describe. One body posed like Christ with a rotating crown of heads; well, it sounded too crazy even for County Road F.F.

We waited in silence; I watched the corpse through the windshield as if it was a hallucination that might suddenly vanish. Dave poured coffee from an old thermos into an even older metal cup, the kind my grandfather had owned. He drank, his head tipping just enough to show the golden cross at his neck.

"Recognize any of them?" Dave asked, still watching out the window.

"Not so far. Looks like Halloween masks from here," I answered, twirling a pen. "You saw something like this before?" I asked.

"Nope," he answered. "But I have seen some fucked up shit."

"Who would do this, you think?"

"A fucked-up shit bag."

Dave screwed the lid back on the thermos.

"Like...?"

"Fuck, son, you know the drill around here. The hippies, the new agers, the pagans. Once I picked up a guy who was selling puppies to sacrifice for cancer, sign, and everything," Dave turned to look at me, "ten dollars a pup."

Dave had the hint of a smile at the corners of his mouth. "Wasn't clear if he was selling for the disease, a cure, you know, or just to cancers like the astrology sign."

Way down the road, flashes of red and blue appeared in convoy. I could make out the bucket truck bouncing along the barely paved road and wondered if it was from the electric company. Some poor civilian would see something that would stay with them for the rest of their life. I also wondered who was going up in the bucket, and it turns out it was me.

The bucket was only big enough for one man, and I got a quick course to operate the levers. I looked down, trying to arrest the dizziness as best I could. I hated heights and felt demonically sandwiched between the ground that was falling away and the corpse above. I looked to the horizon to center myself, letting my eyes loop the San Juan mountains' curve.

The bucket didn't go up smooth. It jerked and bumped around like it was trying to decide if it was going to rise another foot. The wind had picked up and had flakes of snow mixed in, stinging my face, already pinched with cold. I didn't look up until the arm of the bucket cranked fully extended.

I could smell the rotting flesh before I raised my eyes. It was below freezing today, but the last two had been fifty degrees, just warm enough to hurry along with decomposition. I had to look up to get the job done. The sight from the ground had been enough for me, and I could feel the unease building in my gut. I closed and then forced open my eyes. The body seemed normal enough dressed in REI gear. I reasoned that the dead body at least had money to spend on a parka, boots, and fancy pants. I closed my eyes again.

"Come on, Deputy Larson, it's cold enough to freeze the balls off a snowman," Dave shouted.

I looked down at Dave, leaning against the car with coffee steaming. Off to the side, a deputy was walking around with an old camera snapping pictures. I saw Dave point up to me and mouth some words to the deputy, who, in turn, laughed, angling the lens in my direction.

Fuck you, Dave.

I wiped my gloved hand across my face and then raised my eyes by small movements up the body. I could hear the rattling and meaty thumps above me as the heads caught the wind and spun. The heads looked out on the valley in a full grimace, unnaturally showing air-dried gums and teeth. The ones facing me were too far gone to ID by anything but teeth. I thought, standing there in the swaying bucket enveloped in the cold air, I might have the same look momentarily.

The heads spun again, and a female visage looked down on me; her mouth had been slashed from ear to ear exposing her teeth that were opened wide enough for her shriveled tongue to peek out, hard and crispy. Her eyes gouged out, but it was unclear if it had been by man or bird. Then it hit me that it was Liz Hall, a girl I had taken up with a time or two.

Suddenly I felt dizzy, ready to hurl. My feet unwittingly moved backward, causing the bucket to wobble and my top half to arch dangerously over the side. I grabbed the edges to steady myself, swallowing the vomit in my mouth.

I turned cautiously to look down at the assembled men below.

"Liz Hall," I shouted.

"What?" Dave shouted back.

"One of the heads," I pointed up. "Elizabeth Hall, the teacher."

The deputies below looked at each other in horror. Dave nearly sprinted around the car to presumably call in the information.

I pulled the wire cutters from my pocket and proceeded to cut away the wire, and slowly put the heads in the bucket. Occasionally, I looked down at my boots, now surrounded by faces that seemed to be frozen mid-scream. When it came to the last one, I had to remove my gloves to pull the wire inserted through the ears. I pulled the wire, feeling it catch whatever was in the skull. I pulled again and felt the wire grazing bone and cartilage and then something soft. My hands got so cold that my fingers turned into rigid hooks. I couldn't feel them or sense how hard I was pulling. The head came loose with a sick pop, and I scrambled to catch it in my frozen hands. The head tumbled out of reach, plopping onto the dirt like an overripe melon. I didn't realize the body was affixed to the same tangle of wire until it slid free and hit the ground with a revolting thump.

At that moment, I felt like such an incompetent rookie that my disgust subsided enough for me to lean from the bucket and shout an embarrassed, "Sorry!"

"Jesus, Larson!" one of the other deputies yelled up at me.

I lowered the bucket, aware the entire time of Liz's eyeless stare from her destroyed face.

As soon as the boom was down, I climbed out of the bucket and clambered down the truck. Weak-kneed and faint, I told the others they could finish the job. I tried to make it around the truck to puke, but too late.

Dave met me with coffee when I walked back to the car. I just sipped, trying to wash the taste of vomit out of my mouth.

"Elizabeth Hall, huh?" Dave asked after a few minutes of silence, watching the others take pictures and bag the various parts.

"Yeah, I mean, yes, sir."

"Does she come over on this side of the valley?"

"I don't know; she used to crack jokes about it with me. She's not the new-age type." I thought about it a minute. "More sensible teacher type."

"Oh yeah, teaches over in town," Dave asked, then his eyebrows came together in thought. "It's winter break, right?"

I nodded.

"So, if we can place her at school in December, then that means these folks were probably killed in the last two weeks. Almost no one uses this road in the winter." He said this as a statement, not as a question, so I didn't feel the need to add anything.

"Did you date her or something?"

I looked up, "We were friends. I saw her in town about three weeks ago, I think."

"Did you kill these folks?" he asked casually, joking.

He must have seen my face go pale because he smiled, "Aww, Larson, I'm just fucking with you. Whoever did this possess a much stronger stomach than you."

He slapped me on the back and walked over to supervise the bagging.

By the time the remains were bagged and tagged, we had one body and six separate heads. Though we searched the area on foot and by drone, we did not locate the five other headless bodies. The electric company had to replace the pole with a new one, and the old one was tarped and secured for evidence, then put on the back of the bucket truck, the driver of which seemed to be doing as well as me. Probably wishing he had slept through his alarm this morning.

When we got to the station, I locked myself into the bathroom. I splashed cold water on my face. My reflection seemed to belong to someone else; I just kept looking at my eyes, looking for some sort of change. I took the job, always wanting to be the one who could change things for the better. This stemmed from my sister Kim found raped and murdered in the mountains. It was a youth camping trip, and I had been there too. No one saw her wander off, and the perp was never caught. I had my suspicions, so did the department, but mountain towns keep their secrets.

Kim had been laid out like a gruesome satanic sacrifice with flowers and rocks positioned in a wheel, her blood everywhere. They had searched the mountain for the killer, searched where they had found other bodies. The autopsy came back, removing any doubt that some sick fuck had brutalized her.

I willed my brain to stop and splashed more cold water on my face.

I turned the tap to hot and wiped the remnants of death and vomit off. I felt the panic building but shrugged it off best I could. When I went to my desk, Dave was sitting back with his boots up. I marveled at his calm and wondered if I would be as calm about death and decapitated heads after years on the job.

"Elizabeth seems to be the only local; the others will be hard to I.D., we got to send in teeth to CBI. The body has fingerprints, of course, so we are waiting on that before releasing anything to the press."

I took off my hat and put it on the desk, sitting down slow to not jar my stomach.

"Sorry, son, that has to be particularly difficult with your sister and all."

I looked up at Dave, a bit surprised by his concern as it broke with his steel character.

"I'll be alright," I answered back.

"You want to make some calls and see if we can figure out what Elizabeth had been doing?" Dave leaned forward. "I checked with Shirley, no missing persons have been filed on her. By the way, did she go by Elizabeth or Liz as you call her?"

I shrugged, "Both, I think."

Liz was a Colorado transplant; her family was all east coast, so her not being called in wasn't that strange. She was a careful person, well, except when it came to me. We weren't dating, but we weren't not dating. It was complicated.

I made a few calls but didn't find anything new and stood up, grabbing my coat and hat.

"Where are you going off to?" Dave asked.

"Well, I was thinking of Liz's house to start."

"I'll come along, and we'll get lunch."

I was amazed that he could think of food. Dave barked out orders in his undersheriff way to other deputies working on various early angles of the case. I followed him out the door like it was his idea all along. We stopped by a café, got takeout, and I watched him navigate a massive burrito with green chili through his handlebar mustache while I drove to Liz's house.

"Do you pray, Larson?"

I glanced at Dave and then back at the road before me. I didn't believe in God. A flash of my sister's pale body, half wrapped in a sleeping bag, reminded me of what had killed off the last of my faith in the Almighty.

"No."

Dave took another bite, chewed. "Believing in God might be old-fashioned, but it has saved my sanity in this job." He swallowed.

I simply nodded.

The office and Liz's house were in the town of Cottonwood across the valley, about 35 miles from where the corpse and heads were found. Our department was responsible for a cut of Colorado that was 1000 square miles of barren high valley bounded to the west by the San Juans and to the east by the Sangre de Cristo mountains. In the summer it was hot and in the winter cold with temps that could drop from 60 degrees to 18 below zero in the time it took to drive to the closest store and back. I never understood why folks came here to this harsh environment; I was born here and could never shake myself loose. Even when I got old enough, I stayed, mainly to find my sister's killer and partly to care for my mother, who had died four years previous. There was no one here for me. I suppose I stayed because I couldn't see beyond the ghosts that walked with me.

The winter landscape was brown and rocky, patched with rags of snow. The road curved around one of the low-slung hills that made up the San Juans' foothills. We passed the cemetery, with each of the graves surrounded by a fence to keep animals out. Some graves were fresh, littered by the remnants of tattered cloth flowers left by the family. The wooden crosses were often painted in bright teal, yellow, and red, a testament to the Chicano culture that inhabited this valley. The road opened, and except for the cattle haloed with dense clouds of breath and the mountains' surrounding teeth, nothing else stood out beyond the barrenness. We did not speak during the drive; instead, we listened to the radio's chirping from other patrol cars in distant corners of the county.

Liz's house was a squat adobe that she rented just outside of town. Two cottonwoods stood like dark, twisted hands on either side of the drive. I pulled up close, just behind her Subaru. Dave and I got out, and each of us took a slow walk on either side of her car. I investigated the passenger side just as Dave popped open the driver's side.

"Well, it's open. Is that something she would do, leave it unlocked and all?" Dave asked.

I was minorly annoyed that I had become the Elizabeth expert.

"She's from the east, so I assume she would still be locking everything up," I said but then added, "It's not like I knew her that well."

Dave's bushy eyebrows hooded his gaze. "Well, let's look at the house. She rents, right?" Dave asked, smiling, seeing if he could make me uncomfortable.

"You know Dave, I don't have that information, and for your own, we always went to my place. I have never been here."

Dave closed the car quietly and joined me on the walk to the front door. Nothing looked out of place. We knocked, not expecting an answer. I reached for the handle, and the door swung open without any turning from me. Dave whipped out his gun, getting tense, and nodded for me to draw my pistol. As soon as we were both armed, he pushed the door open with his boot. I entered cautiously with my gun up and Dave just behind. The slant of light from behind us seemed to disturb something.

A shadow or enormous spider skittered quickly out of the light. I thought I heard its appendages on the wood floor. Startled, I took a step back, feeling Dave's gun and his exclamation of surprised annoyance.

"What the hell, Larson!"

"I thought I saw something. A cat, maybe."

"Well, the cat almost got you gut shot!" he whispered harshly.

Something pooled dark and thick on the floor. Above me, a light came on. I turned as Dave's hand lowered from a switch by the door. His eyes got big, and I turned back. The smell was like pennies and old rancid parmesan cheese. The dark spot was brick red now under the light, a whole body's worth of congealed blood. The same waves of nausea from the morning hit. I sunk into a crouch to have a closer look but mainly to keep from messing the crime scene with vomit. I pushed my gun arm elbow into my stomach and used my other hand to cover my nose, stifling the smell. My eyes ranged across the room, looking for what I was now hoping was a cat.

Dave joined me, dropping low. I could see his professional mind taking in the whole scene. He noticed before I did that the blood was oozing up from between the floorboards; it came in small spurts like a heart pumping.

He didn't say anything, pointing to the floor. I'm not sure what unnerved me more the pumping blood or his fearful expression. Dave was many things, but if he was ever afraid, it never showed.

We both became aware of a scratching sound that I prayed was mice below the floor. Dave reached down with shaking hands to try and pry a board loose. Having no success, he stood up, leaving me alone in the house presumably to get some sort of tool.

The noise grew louder, scraping like nails. I stared at the spot, unable to move. In the corner of my eye, I saw the movement again, shadowy, and as I turned, I saw the thing skitter up the wall and across the ceiling down the hall. It had the sheen of oil and didn't make sense in my mind. I felt frozen but would have run if I could have moved.

Behind me, Dave came in brandishing a crowbar. I closed my eyes tight then opened them, somehow feeling better with him in the room.

"Move back," he said, gloves removed, gun holstered.

I looked up at him stupidly. He made a prying motion indicating his intention, his eyes wide, determined.

I forced myself to stand, gripping my gun, my heart fluttering fast. Dave shoved the sharp edge between the boards and pulled hard. The board came loose and flipped over, resting a couple of feet away. We both leaned over.

Below those boards was a headless dried-up corpse, its arms, and one remaining hand curled into claws. The skin was cracked and pale, indicating it had been under the floor for over a week. Parts of the body had a black oil sheen, especially around the shoulders and neck. We looked at each other for a minute, feeling foolish.

"Come on then," Dave said, pointing the crowbar at the corpse.

I crouched down to have a better look. I reached out a hand touching the cold skin.

"Definitely been dead a while," I said more to myself than Dave.

I looked again, covering my nose with my free hand.

I knew that body.

The curled fingers twitched, and I nearly came out of my skin, falling hard on my ass.

I didn't think.

I aimed and shot. Once, twice. Three times.

The body convulsed, and the hand dropped, fingers curled tight into its palms. Something down the hall screamed. Dave yelled at me, but I couldn't understand him with the gunshots ringing in my ears.

It happened so fast. It didn't seem real.

We both backed up near to the door. I kept the gun trained on the body, and Dave held the crowbar like a club.

"What the fuck was that?" Dave said, his voice higher than usual.

"Pretty sure it was Liz." I kept staring at the headless body, unbelieving. Nothing ever looked more dead than that corpse—yet it had moved. I saw it. Dave saw it.

I watched Dave reach up for the cross at his neck, pulling it out from under his collar, kissing it. He mumbled a prayer under his breath.

We crept slowly forward as if trying not to make the thing animate again. Dave grimly popped off more boards. What lay below was an intact body minus a head. The image of Liz's head between my feet cut into my brain.

We stared incredulously at the body. Neither of us could explain how it had moved. Neither of us wanted to.

"We'll say it was a rattlesnake in the floor."

"Huh?" I asked, shaking my head.

"To explain the bullets."

"Oh."

We crouched again, cautiously over the naked body covered in human-looking bite marks. The jagged stump of her neck looked like her head had been chewed off. The odor was intense, overpowering, and I thought I would never smell things normal again. Dave turned green and threw up, barely turning his head away fast enough.

"CBI is gonna love that," Dave said, wiping his mouth.

A scratching noise came from the rooms down the hall. Dave didn't seem to hear the noise.

"I'm gonna check the rest of the house," I said.

Dave just nodded his eyes still staring at the thing in the floor.

I stood and raised my gun, walking slowly down the hall.

Nothing seemed out of place; no shadow or spiders crept from the corners. There was no oily trail to follow down the hall. Her bed made up in a pale pink velour blanket, and pillows lay undisturbed. The bathtub was filled with icy cold water in the bathroom, and on its edge, a fresh scented candle stood ready beside a fluffy white towel. The bathroom appeared pristine like her bedroom, untouched by the dark thing I had seen scurrying in this direction previously. Nothing screamed danger here.

I looked in her mirror, leaning over pink and peach bottles of feminine mystery. My eyes were sunken in and a sick color of bluish-purple. Still paranoid, I couldn't help looking over my shoulder, wondering if what I had seen slithering back here was something only visible in one's peripheral vision or as a reflection. I waited, holding my breath, my chest rising and falling in expectation of a killer.

"Larson!" Dave yelled from the front room. "Anything back there?"

I had one last look around. "No, nothing back here."

I steeled myself to cross the barrier of light into the slaughterhouse of the front. But my feet seemed cemented in place, stuck there between light and shadow.

Eventually I forced my feet to move walking back to the carnage of the front room. Dave looked sick.

We went outside, both of us huffing the fresh air. A car drove past, and I could see the normal-looking family through the windows. It seemed impossible that something normal could be so close to something so unexplainably horrendous.

Dave got his stomach under control and called it in. A report had come while we were in the house—one of the heads was positive for Elizabeth Hall. So, one body was now accounted for, two were unknowns, and two headless bodies were found fifty miles across the valley near a fire pit the locals used for full moon parties up on the mountain.

Shirley paused over the radio, "Dave, the two on the mountain were cooked and partially eaten."

Dave looked at me, then looked at the house. "I think that Ms. Hall had a similar circumstance."

The radio clicked, then went static. I suppose Shirly didn't know what to say.

"Send a team in, will ya."

"Sure thing, Dave."

Dave looked at me, "We aren't going in there again until we have a team."

A week passed with Dave and I working on the case. The coroner explained the animation of Liz as rigor mortis combined with built-up bodily gasses. The coroner didn't buy our rattlesnake story and had a good laugh when Dave finally admitted what really happened. Anytime I tried to offer a differing opinion, Dave shut me down as having a superstitious mind. I never told him about the sounds or shadow I'd seen in the back of the house; he wouldn't have listened anyway.

The town folk on the mountain remained tight-lipped while ours in Cottonwood were buzzing with satanic rumor. Cottonwood was a God-fearing town and had a natural inclination to suspicion for those who lived on the mountain.

When we questioned those on the mountain about Elizabeth, they just shrugged. They all claimed not to know the teacher from across the valley, or if they did, they were not saying so. A couple of them even took off running up into the woods when they saw me approach. Dave had laughed and suggested I might smell bad or something. I just figured they had drugs on them and didn't feel like being hauled into jail. But their eyes, the way they looked at me, verged on creepy.

I dug through her social media; it amounted to the mundane, filled with educational posts, recipes, and crafting ideas. All posts ended on the twenty-first. I went through her settings and found a section for something called «secret messages».

There was only one message there. I clicked it and saw my profile picture looking back at me. My finger hovered above, tremoring, the rest of my body stiff. I looked around the office, suddenly worried. Everyone in the office was either bent over work or chatting over coffee.

I clicked the message dated from the twenty-first.

> pick you up around eight party's up on the mountain
> snow and a big bonfire should be beautiful

I read it twice, unbelieving. It had my picture; it was sent from my account. I quickly hit the X, minimizing the screen. I reached for my phone, almost dropping it. Dave turned in his chair, shuffling through some papers across from me, then looked up.

He cocked his head, "Something wrong Larson? You look kinda fucked up."

My mouth filled with bile that I swallowed and then shook my head, feeling the burn.

I lowered my hand into my lap, quickly tapping in the code to unlock the screen. I opened the app, trying to find the same section on my phone. Sure, enough the message was there as if I had sent it. I didn't hesitate to break my vow as a deputy and erased it, breathing hard and feeling sick.

My hands were shaking, and I licked lips that had suddenly gone dry. I pocketed the phone and clicked the computer screen back to life. Quickly I deleted the message from her account.

Dave's phone rang, he answered it, replying, "I see," and "OK," while looking across at me.

He winked. He fucking winked at me!

My body began to shake.

"Hey there, son, cut that out. You're rattling my desk!" he said pointing at the phone next to his ear.

I decided to make a big deal about the last public post to cover my screaming insides. Sweat dripped down my neck. Dave hung up the phone, scratching out a note to himself that he folded and put in his pocket.

"Liz posted last on the twenty-first. After that, nothing, so I figure she must have been killed around then." I kept my voice even and monotone.

He just looked at me. "That what got you looking so sucker-punched?"

I shrugged, not sure what else to do.

"Good work. I sure don't know how to do that internet sleuthing." He looked down at the papers spread across his desk.

"You hear anything new?" I asked, worried.

"Naw, it was just the wife with a grocery list."

I felt myself relax in the chair. "If it's alright with you, I'm gonna go on home and get some rest." I stood up, slowly grabbing my hat.

Dave nodded. "I'll pick you up around seven in the morning. We can go out there then. I have a couple of other places to hit after if that sits well with you?"

"Sure, Dave," I said over my shoulder, heading fast out the door.

At home, I paced the floor; my face lit up in the dark by the phone as I went through the messages.

Nothing.

I drank too much whisky and fell asleep, awaking tangled in my sheets. I couldn't figure out where I was, still feeling caught in a nightmare. I was running on all fours like a dog, and then I was pushing the wire through warm meat, hitting bone, and twisting the wire until it pushed through with a sick pop.

My phone chirped a musical tone. I rolled over and got it expecting the office.

It said Messages.

I clicked the screen.

A thumbnail picture of Liz popped up.

I struggled to sit up, my body suddenly awake. I swiped the screen open.

Mountain at midnight, god, it's beautiful—

I just stared. I hit delete.

I launched myself from the bed, pacing a rut in the carpet, ending up in the bathroom. I leaned over the sink, looking at my exhausted face in the mirror as if checking for the dream. My eyes were dark-rimmed and sunken, my face almost skeletal. I knew that I had not been there; I had been home sleeping. But there was a ghost in the machine speaking through my phone. It was speaking through a dead woman's phone. It couldn't have been me. I had taken my oath with all seriousness to uphold the law and protect.

I heard my phone chirp again and felt the breath sucked out of me.

I kept looking in the mirror—like I did at Liz's house, expecting to see someone behind me. I went to the bedroom, just staring at my phone; the screen lit up and vibrating. I reached out, my hands shaking.

I know you're home

I could see the ellipses in movement like someone was typing more. They stopped; a picture flashed. It was Elizabeth's head, freshly cut and still life-like, laying in a crimson pool of blood.

I'm feeling pretty

I jumped, dropping the phone, hearing it crack. Breathing hard, I stumbled to the bathroom and threw up in the toilet. The breath in my lungs felt constricted. Everything after was a twisted blur: pulling on my uniform, strapping on my gun, starting the car, driving.

I wanted to find the fucker no matter how scared I was. In my mind, Liz and my sister were blending, stitched together. I remembered part of my nightmare then. It was Liz's adult head set upon my sister's teenage body. I just couldn't shake it.

I drove the fifty miles across on Highway 16, the moon lighting up the valley in false twilight. Someone was trying to frame me, and that someone was on the mountain.

Spanish Peak was quiet at two in the morning. I took the last bit of pavement for a mile before turning onto a pitted washboard mountain road. I slowed to keep control of the car.

Pinyon and aspen lined both sides, easily hiding anything that might be crouching there. I didn't know what I was doing, lacking any kind of plan, acting in panic and desperation. I parked and got out of the car, still in some sort of trance in an area just before the old service road that twisted up the mountain.

My hand went unthinking to my holstered gun, pulling it out and holding it at my side, its heft comforting. I could see well enough up the service road that led to the fire pit. Nothing moved in the darkness, and I took careful steps checking both sides. Only a few coals simmered in the fire pit, the locals ending the bonfire early on account of the cold. The frigid mountain temperature clawed deep in my bones as I crouched, disturbing the ashes that still held some warmth. Beer bottles and nubs of joints littered the periphery.

Footprints pressed into the sand and remaining snow. I got out my flashlight and looked around, deciding that I was alone. Most of the prints followed a haphazard revolution around the pit.

One set, however, trailed off; I looked back in the direction of my patrol car, weighing my options. In me, the law officer cautioned my next choice, my guts screaming to call it in despite the incriminating messages. Dave would have called it in requesting backup. That's why he was still alive and pissy.

I placed one boot into the first print and then the next. All my training went out the window as I struggled up the sandy path that led up the mountain. It seemed to go on forever, the sand making for slow progress laid open like a woman's back bent, absent of vegetation or snow. I had the overwhelming feeling that there had been no choice at all. That this place had been here since before man had ever walked, and it was pulling me up the terrible mountainside. There were stories of mountain madness—cannibalism, witches, and cults. I guess on the job, I had seen some of it, but nothing compared to the sick feeling that was developing in my guts as I climbed.

My mind filled with visions that felt like memories. Liz running naked through the trees, my bare feet in the cold sand. I shook my head, willing the movie in my mind to stop. I tried to focus on the path, but still, they came; flashes of chasing others, bloodlust of the hunt, and then glitching back to Liz, begging me to stop. I shook my head, clenching my eyes shut. Blood, so much blood, covering the snow and then evaporating when I opened my eyes. Everything was blue-lit in the moonlight.

A keening sound floated down to me, echoing from the unseen top of a rockfall at the base of the mountain. It sounded like a baby screaming. I dropped into a crouch breathing hard.

Peering into the darkness of the forest on either side of me, I held my gun in shaking hands.

Again, the keening baby-like cry filtered down the mountain. The sound was so wrong in the inky darkness. My arms shook as I peered blindly ahead and then back the way I came.

Mountain lions made similar sounds and didn't sleep the winter through. Suddenly not knowing if the monster was real or if I was the killer on the loose. I refused to believe it had been me.

I had been home. I had been asleep.

My boot hit something. I shone my flashlight beam downward and saw a phone that was encased in pink as I remembered Liz's had been. I had made fun of her the night we hooked up, and she had tapped my number into her contacts. I picked it up and was shocked to find it on, fully charged.

It made a chiming sound and lit up with my name in a notification bubble.

I'm coming, just a little bit farther, and the climb

"What the fuck!" I cried out. "No, no, no…" I kept whispering to myself.

I dropped the flashlight and pulled out my cracked phone. The message was there as if I had casually typed as I hiked. I threw my phone as far as I could, hearing it clatter against a rock, and then did the same with hers in the opposite direction. I screamed curses as I paced on the sandy trail. I leaned over, picking up the flashlight looking up the path lit like a sandy dais to hell.

Someone was fucking with my head.

I made myself walk. No choice was mine; someone else was holding all the cards in this sick game. I kept climbing upward until the path disappeared into a wash of rock and boulders. The footprints stopped here.

The light fell on the rocks jagged and locked together for eons. Some of the stones had a deep liquid sheen, and I reached out a trembling finger still holding my gun. When I turned it for a better look, my glove was stained in fresh blood, considering the frigid temperatures, the blood should have been frozen.

If I shimmied up the rock, I might be crawling right into a mountain lion den or worse. I turned to look down, the valley's lights scattered in the darkness like a blinking galaxy. I was a couple of thousand feet above where anyone lived. My lungs were struggling for air.

I holstered my gun, put the flashlight in my mouth, reaching with a hand, trying the rock. I felt something firm but not the expected stone. I pulled at it. I turned my face to illuminate my hand as I dropped it to the beam of light.

In my hand was the cracked end of a bone; it looked like a straw with red bits shoved inside. Around it was gnarled flesh and rolled skin.

I felt myself falling, my flashlight leaving my mouth as I choked on a scream. My hand tightened around the thing as I hit rock and sand, landing on my side, and rolling, hitting a few more rocks on the way. The flashlight bounced and then hit a rock but thankfully did not go out, casting its light down the sandy path.

The stars and satellites above me blinked in and out. The moon appeared so large I thought I could feel it pushing me down. I tried to sit up, but searing pain raced through my body. I pressed a gloved hand into my upper chest and decided I had only bruised some ribs, not broken them. I bit down on the pain best I could and hurried across sand and gravel to the flashlight, acutely aware of what I still had in my hand.

Grasping the light, I placed my other hand in front of me. I wasn't surprised this time that I held a woman's hand freshly chewed at the wrist. I think I was numb from everything because I just stared at it.

I took off my glove with my teeth and, with my bare fingers, felt the flesh, finding it still pliant and warm to the touch. The very tip of tattoo ink showed in the rolled-up skin that I pinched open. The nails weren't painted, but there were crimson bits underneath the jagged nails.

This hand had fought back.

I put the hand on the ground and struggled to stand. I holstered my gun, deciding then to climb. I grabbed the rock, hauling myself up, using only my boots' tips to push upward. My ribs felt loose, and like they were jamming into my lungs. Each handhold came slowly with the expanding of my lungs under injured ribs. I pushed upward with booted feet and shaking thigh muscles. My hands finally felt a leveling off above me.

I considered my gun, wishing I could both climb and have it out. I slithered up over the lip of rock and rolled, biting my lips, and tasting blood. My chest felt like blades were piercing through skin, and I hoped it wasn't the ribs. I pulled my gun and flashlight without thinking, sending a beam of light against the mountain side.

Against the rock face, a hole gaped open like a mouth, big enough for a person to crawl through. A mountain lion would not explain the bodies we had found, nor would it explain the messages. Yet I found myself praying that it was a lion there in that impossible dark. You could kill a mountain lion with bullets.

My flashlight felt small and thin, like the courage in my belly. I kept thinking about the reanimated body, the heads, and the shadow creeping in Liz's house. The hole looked like a dark womb for such things.

I hesitated, and from that hole came again the terrible sound of a baby screaming. The sound grew in crescendo and echoed off the walls of the cave. I winced and curled into a ball, covering my ears with full hands.

Lights started bouncing off the side of the mountain. They were coming from below the rockfall. I panicked, not knowing how I had missed an entire posse behind me. I wondered if I had lost time or if they had been lying in wait under the trees.

"Deputy Larson, we need you to come on down!" A voice belonging to Dave Blackwood called through a bullhorn.

I edged over to the lip and peered down, a spotlight catching my face and blinding me for a moment. When my vision cleared, I saw Dave and other deputies gathered below, guns out.

"The CBI read your messages; we know you done it, son."

I blinked, and belly crawled backward, my boots scraping against the mountain.

The cave's sound was building, yet the men below didn't seem to hear it as they shouted for surrender.

I cried out, adding my voice to the screeching coming from the cave as it echoed across the valley.

It seemed to awaken something above me; a shadow darker than the blackness of the hole skittered across the surface, dislodging rock from the side of the mountain. It moved like a giant stain, moving downward with incredible speed. It paused and then darted into the hole in front of me.

I chanced a quick look at the men below, making my decision. I didn't fully understand what made me go there, but I did know I didn't want to go away in cuffs. Whatever was in there had killed. I needed to know. I needed proof that I was not the killer, that something evil had come off the mountain. I put the flashlight back in my mouth and then belly crawled to the opening.

I thought about my sister all those years ago. We had been camping only a mile away from this location; her body found not far from here. Liz's dead face existed behind my eyes when I closed them. Someone had sent those messages; someone wanted me to know what they had done.

I wanted answers, and I would die for them if necessary.

The smell of ammonia hit me first, the hole's bottom covered in bat guano was slimy. I could only manage to rise enough to crawl and had the overwhelming thought that I was navigating the throat of the mountain. The going was rough, and claustrophobia was pressing in on me as much as the pain in my ribs. It remained tight for twenty yards then suddenly opened to a man's height. I took the flashlight from my mouth and struggled to my feet.

The screaming had lowered to bass-like droning and was unlike any sound I had heard before. It was unsettling, reminding me of a woman in labor. The farther I went, the more the sounds felt like they were affecting my body. The air was ammoniac from animal excrement and thick, burning my lungs and eyes. It was growing warmer, and below my gloved hand, the walls felt alive, rising and falling as if they were breathing. Sometimes I thought I heard someone shouting my name from behind, but the farther I went the more I felt detached from my body, the building smells and heat disorienting me.

Something inside was reacting to the primal nature emanating from within the cave's tight space. The smooth and circular walls curved and went on before me, swallowing the thin beam of the flashlight. I forced myself to put one foot in front of the other, stumbling through the thick guano cave.

A sound like teeth clicking together began to fill in the spaces within the droning. My flashlight began to glitch and then finally failed, leaving me in the dark. I thought as I felt my way that something was beside me, touching me with delicate fingers. I turned and reached out in the darkness, finding nothing. I took a few steps more, testing with the tip of my boot, afraid that there might be a chasm that would swallow me whole. There were plenty of stories about this happening in the caves and mines that dotted this mountain.

Something moved in the blackness; I could feel that it was large enough to displace the air around me. A heavy feeling of dread impressed upon my body. Rock was scooted around in the darkness; something like claws skittered down the sides of the cave. My resolve melted, and I tried to back up, falling to the hard-slimy floor.

I felt something touch my head, and the dream-memories on the path flooded my mind. Liz smiling at me over the bonfire, our naked bodies entwined, making love, stepping over other couples, the stars so huge above, rolling away from her, cocooned in the sleeping bag. Hearing twigs breaking, something out in the trees. Warm suffocation and something filling my mouth, choking, drowning on the cold sand until things went black. The hunger. Liz sitting up screaming. Looking up as I fed upon two bodies, hot blood in my mouth. The phone in her hand lighting up her frightened features. Her running. The taste of her neck. A blackness that had the sheen of gold.

A terrible scream brought me back.

I attempted to stand but landed hard on my knees, trying with desperate movements to crawl. My gun had fallen out of my hand. I still had the flashlight and frantically banged it on the floor of the cave. The screaming continued just behind me. The flashlight finally flickered, giving a weak beam, showing the narrowing just ahead.

I managed a few yards and turned; something was oozing up and around on the ceiling. A slick shimmer of gold played on the percolating blackness. The oil-like substance dripped down pooling on the cavern floor. I crawled through it, scooting and pulling my way towards the entrance. The thing above tried to grasp at my legs, then recoiled back into the mass as another arm of oil would form and drop.

I had to get away—draw it out so the men would see the monster wasn't me.

My elbow slid out from beneath my belly, hitting rock and sending me sprawling on the floor of the cave. I struggled to roll over, realizing that I couldn't go any farther. The flashlight wavered on the morphing ceiling.

I lay there looking up into the strange growing black gold. The liquid arms that fell from it grew longer with fingers that curled, snatching at my body.

Above me, it bubbled, then covered more of the cavern's surface, stretching and sticking. I shone the light down the tunnel seeing no end to the oil-like thing as it snaked into the dark. The blackness above me morphed from my shadow face to Liz and then glitched into the faces of the others and then my sister.

"No," I whispered.

It flattened as if a great hand was wiping the morphing features away and took on the shine and reflection of engine oil. I tried to use my elbows to scoot further down the tube. I could smell the cold mountain air.

I was close to the opening.

The screaming stopped. I couldn't help but look upwards mesmerized, any thought of self was fading.

The thing slowly dripped from the ceiling like a slimy membrane. I tried to scream but felt my mouth filling with the substance. I was choking as it wiggled into me like water swirling into a drain.

It filled me with terrible things.

My mouth sucking and biting Liz's neck, biting until it rolled off her body in the sand. My sister is running so fast, my hands on her back pushing her off the cliff. The sick sound of her head on the rocks. My hands, my bloody hands.

My eyes opened, and I looked through a shimmer of oil. My body covered in the oil, and as I moved, it moved with me. I crawled through the tunnel, tumbling out of its mouth, my mouth opening and closing.

"Get a light up there, every light, and don't shoot. I want him taken in unharmed," Dave yelled below.

I screamed, the sound bouncing off the mountainsides that enclosed the precipice.

The minutes were razor-sharp and cold.

"Larson, come on down and let us get you some help, son!" Dave yelled.

A small part of me realized that the older man cared, but what I used to be was being siphoned back into the black pit of the mountain. I felt inhuman strength pulsing in my body. I remember climbing the pole, dragging first the body and then the crown of heads, shoving Liz's body in that hole dripping in the black gold, reanimating her headless, clawing corpus. The shadow in the house was only me, the shadow me that I was becoming.

I roared, launching myself at the men, blood and the terrible oil soaking the ground. Dave fumbled with his light; the other men fired blindly as I sunk claws into the nearest deputy. I drug the man screaming back up onto the lip of the cave. Dave Blackwood stared helplessly; his gun pointed in shaking hands. I could see his struggle, and a part of me wished he would do it.

I fell backward into the oil, the man in my hands screaming.

[7]

White folks mostly lived in the flatlands. They were suspicious with dreams of living out on the frontier. They purchased the land tracts by auction or online for cheap, believing they got an unbelievable deal. They would pack up out east and come here in old campers, sometimes tents realizing quickly that the land was barren and water scarce. They came out with families, guns, and dogs, and the desolation would eventually drive them to a certain kind of valley madness. In the mountains it could be worse.

You saw too much of it, the barefoot children running through the rattlesnake-infested brush, mothers trying to grow their food while they starved. You have pulled up to conduct safety checks and had shots fired right over your head by men tweaking out on meth.

The influx of newcomers you have no power to stop. It has been this way since the land was first invaded by the Spanish and later by Manifest Destiny and the goldrush. You know intimately that the ground was never meant for Anglos to inhabit. The valley asks each of its inhabitants to fulfill needs that cannot be maintained alone. The aloneness that man craves here is a lie, even for you.

You reach for the radio holding it up to your mouth; you have words crunched up there but cannot spit them out. Patsy Cline plays softly, and you think of Sandy sitting alone at the dinner table. You feel awful about it but would feel worse if she saw where your mind strayed now. These moods scared her.

Strange lights start strobing on the mountain. They twinkle and glimmer reminding you of the angel fire you saw once out east. They say such things happen the world over, but not like here—never like here.

You've seen them before, even chased them up the trails when you were younger, never finding the source. Now you just watch them, radio in hand. You don't report them.

SNAKE MAN

"Sir, did I just hear a rattlesnake?" the officer asked, the colossal wall of Mt. Blanca framing his head.

I didn't want the full-on say yes, but I could not deny that the officer heard not one rattlesnake, but rattlesnakes—plural. I blinked up at my reflection, tinted blue in his standard issued aviators and smiled.

I could have said in chorus with him the next bit as he leaned into my rolled-down window.

"License and registration, please."

I was hoping Susan, my sometime girlfriend, had not been fucking around in the glove box. If she had, then the papers might not be covering my gun. Swallowing I turned real slow, hoping luck was on my side.

If she hadn't, then the Glock nine mil would still be discreetly covered by papers and wrapped in a red bandanna. I tried to remember the last time she had been in the car, and if we had argued. Susan was a bit rough around the edges and liked to slam around my car when she was pissed off. I decided it had been a month or so, and I had used my gun since then. I packed illegally, my rap sheet a bit longer than I liked. Bad luck seemed to follow me in a hopscotch pattern of years.

I glanced at the stern face of the sheriff's deputy who was a long way from Cottonwood. I swallowed spit and reached slow, popping the latch. The glove box door swung down as I held my breath. The wrapped gun was thankfully covered and out of sight.

I snagged the papers and handed them over. I always kept my wallet on the dash. I guess you could say I get pulled over a lot and through force of habit, found it an excellent idea to have it close rather than in a back pocket. Cops are generally jittery out here in this valley with the tweakers, hippies, and aliens.

I gave him the license. He studied the plastic card and flipped through the papers like they were his very own divorce decree. He glanced between

114

the card and my face and did not seem to see the resemblance. Which there would not be as the guy on the card was not quite as good looking.

"Bill Hardy?"

"Yep"

Behind me, the snakes were getting testy like they had taken offense at being pulled over. I wasn't too sure of the count, but at least six were jammed in a box across the back seat. I had covered it in a burlap potato sack, but you just can't hide the racket that a full box of rattlers can produce.

"Do you have a commercial wildlife permit for the snakes?"

"For what?" I asked, stalling.

The corners of his mouth rolled into a downturn. The snakes hissed and rattled behind me. I glanced back, sweat dripping down my brow.

"Um, no officer," I said as casually as possible. "They're pets…"

He leaned in; his face set grim. The devilish sun radiated down, making the mountains waver like oil through the windshield.

"Sir, in Colorado, it is not permissible to have rattlers without a license."

I just shrugged. I knew the law but also knew my purpose in having them.

"Please get out of the vehicle, sir," he said, stepping back.

Behind my seat, the rattlers buzzed. I shook my head, realizing that the good day was quickly going sour—nothing like the law to mess up a man's day. The trooper shifted on his feet, unable to hide both his anxiety and his annoyance.

"Out of the car, sir."

I popped the door, showing my hands. There was no sense in getting the officer all worked up. He searched me, lifting my Hawaiian hibiscus shirt to find a knife at my waist and in my boot, and then cuffed me, leading me to the back of the car. The officer looked pissed, especially when I smiled at him. He went to his patrol car, watching as if daring me to do something stupid.

I didn't.

I was sweating balls when he finally walked back, calling in on his shoulder radio. He headed on past me to my driver's side door. I think he meant to search it as he leaned on the driver's side. I just watched, somewhat bored and fucking hot.

I was staring at Mt. Blanca tripping out over a dust devil to the west when I heard him scream. Quick as shit, I saw his body go stiff, and then he fell backward, holding his neck and right after slithered one of the snakes. The snake must have been all riled up because it went directly after him, like its feelings were hurt.

The officer rolled around, trying to use his legs to push away, all the while grasping at his neck. The snake rose, swaying like one of those king cobras. It paused, then launched at the man biting him over and over.

I screamed like a bitch. I'm not sure it hissed or if my brain just added the sensory overdub to make it more frightening. Either way, I almost pissed myself.

The officer cried out, his mouth wide open, looking at me with crazy eyes. I shrugged at him, kind of jumping up and down, wondering what he thought I could do now. The truth was, I could do nothing at all with my hands cuffed behind my back. Well, I could do something, but snakes in this sort of mood are beyond dangerous, and I didn't want to die today.

The snake was acting like a rabid animal biting him all over his body. I had never seen anything like it. I finally decided I should probably do something and inched closer. I moved slowly because snakes are a bit like an officer of the law in how nervous they could be, and I respected both—mostly.

I followed the crazy movements of the reptile. If I made a mistake, both of us would be bloated ant-covered corpses when the deputy's coworkers found us. I waited until the snake had its head on the ground and stomped it. Typically, I would have cut the head, but my knives were on the hood of the car, and my hands were useless behind my back.

The officer had stopped me out on road G, which was a little bit of gravel and a whole lot of sand. I chose the shitty road because the police usually wouldn't try their tires or luck out here. The back roads required that you let the air out of your tires to get some decent traction. Right now, it made killing the snake under a boot a bit more complicated, and the snake was pissed off royal. Every time I tried to smash it; it just went further down into the sand.

"Yo, Officer, you gotta roll off a bit!" I yelled, the full body of the snake wrapping up violently around my leg. It, for sure, did not want to die.

The officer moaned and shook, his body writhing in pain. I had thought of letting up the pressure and jogging backward, seeing if the snake would just slither off. It seemed, in this instance, to be the only option.

"Come on, man, move!" I yelled.

The officer tried, screamed, and then collapsed in a concerning stiff, nonliving sort of way.

I cursed at the snake that whipped around my leg, the infernal rattle droning on. I stood for close to half an hour, my skin turning red under the blistering sun. Nothing seemed to move around me except the damn snake that was finally growing exhausted. Some vultures swooped overhead for a bit, impatiently waiting for me to move away from the body of the officer.

I wondered if I could be prosecuted for the natural behavior of the snake. I know I had locked the box, and it's not like they were dogs who could bite their way out. It probably didn't matter, because now with the sun-cooked corpse of a dead deputy on the road and a lanky forty-something in a Hawaiian shirt, hands cuffed, standing on the head of a snake the next ridiculous problem was crystal clear. The situation would be funny if it weren't so sad compared to what I had set out to do.

A man needs to question his choices when stuck in a situation such as this. I calculated that it would take about an hour or more before the sheriff's department sent out another car. The county was huge and sparse; that's why people like me came to this part of Colorado; it was easy to stay under the radar.

I thought about the explanation I would have to tell the next officer. They already had one of my aliases called in by the dead stiff in the road and the make and model of my car. The plates were stolen, and my actual name was Mike, so I had that going for me.

I still had cuffs on and a batshit-crazy rattler below my boot; two problems that needed fixing.

I decided on raising my boot and scuttling back as quickly as possible. The snake would move fast, but I hoped it would head for the rabbitbrush and not me.

I waited for the snake to unwind from my leg, then let up and jumped back. I like to think I am relatively agile; after all, I caught the damn snakes on my own, but my feet tripped me up, and I fell hard, landing on my back.

I lay on the hot gravel and sand stunned. Shaking my head, I looked over to where the snake seemed to be waiting.

The rattler skittered off a few feet then coiled as if it knew I was the cause of all its problems. Helpless on my back with my hands cuffed below me I tried to push further away with the heels of my boots. The rattle of the snake was loud, and it was shaking out a song of retribution.

I rolled, catching my boot on the back tire. The snake uncoiled, slowly slithering in my direction. I could see the venom dripping off the bastard's fangs. I clenched my eyes shut, then opened them again at the sound of the dead officer's corpse letting off gas. It was the slow wet fart of the dead man that startled the snake into the brush quick as shit.

I have experienced many things in my life but being saved by a dead man's fart was a first. I waited to see if the snake would return, but it didn't. I labored to get on my feet and went over sitting down hard next to my corpse savior. I had to turn my back to try to get my hands close to him, angling my fingers into his tight pockets. Finally, finding the key, I pulled it out with my fingertips. It took acrobatics to get the cuffs unlocked and off my bleeding wrists.

Standing up, I looked around; sweat rolled off my body. I glanced west and east to both mountain ranges looking for dust heralding the approach of the reinforcements. Seeing nothing but sage, blue sky, and the infernal sun, I allowed myself a sigh of relief then stumbled back a couple of feet bent over, trying not to vomit.

I got back into my car, checking to see if the other snakes were secure. I lifted the burlap to find the critters sluggish in the heat of the vehicle; all but one accounted for. I looked over the box, hinges and all but couldn't figure out how only one got out. I didn't question it though; it was an odd sort of saving grace.

I jumped back out and snagged my knives, stashing them in their hiding spots. I would have been pissed if I had left my prints for the sheriff's department.

I started the car up, driving off-road around the body. I hit the gas, kicking up gravel and dust while fishing around on the floorboard for my whiskey. Never did a drink hit the gut with more pleasure. I took side roads watching the rearview mirror for pursuit, but none came. After zigzagging across the valley, I finally reached my old Winnebago.

My dog Dirt was happy to see me as I pulled in. He jumped around my legs as I unloaded the snakes, shoving them under the trailer. I wouldn't get paid if the snakes were cooked. The customer wanted them fresh and alive. I then decided that throwing a tarp over the car might also be a good plan and bungee corded one over the old Ford LTD. I wasn't too worried it would be spotted, or even if it was, connected to the incident as there were quite a few of them in the valley. Exhausted, I pulled the door of the trailer and climbed the three steps, Dirt just behind. Grabbing a cold beer from the fridge, I threw myself on the couch.

I petted the mangy dog and replayed the day in my head a few times. Snakes generally bit once and slunk away. Snakes also typically didn't go full-on bat shit. While I considered the reptile brain and all, getting the box open and just launching an attack was over the top. It was like the rattler exhibited higher-order thinking, and I got to wondering if the box of snakes was some lousy mojo waiting to further shit on me. I needed to get them delivered quickly.

My cell phone rang in my pocket, giving me a jolt. I fished it out and flipped it open, taking one more swig of the beer before talking.

"Mike?"

"Yeah?" I replied.

"Running late?" the voice asked as much as presumed.

"Yeah," I said, setting down the beer to scratch an armpit. "I ran into some trouble, but I got em."

"Gonna bring them over?"

"Yeah, man, after dark if that's ok?"

"Sure, Mike, sounds good."

The guy hung up, and I traded the phone for the beer. I didn't know the dude, but he was paying me for as many snakes as I could rustle up. I generally didn't ask questions. I made my living picking up stuff no one else would and delivering it to folks no one wants to know. This week it had been wrangling rattlers in Penitente Canyon. Illegal as hell, but seriously, who cares? I just looked like an old hippy trying to find crystals from the rock holes and old mine shafts to sell.

The promised pay wasn't bad either. I mean, you should get paid reasonably well if you're sticking your head down an old mine shaft. Dark holes in this part of the country can kill you with noxious gasses and dens of everything from rattlers to mountain lions. My work gave a certain kind of freedom you can only find in this part of Colorado. I wasn't the only one, nor was I the craziest; my customers usually put me to shame in that department.

I drank my beer, then popped open another. Dirt finally settled down on the floor at my feet; it was hot, and neither of us wanted to move much. The real shit show would start later when I loaded the box back into the Ford, heading out to deliver it. There was always a bit of danger in that, especially when I barely knew a customer.

After napping through sunset on the San Juans, I loaded up the snakes, fed Dirt, and changed my shirt. I switched out the plates used during the snake incident to some rusted ones I stole in New Mexico. For some reason, if you had a crappy car from New Mexico, they didn't bother you.

I headed north on 17 and took a few different shitty roads to the address if you could call it that. All I found was a big old cattle gate, brown rusted since last century. I parked the car and got out with my bottle of whiskey, tired of the ominous buzzing of the snakes. The cloudless sky was choked full of stars. I leaned against the car, waiting for the buyer.

After a while, I could see headlights headed my way on the gravel road beyond the gate. It was some sort of ATV. As it got closer, I made out two riders, one of which had a rather imposing silhouette. The ATV stopped, with a plume of valley dust further obscuring my view. The big guy got off, unfolding his frame till he stood a whole foot taller than me. I was a bit blinded from the lone headlight, but soon enough, the ATV turned and headed back up the road leaving only starlit darkness.

The big guy unlocked the gate and came through. He looked a bit like Kenny Rogers in the Gambler days with big beefy hands and the white beard. He smiled, and I'm not sure why, but this bothered me a bit. We shook hands wordlessly, and he looked in the passenger window, not in the least bothered by the buzzing.

"I'm Lonny," he said, his voice sounding like it had on the phone.

"Mike."

He snorted and then spat on the ground. "Damn allergies," he said before continuing. "I thank you for getting them. The snakes I mean." He said it with a reverential tone like I picked up his children for church.

"Yeah, no problem. Uh, how are you getting them wherever you need them?"

"I was hoping you wouldn't mind driving them up." I looked in his face to see if I should be worried and decided that I should be a bit on guard with that smile.

"Uh, sure. Yeah, no problem."

"It gets all confusing on the roads, best if I drive up," he said as if reading my mind.

He got into the driver's side; never mind if I cared to drive or not. I took a big gulp of my whiskey and got in the passenger side, comforted in part that my nine mil was right at my knees.

We started up the road, only pausing so I could lock the gate for him and then continued driving on what hardly seemed to be a road at all. My car was old and not up to the punishment, and I could feel myself wince at every rock we hit, and we hit quite a few.

I looked over at Lonny driving my car, still grinning in the most disturbing way imaginable. It was like he got the smile out of a box and slapped it on his face. Usually, this kind of arrangement was not to be done as I had a healthy reverence for life most days. The folk that lived this far removed from the main drag were, like me, wanting to hide something. Figure in the snakes in the back seat, and you had yourself a character who was not the sort you would be kicking back a beer with on a slow Sunday.

"Your place far?" I asked.

"Naw, not much further," he answered, looking at me with the stupid grin.

Lights dingy and yellow showed as we crossed a hill, but they seemed to be coming from below the ground. We pulled up and parked next to a bulldozed pile of dirt. The rise of ground we parked in front of was the top of a berm above a deep dug pit that contained what appeared to be Earthship buildings. This was not uncommon, especially for those who wanted privacy. People out here dug deep in the ground building homes, usually out of old tires and bottles, and they covered the structures with dirt and adobe. They called it an ecological building that was earth-friendly, and I suppose it was. However, I embraced caution as this man might live in the same sort of way the snakes did. The only way you would know they were here was by air, and I guessed they shot down any drones that came by.

"Nice place you got," I said.

Lonny just grinned wider until I thought it might crack the shell of his pumpkin-like face.

He got out, and I followed real slow, waiting until he was going around the car to snag my gun and tuck it in the back of my belt, pulling my shirt over it.

We worked together to get the snakes out, walking the box to a gate that surrounded the place on top. He opened it, and we carried the snakes down a long set of steps made from railroad ties and dirt. Four structures were painted up on the front in rainbow colors, and sugar candy skull faces. It was nicely done but creepy as fuck.

A woman came out of one of the structures with dirty blond dreads piled on top of her head. She was somewhat pretty, but as she got closer, I noticed her eyes were a bit crossed and the kind of blue you associate with psychotic tendencies. I know the type.

She had the same kind of smile as Lonny, and this worried me. She pulled a goat by a rope behind her and tied it to a small post in the yard. She whispered some words to the animal then walked over to where we stood, the box at our feet.

"This here is my wife, Kitten," Lonny said, throwing a fat arm around her. Their eyes met, and they looked like they were trading messages using telepathy.

Kitten was considerably younger than Lonny, her face unwrinkled, and her lips still pert, and I wondered how he had found her. Unions here were often of the oddest sort. Many men in the valley had this old west notion of seeking a younger partner and pushing out babies as if they were raising the next generation of humans on their own. Such couples were usually lopsided, wrinkled old dudes with barely out of childhood young women. To be honest, it creeped me out, but that might be my inclination to tangle with women in my age bracket. I mean, it's nice when you can recall the same toys from childhood rather than buying them for your mate.

I'm jaded, I know.

I looked but didn't see anyone else, so I assumed she had been the ATV driver from the gate. I nodded to Kitten and looked around; it was late summer, so everywhere were the sunflowers that popped up this time of year. There were organized piles of recycling and a large fire pit prominently located in the center of the compound.

"Earthships are great except for the mice," I said, giving them a reason to explain a need for the rattlers.

"We ain't got no mice," Kitten said, smiling up at Lonny before squatting down beside the box and whispering, "Hello, sweet babies."

"Come on, Mike, I'll show you around and get ya paid," Lonny said, using an arm to direct me down a narrow path.

I followed, turning my head long enough to see Kitten weaving her head near the snakes. For a moment, I swore I saw a forked tongue come out of her mouth and then thought better of it. After all, I had been dealing with snakes all freaking day.

"Uh, your wife safe with all those pissed off snakes?" I asked Lonny as I followed him.

"Oh, she loves snakes," he answered nonchalantly.

The first structure we came to is what I would call the big house; it had a kitchen, living room, and a bedroom. I had to admit it was well built, not at all like a dark hole in the ground. Lonny seemed proud of it and pointed out the stone fireplace and stone cut floors. It was full of plants and almost seemed jungle-like with vines going everywhere. In a way, I felt like I was in a large terrarium full of humidity and flowers. It reminded me of the Brookfield Zoo back from my childhood Chicago days. When I looked closer, I saw all kinds of lizards and snakes hidden amongst the foliage. They were free to roam the place, and I had to wonder if the couple woke up with them in their sheets. I saw many webs in there too and didn't want to know the spiders that belonged to them. I hated spiders.

We went into another structure that was a certified greenhouse with the expected flowers, herbs, and pungent weed, of course. Everything seemed beyond my imagination in size and health. I wondered what kind of plant food they used to get marijuana the size of pine trees. I suppose if I was a weed smoker, I would have been in heaven and might have requested my pay in pounds of the stuff. However, I didn't partake, finding weed just made me trip balls like I had ingested some psychedelics. Beer and whiskey were my preferred mode of relaxation.

Next was the well and battery house for the huge solar panels south of the compound, as Lonny explained. This structure was more of a hole in the ground that seemed less hospitable with a gnarly mass of black widow webs all over. Lonny went on about sustainable living and solar power, which was apparently how they had lights on way out here. I asked the expected neighborly questions and kept waiting for the man to pay me. Outside,

Lonny paused, the smile finally sliding off his face; he shoved his hands in his pockets, looking uncomfortable.

Of course, I thought, this is where he tells me he doesn't have the money. I hated it when this happened cause I had to bend my usually chill personality into that of an asshole. I watched him struggle for words, then, after pausing, he smiled, and gestured for us to continue the walkabout. We came to the last structure, which was a smaller version of the house. As we went in, I noticed it had been abandoned for a long time; it was dark with only one tiny window about my head's size and smelled of mouse shit. I turned around in the place, beginning to form a question. Before I could speak, Lonny explained that this had been their first home, his voice warm with remembrance.

While my back was turned Lonny hit me with a shovel; I had missed him picking it up. It hit hard, pain jolting through my skull, sending me to my knees. Blood trickled down my head and out of my mouth. I spit out a tooth; my brain was full-on rung.

"Fuck you, Lonny! What the fuck!" I yelled, putting both hands on my head.

"Sorry, friend-o," was all Lonny said, as if he were straight out of a Cormac McCarthy novel. He patted down my waist, found my gun, and snatched it. He then saluted me, turned, and exited, throwing the door closed. Outside I could hear him setting a lock. I struggled to stand, my head pounding and grabbed at the window ledge. I could see his back as he walked away, dragging the shovel.

"You better fucking let me out of here!" I bellowed, beating on the crumbling adobe walls.

I kept at it for a while, but no one came back to let me out with an excuse of it being a joke. I tried kicking the door, but it wouldn't budge. I paced a bit, trying to figure out a way of escape. I reached for my knives but then remembered that I had left them back in the Winnebago when I had changed my shirt. I cursed myself for being so stupid.

Beyond the window, I could see the beginnings of a fire glimmering. Lonny walked around it, throwing on wood and gasoline, making the flames lick high. Several things ran through my mind, and none of them good. If they were going to cook me, then I needed to scratch up a plan. I didn't want to die tonight. Not at the hands of these assholes.

I have lived here in this valley long enough to see what it does to people. The lack of law enforcement and the miles of nothing made ordinary folk go a bit crazy. I couldn't even begin to count the number of people who went missing yearly. I wondered how many came to Lonny's delivering snakes and never went home. I damn well was going home, if not fully paid.

I couldn't see anything in the strange environment, just the scene beyond the window, and it was getting bizarre. Kitten had taken her strange head weaving dance and applied it to her hips; she was starting to prance around the fire and was breaking out into an unintelligible song and yelling. This went on a while, then she launched herself on Lonny, who was laughing, and they started acting like a couple of teenagers getting frisky. I sat down to figure out the damage to my head. I had a pretty good gash above my ear, and my face felt tender. My mouth stopped bleeding, and I tongued the space where my tooth had been.

I got up and paced some more, hoping to rid myself of the headache. I wondered if this was part of some redneck practical joke gone a bit south. I looked back out the window; both Kitten and Lonny were naked. Their white asses shining in the moonlight like wet melons, their arms outstretched like they were doing voodoo.

Lonny dropped his arms after a while and walked over to the goat they had tied up when I first came in, undid the rope, and brought it over to the fire. I just kept looking, half expecting them to throw it on the fire or some other crazy shit. It's when they both started prancing around and petting the animal that I got worried for the goat.

Their heads rolled back in unison, and when they dipped back down in the firelight, I saw their mouths crowded with impossibly long fangs that had not been there before. Lonny and Kitten both lunged for the goat, sinking their teeth in.

"F—ucking no way!" I whispered

I bit my lip in replacement of the cigarette I wished I had to smoke and went back to the window. The couple was not eating the goat but suckling on it. Blood glistened down their bodies as they just sucked and laughed.

I felt vomit in my mouth and tried to swallow it down. It quickly became apparent that I was next on the menu.

I dropped to the floor, feeling around the perimeter searching for anything to pry the door open. Though locked, I had absolute faith that the door was not as sturdy as it ought to be. My finger rutting around, I prayed hard none of the black widows would see me as a threat. I was pretty sure

I felt a couple skittering around as I groped in the dark. I also tried not to upset the dirt so much since it would mean nothing to escape if I came down with the hantavirus. Finally, I felt something metal and bumpy like rebar and pulled it out from under an unfinished wall.

I stood up and felt along the door frame, looking for the hinges. They were rusted as I had hoped, and there were only two. I used the rebar to pop out the hinges as quietly as possible, pulled open the door, slipped out, and slipped the half-ass door back on the hinges.

Kitten and Lonny were still doing their weird blood-sucking shit, so I moved as quietly as I could to a large chamisa bush. The gate I came in was wide open, but it was also fully exposed. I figured I could try to take on the couple, but they might be on some drugs that gave them super-human strength or not feel pain. I also knew that places like this had stashes of illegal guns, gun control notwithstanding.

Across the way, I saw the now bloody nightmare of Lonny go for the snake box, dragging it near the fire. Kitten, with blood dripping down her chin, started her weaving dance again in the direction of the box.

I guess I was going to find out what the damn snakes were for after all. Kitten opened her mouth with crazy teeth and rolled out a forked tongue. This was not the type one gets in somebody's modification shop. Nope, this was identical to what comes out of a reptile's mouth.

"What the fuck kind of vampire, fucked up shit is this?" I said under my breath.

I crouched down and crawled closer to the gate, still trying to keep an eye on the devils by the fire.

Kitten opened the top of the box, and the snakes sensing freedom slithered out. At first, I was overjoyed. After all, if the snakes bit them, then it meant I could just look for my money and walk right out. But instead, the snakes just coiled up at their feet, docile as pet dogs. One of the snakes, Kitten just picked up like a cat and rubbed it all over her face. The snake seemed to like the cuddles as if its mamma had picked it up. I about fell over; nothing was right in this world as far as I was concerned.

I knew I should be trying to exit, but the scene before me was tripping me up. Lonny turned, looking to the door I was supposed to be locked up behind. He was still smiling, but some kind of frothy goo was seeping out of his eyes and the corners of his mouth. His head swiveled back and forth, reminding me of the officer writhing when the snake struck earlier. Something was very wrong about this whole deal.

The goo kept coming, and the scene was so disgusting that I got the heaves, choking, and trying to hold it back, not wanting to make a sound. Within seconds more of the shit was coming out of Lonny. His mouth seemed to be elongating from ear to ear like something was trying to slip out.

The same thing was happening to Kitten. I watched horrified as the dreads on her head started slipping off her skull, pulling the skin with them. I have to say, I often wondered if dreads fell off when they got too heavy, but this was unnatural like she was slipping out of her skin. It was not only her but Lonny also; their flesh was just stretching and rolling down, leaving a metallic sheen of greens and blue ridges in replacement. The skin just dropped, sloughed loose, like sludge pooling below both of their knees. The rattlesnakes around their feet raised their heads, trance-like, cobras out of a basket.

I closed my eyes, wondering if I had been hit on the head harder than I thought. I had to get out of this place. I didn't want to see what was coming up next. I opened my eyes and forced myself to move in a crouching sort of walk towards the gate.

I chanced a look and saw that what had replaced Lonny and Kitten was sort of reptile in its iridescent scaly skin. They moved in the way the rattlers did, coiling just beyond the firelight. My heart was pounding out of my chest, and my brain was frying, not able to rectify what my eyes were seeing. The human flesh just continued to drip down with an audible squishing sound, and the demented forms left just flopped on the ground.

The buzzing rattle sound I had come to hate today got louder—supplemented by new, high-frequency metallic sounds of the recently changed Lonny and Kitten.

They moved in wet floppy motion towards the building I thankfully no longer occupied, smashing down the sunflowers as they went. One reared up and began pressing against the door as if it knew how to open it. The moonlight shone across the head just right, illuminating fangs as long as my hand and dripping venom and goat blood.

I shrieked in horror, it was not manly, but there was no other way to express how I was feeling just then. I screamed, and I sprinted for the gate, whipping it open and making a beeline for my car. I could hear the creatures behind me slithering faster than I would have thought possible. Things were crashing behind me and hissing, and yes, they hissed as you hear in a B horror movie, but this was real, and way more fucked up.

I ripped open the car door and got the engine started. It roared to life, and I slammed it into gear, but not before those monsters had launched themselves at my car. Their bodies were massive, as wide as car tires, and I could hear the metal frame of my LTD screeching under the weight.

Big loops of snake body covered the windshield, oozing mucus on the glass, as they beat their heads on the side windows. My car was old and not outfitted with the new fancy glass, so I watched in panic as small fractures began to form. I hit the gas, hoping they would just slide off; I could barely see as I tried to stay on the road and not hit every rock the mountains had thrown off eons ago.

I felt the old Ford shudder sandwiched between rock and snakes. The vamp snakes continued to attack the windows, and finally, the driver's side shattered. I grabbed my bottle of Jack at the neck and started beating the heads of the things, hollering as I wildly turned the wheel. I had very few options, and one of them was death. I kept screaming and cursing, but it was impossible to keep up my assault with the bottle and drive.

"Fuck you, cocksuckers!" I hollered, hitting one of the creatures square on a fang.

The curved oozing fang busted and ricocheted across the car. Venom, and I suppose lizard and goat blood, dripped on the inside of the door and sizzled hot like battery acid. Some of the poison sprayed on my arm, causing my skin to smoke and cook. I was full-on driving and crying, slapping at my arm, and veering off the road. My driving was erratic, and I wasn't sure how I managed to stay on what little road there was. The pain was unbelievable as I watched the meat of my arm disintegrate and pop like bacon. I started to feel heat boiling in my blood and then a strange numbness creeping up my arm and across my chest.

I saw the gate ahead and hoped my old Ford could take it out. I smashed through the gate, going seventy miles an hour, and watched as my fender flew. We careened down the road as the roof began to give from the weight of their serpent bodies. I ducked farther down; my chest was clenched in what I was sure was a heart attack. The pain was such that I was quickly tunneling into unconsciousness. All I could hear was the engine's crunching and the rattle and hiss of Lonny and Kitten.

In the distance, an orange band of light across the horizon heralded the dawn.

The vicious heads of the things were snapping at me as I beat them continuously with the bottle. I wasn't even sure how my arm was still working and even less sure how the bottle had not shattered.

I got about one hundred more yards, and the most peculiar thing began to happen. Lonny and Kitten started screaming. Their bodies were beginning to smoke and sizzle. I looked at the sun and then back at them, realizing I was not the only one who got so caught up in shit that I forgot something else on the planner. I watched as their shimmering skin boiled, flamed up, and then grew ashy. We all know how vampires feel about light—turns out it's all true. Bits and pieces of Kitten and Lonny began to float off in the air.

It would've been tragic as hell if they had not been hunting me right then. They started screaming in vocalizations that were much more human the more they melted away.

I don't know if it was on account of the sunrise coming or some witchy boundary I had crossed. Either way, they continued to dry and then curl like snakeskin you see on the side of the road until they were light enough to just float off the car in big sheets, peeling in layers.

I hit the brakes, clutching at my chest. Within minutes their bodies just fragmented and fell away from the car. I sat in the Ford for a minute, too afraid to move, and opened the bottle of whiskey. I looked in the rearview mirror, checking the damage to my face and then down at my melted, bleeding arm. I was dizzy, and my chest was seizing in pain. My arm, hurting like hell, was black and plastic-like in places, but no longer smoking.

I got out, and the hazy sun was a welcome sight. I walked behind the car a considerable distance and saw big flakes of snakeskin in chunks as I went. I picked it up and found it just came apart in my hands. I walked farther and came across the rattles that looked more like abandoned beehives at this point. I considered picking them up and throwing them in the trunk but then thought better of it as I wanted no chance of opening it later to find bits of Kitten and Lonny's asses there.

I drove home, bumping along with a flat tire and a bent frame. Dirt waited for me in the road and followed, barking up a storm as if telling me what a dumb shit I had been. I had heard stories like mine in some form, mostly about aliens and cattle mutilations. If someone had told me my account of events, I would have smiled and wondered what drugs they had been on. I wasn't even sure I trusted my mind.

I got out of the Ford and stepped back, looking at the mangled mess of twisted metal. Dirt ran around excitedly and disappeared around the back end. I called for him, and he returned with a bit of the skin hanging from his mouth. I squatted down and put out my hand; Dirt dropped his trophy at my feet.

I picked it up, swearing to myself that I would add snakes to the undeliverable list. Standing up, I let the scaly skin disintegrate in the sunlight. I looked up and westward to the San Juans and then turned east, taking in the distant sand dunes at the foot of Mt. Blanca. I shook my head a bit mystified. This whole valley was like the boot of the devil, stomping on men like me.

[8]

You feel the land daily as it shrugs its body, trying to toss off the white parasites, yourself included. Your grandfather and his stayed, tied to a place that didn't want any of you. Your grandfather said it was the mountain, but you never felt real sure which one he meant. You recall that he always spoke of the mountain as a woman, and now as you look up, you know the range has always been feminine in your mind.

Suicides and disappearances are regular occurrences here. Never does a week go by that you aren't working a case, trying to find someone. You told the Colorado Bureau of Investigations that they should open a field office here, but they didn't think it was funny. You weren't joking though. They come over from Pueblo, leaving you to hold a crime scene down for hours while they take their sweet time. You stand with a family under the hot sun, holding back family members who are either trying to get to the body or are busy accusing the neighbors of murder.

Six months back, you made the poor mistake of joining the younger deputies on a mountain search and rescue, pulling your bum knee out of alignment. The team went after the missing hiker; you stayed with a cliff edge before you and a tangle of cottonwood and pinyon at your back 10,000 feet up. At first, it felt like nothing, but as the hours ticked on, you felt eyes on your back. You clutched your gun tighter than you do now. Each moment and shadow taking on the shape of a mountain lion or bear. Sometime in those hours, you started to nod off, the pain numbing with sleep.

A scream pierced your dream jolting your body and knee with pain. For a split second, you saw something. Something that left a depression in the sandy dirt beside you. You lifted your gun with shaking arms, pointing it into the climbing shadows, recalling the terrible creatures your grandfather swore haunted the mountains.

Then you saw it. Something so terrible you couldn't name it, nor could

131

you describe it to Sandy later at the hospital. It let out a sound like an elk bugling, but it was wrong, warped.

That is how the team found you. Your eyes wide and frightened, helpless as a child. They lifted you on the stretcher meant for a body they never recovered.

INK POISON

Caroline's brains were sprayed across the wall. Dried dark crimson chunks of brain matter and skull bone had slid down and withered into macabre abstract. I stood with a bucket in my yellow-gloved hand and a sponge in the other, quickly realizing that I would need more supplies to get that shit off the wall. It was surreal as fuck, and I was as detached as a fingernail ripped right out of a finger.

How does anyone look at such a thing and just stand there? I felt outside my body like I was looking through a camera lens all fisheye wide. I couldn't ascribe what I remembered of my sister's face to what was splattered on the wall and down into the carpet. I felt no connection to the bone fragments that I could feel crunching under the soles of my boots. There would be no tiptoeing respect for the dead here; she was everywhere.

My sister, they said, committed suicide, but this was something different; I didn't care what Undersheriff Blackwood or the coroner said. I didn't go with my parents to the morgue to ID the body; instead, I stayed here to scrape up the bits left behind. They said it had been a gun, but no weapon was located, no matter how many evidence sweeps they attempted around the house or in the woods.

Everything in the room was turned upside down, a combo effect I was told, of the Sheriff's department, EMTs and my sister in a rage before she pulled the trigger. The investigation stalled for three hours that morning as we waited for the Colorado Bureau of Investigation to show up from Pueblo only to come to the same dead wrong conclusion.

I wanted to see what triggered Caroline, see the note they said they found. I looked down into my bucket of bloody water, and it occurred to me that only a few hours before, this blood had been flowing through her arteries.

But they never found a gun—there was no gun.

Blackwood said, "it will turn up," and he suggested it might be outside in the pinyon and cottonwood that surrounded our house.

I asked, "How can a gun carry itself to the woods?"

He just looked at me like I spoke nonsense.

I walked to the bedroom window and stared into the woods that pooled with shadows. The sun setting behind the San Juans to the west.

I suppose they didn't have an explanation, so they decided to feed my family some bullshit. My parents ate it up.

I looked down at the mess—it wasn't suicide.

I scraped pieces of my sister into a newspaper, then set to work scrubbing the walls. With my hands, I felt along the bone-white, splatter-painted stucco, trying to find a hole, bullet casing, something that would tell the story. I felt the drowning sort of numbness that comes after horror.

I intended to bury what was left in the woods under our special tree. I lost track of how many times I had to empty the bucket. Each time I took it out to the tree line and poured it where my sister and I had sat and smoked at night. It seemed poetic in a way, but I couldn't come up with any coherent words to say.

"Here is the elixir of my sister," I said aloud to no one, my voice sounding hollow; my mind tripped back through the day as I dumped the blood-stained water onto the ground.

When I had arrived, a deputy was vomiting behind his patrol car, red and blue lights flashing. My parents stood off to the side of the house, holding one another. My mom sobbing hysterically, and my dad staring over her head at the mountain, his eyes vacant. I took hesitant steps toward Undersheriff Dave Blackwood.

"Who is it?" I asked, my chest feeling like it was going to implode.

"Who are you?" he said, pulling out a pen and a small waterproof notebook from his pocket nearest to his gun.

I was surprised he didn't remember me.

"I'm Casey," I said, nodding in my parents' direction.

"The other daughter?"

I had heard that before, mostly from my father and not in a pleasant way.

"I guess, yeah. What's going on? Where is my sister?"

Blackwood's wrinkled face went from stern to a whitewash of pity. His lips pressed together like he was willing the words to stay tangled up with his tongue.

"I think you should talk to your parents," he said, nodding in their direction.

I glanced over just as my mother collapsed to the ground, my father going down with her, unable to hold her. Or perhaps, I thought, unwilling.

"Is it Caroline?" I said, my voice wavering.

He closed his eyes, his lips tighter.

I pushed past him; my mother, finally realizing I was there, began howling. It was a sound that I had never heard her make, like an animal. I ran up the porch steps whipping open the door. I got over the threshold and skidded through something wet, almost losing my balance. Below my feet was something squishy like raw hamburger. I lifted my shoe and stepped back into the wall that was wet with blood. The gorefest was everywhere, helter-skelter. Blood oozed on the walls, the ceiling and pooled on the floor.

Stuck to my shoe was something meaty with bits of hair. The blood trail ran down the hallway. I followed it, moving in slow motion. A deputy spoke to me, saying something about an animal getting through the window. I shrugged off firm hands, trying to turn me back.

The furniture of the living room was printed in blood spatter. The kitchen was normal looking as I passed, sterile just as my mother liked it. I continued down the hallway that never felt so long before, the carpet almost black, darker than I thought blood could get.

I pushed open Caroline's door, thinking this was some kind of joke, a bad remake of some Rob Zombie movie. The second thing I thought was that the strewn body parts were things I knew. The dismembered hand and arms were hers. A half-face nose and part of a mouth lay in the corner like a tattered meat mask. The folded bits of brain that I always teased her about not having were strewn across the carpet. Each part of her glittered with glass bits, web-like across the room.

The window was busted out—or rather, in. The same window we snuck out of to smoke weed in the woods or party with our friends. The bed was primarily untouched; the comforter messed up like she had left it the night before. Pictures, still hung in frames, of relatives from the 1920s that she had a fascination with, and her pillows were on the floor with grim red handprints.

I found myself frantically going on about the window, the glass, yelling at the deputies. I had watched enough on Netflix to know windows did not explode inwards if hit by a bullet shot from inside. I was tromping all over their crime scene, calling them incompetent assholes, all the while picking up pieces of Caroline and holding them in my arms.

I started screaming and didn't stop—blood on my shoes and glass cut into my knees where I collapsed. The incomprehensible pieces of flesh in my hands still felt warm like cooked liver. The room spun, the same room that we had shared growing up, talking about boys, and in my case girls, hating on our parents.

Two deputies took hold of my arms; another took the flesh from my hands and dropped it, like chicken, in a baggy. I started hyperventilating there in my sister's room. I couldn't breathe.

The deputies gripped my arms, their gloved hands squeezing hard, pulling me back through the hallway, my heels sliding through red. I fought them kicking, and they got rough, I think, to shake out the shock that had taken over my body. One was yelling at me, but his words sounded like Pig-Latin. They sat me down rough in the dirt, still speaking in crazy tongues and pointing fingers. I clutched my head in my hands, rocking back and forth hysterically sobbing.

I kept this up until my dad walked over and slapped me hard. Every part of his body was tight with stress, including the vivid tattoo of my name and my sister's name on his muscled arm. I looked up, staring at our names, spelling out each letter. He tried to say more, but I couldn't discern his words sounding like some crazy gibberish. Shaking his head, he went back to my mom.

He was always abrupt like that, and sometimes I appreciated it. I felt myself go numb and welcomed the lack of feeling, the absence of pain.

A raven called from the tree above; I remember being strangely fascinated, and in my thoughts, I asked, are you, my sister?

The raven's answer bloomed in my mind, "Not so much."

I laughed like I'd gone insane. Nothing in the world made sense. Nothing was right. I shook my head and accepted that madness might be slipping through.

I smoked what was left of a pack of cigarettes and watched as they processed the scene and searched for the gun. I had seen the window, and I saw the mutilated body; this was not a fucking suicide. The sheriff came out and spoke to my parents, who had not gone inside. They did not see what I saw.

It seems someone had called it in saying they heard shots fired from the road, so the Sheriff's department went in first. What bullshit! Who the hell had been driving out here? No one came out this way. We lived sandwiched between the mountains and the valley desert, and the gravel road ended a hundred yards to the south. The property, mostly dirt until the tree line, didn't have any neighbors nearby. No one ever came out here. It was like living on Mars. This seclusion appealed to my father, the endless vacuum of nothingness.

My parents would stay with friends, and I decided to stay here to erase, the best I could, what had happened. Dad was stoic the whole time the authorities spoke to him. My mom looked broken as they left. I didn't know what to say, so I said nothing.

I'm not sure why I took the job. I suppose I didn't want someone else handling what was left of Caroline, and I guess it was because I couldn't do anything else. The shock had worn off, and I felt like a manic robot with too much energy. A neighbor lady offered to help, but I couldn't stand the thought of anyone else touching the remains of my sister.

I couldn't be with my parents right now. Dad and I would get into it, and the Sheriff's department would be summoned again. Undersheriff Blackwood or some deputy had come out here a few times over the last couple of years, our only visitors, really. I'm sure he had seen the marks but never made an arrest.

Outside the broken window, the shadows were slinking down the mountain's rocky hips. My eyes trailed up along the jagged edges to their dangerous peak. I hated this place, the overwhelming darkness that seemed to radiate off the mountain. Folks here said it was a vortex of power or some such shit, and I decided it was a peddled excuse for straight-up Nordic horror movie behavior. Seriously the crime rate for the actual population was astronomical. I could count four supposed suicides, two murders, as well as a missing woman all in a year, most unexplained. It was like the mountain had a mouth that just ate them up, never to be seen again, or if they were found, they were in pieces.

We moved here when I was fifteen. My dad took a transfer for his job in the Forest Service. He played it up, all exciting, like we were going out into the wild west. Dad saw the move as an investment of sorts, called it an investment in the family. A few others lived out here, mostly hippy or cultish types who bought into the crazy idea of building a utopia. I learned later that this new age bullshit was exactly what my dad was into.

We were never the same. The tension built slowly in our home, and the closeness of family dissipated. I told my sister once after a vicious fight with him that we would never get out alive. I guess I was partly right.

I lifted the bucket, which sloshed red water all over my pants. I took it outside and emptied its contents, and went back. I set the empty bucket by the front door and kicked off my boots. Exhausted, I went into the laundry room, looking down at the handprints on the pillows. They were large, more prominent than my sister's tiny hands. I shook away the thoughts of those hands as I peeled off my clothing and stood there in my underwear, stuffing my clothes in the washer. I picked up the first of the pillows and stripped off the pillowcase throwing it into the washing machine. The other I stared at for a minute before extending my hand, noticing with a chill that the blood-stained fingertips were inches longer than my own, almost claw-like.

Something hit the window with a loud thud and slid down the glass. I gripped the pillowcase in my hand tight; I guess considering the events of the day, I was easy to scare. Blood smeared down the window, and a greasy print of feathers smudged on the glass. In my mind, I only felt partly sure it was a bird.

They never found a gun.

My sister had been torn into pieces, her brains smashed out, and it was with this information that I grabbed a baseball bat from the closet and flipped on the porch light. Biting my lip, I felt better; my fingers curled around the smooth wood. I wasn't fearless, but I was angry and lost in a strange new world where Caroline did not exist anymore. I stood for a few minutes on the threshold, feeling the cold roughness of the wood below my bare feet. The full moon looked sinister, and its effect was that it pushed that rage back down in the pit of my stomach, curdling into my knees. I suppose I was glad I could feel anything at all, considering the events of the day.

I could hear nothing in the darkness as I tiptoed down the steps barefoot. The desert mountain air was crisp, and the woods beyond, dead silent. I had never grown used to the quiet of nature here. Back home in Illinois, one could hear the cicadas and see lightning bugs amid the backdrop of suburbia. Here it was nothingness until the ears began to make up noises to fill the static air.

I paused at the bottom of the porch steps and looked around the yard, illuminated under the bright moonlight. I walked southward along the house's side, approaching the laundry room window that caught some additional yellow pooled porch light. I squatted and felt around in the sandy soil below, finding the warm carcass of a raven; its neck snapped and bleeding. I wondered why a bird had been in flight in the darkness but had no plausible answers. It could have been the light inside that had startled it into flight, but it could have been something else. And as I thought this, I peered into the yard and into the boundary of trees. I felt around in the dark for the bird with one hand, musing that it might be the same one from earlier in the day. I dropped the bat and lifted the still-warm body in my hands, feeling the feathers' rough warm oiliness. Somewhere in the back of my mind, I thought about all the dead flesh I had cupped in my hands in the last four hours. I felt sick.

In the woods something cracked, like sticks or bones being snapped underfoot. The sound reverberated across the yard in that it seemed to be coming from every direction. Alarm seized my body and I unknowingly gripped the dead bird so tight that an almost echoing snap came from my hands. I looked down, horrified, and then out into the woods, sucking in my breath, trying to remain as quiet as possible. I sunk down to the ground, all the while listening, squinting into the dark woods. I laid the bird's carcass in the dirt and took up the bat once again, lacing my fingers around its taped base.

I stood up, trying to not breathe. Whoever or whatever it was would only see a girl in her wife-beater t-shirt and underwear with a bat. It was not lost on me that I was fulfilling every female character in slasher films. Any other time and I would be yelling at the TV, "Run, girl!"

I didn't run; I waited.

I wanted to hear a growl or some killer from the woods heavy breathing, Jason style. I searched for tangible things like the dead raven at my feet. I wanted validation of my sister's death. I wanted to know what had frightened the bird into its death flight and speculated the same thing may have happened to Caroline.

I strained my eyes, trying to see through the under-shadows of the pinyon and crowded cottonwood. Nothing moved in those woods. No one or thing crept around the misshapen trunks and tangle of cactus, sage, and goat head.

The sound came again, causing me to lean forward. I swung the bat twice, letting whatever it was know I meant business.

Seconds ticked, and then as if to break the tension on purpose, a mule deer came careening from the trees and darted across the yard. The pressure in my body melted, and I laughed. It was just a bird hitting the window, a deer frightened by the porch lights.

I lowered the bat deciding that my mind was playing tricks. I climbed the steps and retreated inside, flicking on every light and turned on some loud music. My nerves were fried.

Satisfied that I had muffled my senses with light and music, I went to the kitchen. I searched for some food, finally settling on a bowl of cereal, scooping up mouthfuls with blood-stained hands, too exhausted to wash them. The kitchen was the only normal room in the house, clean dishes on the counter, my sister's homework in a neat stack on the table with her bag. I kept chewing, holding my spoon like a wand wishing the players back into the room.

My phone rang; I checked the screen, it read Steven.

"Yeah, Dad?" I said

"Where are you?" his voice asked, ugly, angry.

"At the house."

"What the fuck, Casey? I mean, seriously, what the hell are you doing?"

His voice was rough, his language the only language of love I knew from the man since we came under the mountain shadow.

I hated the sound of my name in his mouth.

"Cleaning up."

Silence, like my dad was gathering up his words, you know, to make them count.

"I can't even deal with your bullshit right now. Your mom is a mess, waiting for her only daughter to get here." He hissed loud into the phone, causing me to hold it away and then set it on the counter.

I wondered if he was getting some sick pleasure from saying, "only daughter."

"I think you got that covered, Pops!" I yelled back.

"I can't believe you—fucking god damn it!"

The phone went dead.

If he had been standing there, he might have slapped me or, at the very least, put his fist through a wall. I leaned against the counter, glad he wasn't there. I wasn't sure what I was doing, but I knew it was for Caroline and my mom, not him, never him.

I finished the cereal and retrieved my bucket from beside the front door, started the washing machine before heading back to the bedroom. I stood in the doorway and looked on the bed where a pile of flesh, bits of my sister's long hair attached to skull fragments, and a single eyeball missed by the cops lay upon the now-soaked newspaper.

The cereal in my stomach lurched. Is this how one gets used to blood, to death? The eye was intact with some strings attached, open forever. I swallowed hard, bending over, willing myself not to vomit.

All I had left of her.

I scrubbed another hour and filled another bucket. I scratched at an itchy spot of dried blood on my face. I think this was my way of loving my sister, caring for every bit of her. Sometimes I cried during that hour, but mostly I set to work, my heart detached, broken. I scrubbed until my raw hands lent blood to my sister's. I added to the pile of flesh as I crunched on my knees through glass and blood.

I will never see you again.

I picked up the bucket by the handle and lugged it to the door. I retrieved the baseball bat and then, with hands full, tottered out to the tree where I emptied the liquid adding to the massive stain of blood that pooled at its gnarled base. I was offering a sacrifice to the twisted roots of the tree. I think Caroline would have done the same if it had been me; we both had somewhat gothic notions of the woods.

I turned back to the house and crossed the yard taking the rough wooden steps two at a time to the door. Behind me, I heard snapping branches again. I froze with my hand on the door handle. I could have sworn I heard a sound like something slurping. Like something was drinking the liquid I had just poured beneath the tree. I stiffened, not wanting to turn my eyes from the lit-up interior of the house. The sound was real enough, and I fought the feeling of wanting to run inside. I forced myself into a slow turn towards the woods.

Huge antlers bobbed above the brush, arching upwards. The antlers were more magnificent than any deer I'd ever seen. Without thinking, I dropped the bucket; its plastic bottom popped loudly. The antlers stopped moving, and the thing raised its head.

The head was human-looking with thin skin that clung to the skull. A long tongue rolled up from the blood puddle and into a mouth full of impossible spiky teeth. The thing straightened, rising like a nightmare, naked, to a height of six feet at its skull. Patches of elk-like fur covered its body, exposing in some places yellowed chicken pimpled skin.

Something very wrong had come down off the mountain.

There was no gun, never a gun.

Black shiny eyes reflected in the porch light, jaws closed, flexing with grotesque musculature. Taut muscles tensed like cords throughout its long limbs. Its snout sniffed the air arching its neck and head; the antlers extended back, dark and velvety. It lifted its longs arms that were so disfigured, almost disjointed. The pale bonelike hands flexed. It snuffed the air loudly, the long tongue rolling in and out.

The creature took a few hesitant steps into the lightened yard, out of the tree line. Its hip bones stuck out in sharp angles as it walked with a splayed shuffle on huge cloven feet. Each movement of the thing seemed puppet like with audible creaks and pops.

I just stood there; the vision of the thing was so improbable that I questioned my own sanity. For a minute, I considered it might be one of the crazy mountain locals who dressed up as Pan daily, as if Halloween were a lifestyle, but it barely resembled a man.

It moved forward, still sniffing the air, its claw-like fingers twirling. It tilted its head as if blind or solely reliant on its ability to smell. A low grunting emitted from the creature followed by a bugling sound like an elk makes during mating season. The hollow reed sound was warbly, building in pitch, rattling my teeth. It was the kind of sound that squeezes your chest like a heart attack.

My hands shook so much that the door handle rattled as I wrenched it open. I swiveled on my bare feet and grasped the handle, pulling hard to shut it, securing the deadbolt. Stumbling backward, I kept my eyes on the door expecting it to be ripped from the hinges. I reached for my boots and quickly pulled them on, the leather stiff on my bare feet.

A clicking, snuffing sound came from outside, followed by a piercing whistling—a loud thud and with it the sound of wood cracking.

I swiped my phone from the counter and tried to dial 911, hands shaking so bad it dropped.

The door shattered, throwing splinters across the room. I stumbled back, catching my hip on the kitchen counter.

The creature screamed, thrashing its body to squeeze its massive form through the opening. Its horrible head raised up, emitting more of the ear-splitting grunts and squeals. Its mouth was full of needle-like teeth, and its eyes bulged out of its skull in rage.

I reached behind me, desperately trying to feel for the knife drawer. I pulled one open and realized my mother had done some reorganizing and all that was in the drawer was spoons, forks, and butter knives. Panicked, I fumbled for the next drawer and was rewarded with blades of all kinds. I wrapped my finger around the first knife and threw, missing the creature entirely. I began throwing the knives as fast as I could catch them up in my hands. I was a poor shot; my throws missed the creature, hitting the blood-stained antique loveseat near the door or skidding harmlessly across the floor. One finally popped it in the chest, but it might as well have been a paper cut. The thing just continued towards me.

I took off down the hall; behind me, its steps resounded with a thud. I skidded through glass and blood, trying to shut the door behind me, but I knew that it wouldn't hold. Getting the door closed, I glanced at the pile of sister meat in the newspaper.

Quickly I asked my sister's forgiveness as I placed it just inside of the door. I kicked out the last of the glass in the window and climbed over the sill, dropping to the ground. I couldn't help my morbid curiosity and pulled myself up to the lip of the window. I wanted to watch what killed my sister.

The door creaked open slowly, not at all what I expected. The creature sniffed the air rolling its tongue in and out of its gash-like mouth. It bellowed again and grunted in guttural tones, then lowered its head in a long arc to the fleshy bits I had left. I watched its tongue roll out over the jagged teeth flicking the meat back into its mouth.

It was hungry.

I felt sick and strangely disassociated, as if everything were happening to someone else. Nothing, not my dead sister, nor this thing eating her remains felt real. Its tongue dropped again, made a sucking noise, and then rolled back up. It stomped its feet in the blood, trying to stir up more bits of meat. I bit my own tongue until it was bleeding, trying to force my eyes away from the thing.

Turning, I ran for the woods. I knew the trails in the dark of night, and even as I stepped from the boundary of light into that of the tangled forest, I felt hopelessness fall over me. I knew it would come. I heard it behind me, still in the house, as it bugled with a voice that was not quite human nor animal. It seemed to use its sense of smell, and right now, I smelled of sweat and blood.

I headed south, ignoring the cactus that cut at my legs and rocks that seemed to be out to sabotage me in the dark. Behind, I could hear the thing crashing through the house. There was nothing this far out in the land grant, only a hunter's cabin that was at least a half-mile away.

I wasn't mountain girl enough to carry a knife. In the dark, my boot caught on something and threw me headlong into the brush. Pain exploded in my head, and I felt blood gushing from my nose. Stunned, I pushed up on all fours and grabbed a nearby tree to drag myself up. I tasted blood and wiped it with the back of my hand.

I ran, limping, blood dripping from my nose into my mouth, in the direction of Half Moon Creek. I heard the angry stream long before I saw it. I tried searching for the log bridge that my sister and I had made in the early days, but it must have been swept away.

I had no other choice but to wade in hoping I could keep my footing even though I was dizzy and nauseous. The water would be ice cold, but the thing behind me would only give searing pain.

I slipped into the creek; the current pulled with icy fingers. The loud rush of the water obliterated the calls of the creature. The arctic cold tore the air from my chest.

My body numbed quickly in the rushing water. The slippery rocks were hard to navigate, and I lost my footing plunging underneath. In the darkness of the water, I choked, the cold water filling my lungs. I reached out, trying to grab hold of anything in the water; everything I grabbed was cold and slick. I couldn't discern direction; my arms flailed, trying to find something to cling to. Rocks underneath the water slammed into me as I tumbled with the flow. My strength faltered as the water shoved me into a crevice between two rocks. I pushed up my head, breaking the surface. Sucking in big gulps of air, I choked back a cough and forced my ears to listen.

I clamored out, pulling my battered body up over rocks. I didn't know how far the water had taken me. I clawed my way onto the dry bank, gasping for breath. I felt dizzy as I reached to explore my battered face. Turning to my side, I pushed up onto my knees, wondering if I could stand. Blood filled my mouth, and I spat, trying to combat the continued feeling of being waterboarded. I looked across the rushing water, closed my eyes, and looked again.

The moon cascaded in a strange slant of light, and from the darkness of the trees, a figure walked forward. I could see long limbs swinging, reaching out. Expecting the creature, I felt terror building and tried to command my body to move. I tried to stand, but my knees gave out. I dug in my heels and attempted to scoot my body farther from the bank.

"Casey?" a voice that warbled across the water asked.

My heels froze, motion suspended with recognition of that voice.

Caroline stood on the far bank. My dead sister ghostly in a torn nightgown; her arms were ripped away and replaced by aspen branches. Blood oozed from her shoulders, trailing down the white bark. I blinked and blinked again, rubbing my eyes, unbelieving. I reached out—then snapped back my hands. She was dead.

"Casey," she sang. "He's coming." She laughed, blood coming from her mangled twig stumps.

"Caroline!" I screamed over the creek, a mix of horror and question.

Her figure was luminous under the full moon, moving like a witch's poppet hung from a tree by the neck. She walked in a circle, swinging her branch arms bird-like in large circles. The top half of her face ripped away.

I sobbed, digging my heels, reaching my hands back to pull myself further into the trees at my back.

Caroline stopped her crazy movements, looking at me, tilting her mutilated face and sweeping a branched arm across her mouth.

"Shhhh, sometimes they eat their own," she said, still in singsong.

"Who are you talking about?" I cried, my voice snapping.

"You're dead," I whispered to myself, then whimpered it again like a mantra.

"You're dead."

She sunk to her knees on the opposite bank, digging the twig-like arms into the wet earth. Behind her, I heard the creature howling and grunting.

It was coming!

"Oh, Papa is back there. Just howling, isn't he?" She arched her back and head backward in an impossible angle, laughing.

"Not real! You're not real!" I yelled at her.

"You see," Caroline hissed like the last breath of the dead, "he promised us to the mountain, and she said yesssss." The previous consonant turning into a screeching note even as her wispy shape glitched.

I wrapped my arms around my knees, burying my face, trying to block her ghostly image out. I wanted to tell myself that she was not real, not there, even as I unwillingly participated in necromancy. I felt my brain jam up with the implications. I know what I had been cleaning up in the house; I had touched her eviscerated bits and watched the body bag being taken away on the gurney.

I flicked my eyes to the apparition of Caroline standing erect, her face twisting into a reflection of my own emotions, her mouth opening into a silent scream. Her wraith turned and dissolved into the trees.

That thing could not be her.

It could not be my Caroline dancing with Titus Andronicus arms.

I sat there, rocking, attempting to warm my frozen body, failing to hold it together. What my senses were feeding me was the prelude to a psychotic break. The last remnants of logic told me that everything aside from Caroline's death was a hallucination brought on by the trauma. People generally don't see what I had experienced; people don't clean up their sister's body parts. My brain had to be trashed. Anything at this point was possible. I should have got into my car and drove home to Alamosa, grieving in the safe walls of my dorm.

I heard the elk-like wail filtering between the trees in an excruciating drone. I rocked harder, trying to cover my ears again with my arms. The grunting scream came wave-like even as it drew closer. I wanted it to stop. I wanted everything to stop.

I suppose my desperation won out because I was standing up on weak legs, wading back into the creek towards the house before I could change my mind. The icy fingers of the stream tapped at my chest, drawing out a painful breath. I pulled myself from the swirling water and clamored up the bank.

Somewhere out in the dark, I heard the snuffing of the creature. I bit my lip hard to keep myself from screaming, low crawling to an enormous cottonwood where I could hide in its thick, twisted roots. I scooped up handfuls of leaves and rubbed dirt on my wet body, dulling the whiteness of my skin. I bent my frame against the bark of the tree, my heart hammering. I held my breath, not sure what my next move would be.

A screeching, reedy sound built into an almost organ-like drone behind where I hid. I shifted my head, trying to see anything under the thick canopy of the trees. An ear-splitting whistling sounded again, only this time closer.

I hunched down, trying to become small and invisible. The cloven hoofs cracked the underbrush as it moved closer. A smell of damp musky fur invaded my nose.

I turned my head in the direction of the thing, biting my lips shut, tasting blood. I gripped the stick closer to my side, knowing it was inadequate protection. Thankfully the moon's light did not slant into the dark roots where I crouched.

The thing clomped out of the shadows. Its horrible form seemed as if it had walked out of a bloody Russian fairy tale. It came closer, moving its antlers side to side, sniffing the air in search of me. Its skin showed various layers of decomposition like a downed elk on the mountain after days of exposure to the elements.

It arched its head upwards as if speaking to the mountain, the antlers curving back, almost touching the ground. The clouds cleared the moon, sending a shard of light down on the creature. It scraped the ground with long arms, causing my eyes to snap back. The creature dipped its head, extending its arms for balance. The powerful muscles rippled, and the moon caught the puckered skin of its upper arm. I could see something there, like letters, ink-like. It was faint and stretched but clearly the outline of a tattoo. The tattoo was only words, but they were words that I knew all too well; my name and my sister's.

My stomach lurched, and I swallowed hard. My heart felt like it might burst. I didn't think, launching myself from my hiding place running. I felt the monster behind me, its loud wailing growing closer and closer. Snapping jaws clicked with hot breath on my neck. Claws reached, grabbing at my shirt, ripping through, slicing downwards along my back. Searing pain made my feet falter. I fell as parts of my back came away in the monstrous claws. I hit the ground hard but tried to crawl away. Tremendous weight flattened me to the ground. With my hands, I tried to pull myself out from underneath. Snapping jaws were at my ear and then lowered, cradled between my head and shoulder. Slowly its claws dug into the meat of my arms, pinning me. I could feel its hot breath putrid with rot on my neck. I lifted my head, attempting to look straight forward, waiting for the teeth and tongue to wrap around my neck.

Bare dirty feet and branch-like arms stepped out of the dark. The creature lifted its head and began its bugling, the noise shattering my ears. Caroline stepped closer until I could see her half-ripped face.

Caroline reached out, gently touching the creature's face above me. It screamed as if in pain and lurched off me, jerking my arms as it rolled.

I scraped forward on my elbows and pushed my body upwards. I couldn't stop my momentum and rushed headlong into the apparition of my sister. My sister's body resisted, then popped like a membrane, her physical body disintegrating like mist and the branches clattering to the ground. I stumbled but kept my footing running headlong for home.

I ran, feeling the wet skin of my back flapping where the thing had laid it open. The thing was at my heels, reaching out its long-clawed hands. I ran towards the porch lights with one plan and locked my eyes on the woodpile at the western edge of the house.

I dove into the pile reaching for where my dad usually left the ax. It wasn't there. Frantically I plunged my hands around the chopping block, finally touching the rough handle. I barely got it to my side before the creature rushed me, its mouth wide with teeth. I swung hard and felt the edge sink into its maw.

The creature let out a wailing bugle that morphed into the scream of a man. It lunged again with tremendous strength, taking me down in its claws. I kicked and screamed, rolling inches away. Crawling, I searched for the ax in the dirt. The creature grabbed my booted foot and pulled.

My desperate fingers touched the end of the ax handle; I stretched, finally grasping and pulling it to me. The creature bit down on my boot, and I felt teeth penetrating the leather. I kicked with my other foot swinging the ax around my head, trying to land it in the flesh of the creature. The ax bounced harmlessly off one of the antlers, jarring my elbows.

The creature bellowed, drew back, shaking its head.

I pulled on the ax and twisted to my side, getting a knee under me for more leverage. I swung upward, catching the creature, the edge bit deep under the jaw, following upwards into the ear and head.

It screamed in the voice of a man as it went down, pulling me with it, my hands still wrapped around the wooden handle. We hit the ground hard, and I let go of the handle, rolling.

"Casey?"

I forced my eyes open; the creature spoke with my dad's voice. I pushed my battered body up and crawled to the beast. The antlers caught in the ground suspending the hideous head in the air. The ax head buried deep in its skull, the handle arching out like a long straight horn.

"Can you see her yet?" he said in gasping breaths.

"Caroline?" I asked, not understanding him.

"No. The mountain," he said, eyes weeping blood.

I felt his faint heartbeat beneath my palms. I trailed my fingers down over the fur and skin, tracing our names on his arm. I said our names out loud.

[9]

In 1975 you were called out to Spanish Creek. A child was found at a trail head abandoned in a car. When you arrived and saw the vehicle parked at Moon Rock Trail, you felt it wouldn't be a child welfare case. You walked around the old Ford Pinto. There were scratch marks on the metal body, scraping signs in the dirt. Someone had fought hard, and blood sprayed up the base of a tree—carnage without a body.

An older couple out on a day hike came across the car. They hiked back into town and rode in the patrol car to show you the location. In the backseat, the woman held the young, brown child in her arms as if shielding the two-year-old from the horror outside. The man climbed out, standing close to you.

"Where are they?" the man asked.

"What makes you say they?" you ask, still assessing what may have happened.

The man looks at you, his face gray, "Why the shoes in the driver and passenger seat."

You nod and tell him to stay put.

You walk closer and pop the passenger door open. A pair of women's sandals lay on the floor, waiting for the return of the owner. It was the same for the driver's side with size ten men's boots, one on the floor and one still leaning against the brake.

"Musta been Indians or the Spanish with the kid being so dark," you hear the man say behind you. "Figures they would dump their kid."

You're irritated but say nothing. The kid would go to an institution on the front range, and this couple would go back to their home with the feeling that they did their Christian duty.

The license plates read Colorado but other than that, nothing.

You revisit the scene over and over, but they, like so many, are never found. Like the mountain just swallowed them down whole.

The mountains now are fading from red to dark slate. The first stars glimmer over the sharp edges, your hand still clasps the barrel of the gun.

WILLIAM ZUNI

We all have our baggage, some carry it around, I bury mine. It only takes a couple of hours to dig a few feet down in an outta-the-way place and throw the body in. I fill the hole and then make a rock arrangement that lends to a medicine wheel fabrication, the reason being that folks in this area follow superstition and look but never touch. Sometimes on the trail coming down out of the mountains I can't help smiling to myself as Anglo hippies dance, tripping balls, just outside the perimeter, believing they are in a sacred place when in reality they are worshiping at the mounds of past mistakes rectified.

I don't consider myself a murderer, it's merely a partitioned way of dealing out absolutions. Anyone I put in the dirt, practically begged to be there. Well not directly. You know how lips lie, but actions are telling.

Today I hunted a baker, not an actual baker who has a business that can be traced. No, this baker only left a French azure plate behind. Funny, the Sheriff's department even offered a lesser sentence if the guilty came forward, but no one did.

Imagine if you will, a potluck spread out across rough-hewed tables community style. Then imagine ten children dropping dead to the ground, flies buzzing on their lips, partaking of the sticky sweetness. The killer was no Jim Jones, but that was the thing about this town and the surrounding mountains, no one felt they were guilty. No one except me.

The mountain tells me things, gives me direction. It is into her embrace that I deliver the goods, she seems to appreciate the feeding, and I feed her often. Sometimes I feel that I am reincarnated, not in the hippy sense but in the theme of one who seeks out the sinful flesh for feeding. If they don't get right, then I make it right.

I spoke to some locals who all had varying opinions, most so fucked up in their thoughts that their words nearly folded over into one another in contradiction. Within those folds I cut out the truth, those tiny details missed.

That's what happens in a small town, but here it was more mixed up with their appropriated beliefs and religions.

They called it an accident, but here more than any other place there are no accidents. In fact, these people lived on their intentions and even stated them loud upon soapboxes that might sound like a farce 2000 feet lower in elevation. In some ways, it might be the elevation that imbued the beliefs that coagulated here. The air was thinner, and for me personally, I could feel the heartbeat of the mountain. Others sensed it but not in the same way I did, a profound feeling like bees that resided in my head, or the scintillating sound of the hummingbird.

I pushed open the door of the local coffee shop, a strange place where Buddhist monks and the New-Age inclined had polite debates on the afterlife and aliens. A white girl with dreads piled on her head led me to a table with a mosaic of dragonflies and iron. I took a seat, ordering a coffee I wouldn't touch, and sat back with my eyes fixed into mere slits. To onlookers, I would appear to be meditating. I was hunting.

I feel I should elaborate on my relationship with the mountain, after all, it sounds crazy, I suppose. I am not insane nor am I given to flights of fancy. In the world, I appear regular enough, but all her best hunters do. I have never met any of my predecessors, but I know there have been some before me. I know from old journals and newspapers going back to the 1870s. I suppose the others would have different tales, but mine is simple, I died for a moment.

Around 2012, I arrived here in the valley and explored the few towns eventually making my way up the mountain to this place, a mecca for the lost and misunderstood. My parents had disappeared here under mysterious circumstances when I was a toddler.

The community embraced me quickly enough, mostly because of my native look. I was half Native American but having never known my parents I also never knew my tribe. The townies didn't care, merely having me around lent to the authentic esthetic they desired in the ceremony. I took on the name Zuni, the first that came to mind. No one thought it was strange and most even seemed to like to roll that name around in their mouth.

The town was big on alternative tourism especially during the summer. I attended many rituals I must admit, as it was the perfect place for information and the hunt. I just sat there silent like a medicine man while they vomited in buckets, hallucinating ancestors that were not theirs. I figured the free booze, marijuana, and sex if I wanted it, was reason enough to be their Indian. Sometimes it paid off in information or my prey who were all too happy to go on a hike with the "sacred one" after a night of illumination from ayahuasca.

I loved the mountains. I felt more at home the higher I went as if a connection was formed with each step. I thought on this a lot, wondering if it was because my past was a locked door that could never be opened.

It was on one of these hikes that I misjudged a trail that was unstable after the monsoon rains. I was told that I fell 100 feet down the side. I was also told I was unconscious for hours, but I wasn't. Something happened that reshaped me, my blood pooling out of my head. The mountain felt my blood soaking into her spongy sides and fabricated a thread of connection as if her tongue sucked and tasted, deciding it was good. I remember being pulled down out of my body through the layers of rock, soil, and root. I could not see her, but her voice as she spoke to me was a terribly beautiful thing, filling me with awe and trembling. In pictures I saw the bloody work required, she had a refined taste and desired those who truly belonged in her belly. I also knew that there were no choices here. Truth be told there was no contrary thought in me, she felt more real than a ghost of a mother. She was the mother.

The coffee came hot and steaming.

Next to me two men spoke in hushed tones, one looked too suburban to be here and the other almost homeless.

"He wants it kept quiet," the homeless one said, his eyes twitching.

"He needs to turn himself in," the well-dressed one added, pressing, "It wasn't medicine, it was a massacre."

"He was trying to spread the love, not kill anybody."

The suburban one seemed to be barely keeping his anger under wraps.

"Besides if he comes forward, the whole church will go down, and you know what that will mean for this town," the homeless-looking one said, shifting in his seat which sent sickening odors of weeks-old sweat and oils wafting in my direction.

I knew the well-dressed one to be Nathan, a member of the town board who hoped to be mayor, the other was known only as Old Bill. I wasn't interested in Nathan, he would be an interest later, nor was I interested in Old Bill.

What I was interested in was the connection. That connection was to the Sacred Buffalo Circle, a supposed Native American church that had nary a native member—all Anglos. There were no words in my language to describe my revulsion for them, but as I had said before, sometimes on the hunt I attended as the token Indian. It was sickening how much they kissed my ass when I visited. The ceremony was an appropriated mix of storybook ritual borrowed from plains Indian, Celtic, and voodoo. I would sit and plan each death and pray the mountain would allow me this honor in my lifetime.

The men seemed to notice me after a bit and nodded in my direction. I nodded back. They didn't expect anything more. I was known for keeping to myself. The community thought I was stoic, but I just fucking hated them all. The men didn't need to say anything more; I knew where to find my baker.

I got up, leaving the coffee. I stopped the blond hippy princess and told her I didn't ask for milk, leaving her looking irritated and less than loved. I headed to my truck. My wolf dog, Ogma was waiting in the back, only getting up to see it was me before laying back down in the truck bed. I'd had fun choosing her name, I decided to appropriate an Anglo name of some god of Irish poetry, fish or something, the assholes didn't even realize it, thinking it was some tribal power word. Some thought she was sacred, which wasn't all wrong, the mountain gave her to me for the hunt, and she liked human blood.

We drove out on the pavement that took visitors to the ritzier holy places, like a mall of various religions and then turned, heading out on gravel roads. The drive zigzagged through prickly pear, sage, and yucca. The valley floor, beautiful in its own way, seemed to say; do not walk here. I spent a lot of time here and even slept beneath the stars on occasion, but it was not a preferred place as the mountain heartbeat became hushed here among the thorns.

Ahead a trashy mix of tepees, tiny homes, and a larger building came into view. The larger building was half a church and half the home/harem of its leader, Thomas Loskva, who was, in truth, Russian. He had five kids with his three wives who all dutifully saw to the internal workings of the little compound. I was usually welcome with some suspicion by the leader. It wasn't that Thomas knew what I was, it was envy for my ancestry and his belief that I would replace him if given a chance that made him keep a long distance. Thomas named the non-profit the Native Church of the Sacred

Buffalo Circle. As I drove in, I thought about how quickly the canvas teepees would burn.

I pulled into the drive kicking up significant plumes of dust and parked. They were armed, so I always thought it best to sit a bit until they came out to welcome me. Militant hippy types were tricky in that they didn't plan on what to shoot at; they reacted to everything like true born sociopaths, a shoot-on-a-whim sort of way. They never practiced with their guns or hunted, most of these folks being vegetarians, and I saw a danger in that.

I rolled a cigarette and lit it watching lazy smoke rise and curl out of the truck window. The turquoise sky was without clouds, and the sun was blazing down heating the cab as I waited. Finally, a door to the building opened and Willow, his youngest wife, came out. Her unnaturally red hair was piled on her head. She dressed like the rest of'em in town in Renaissance getup and a long hemp skirt. Her belly protruded outward; I had heard two of his wives were expecting around the same time. Thomas was a busy man.

She smiled as she came to the window, without a word I handed her my smoke. She leaned against the door letting out a smoky sigh.

"God. Thank you I needed a smoke. Thomas took the truck, so we can't get into town."

Not here, I thought.

"How are you Zuni?" Willow asked stepping back as I opened the door. I stepped out slowly and leaned against the truck with her. She glanced at me under thick lashes reddening from rounded cheeks to the curve of her breasts.

"I can't complain. I wanted to speak to Thomas."

She blew out a plume of smoke while she rubbed her belly. "He went up to the mountain taking some soul seekers on ceremony. I wish I could have gone, but he said it would be hard on the baby."

"Ah," I said. "I agree with Thomas. It's no good."

She laughed, her face almost pretty in action. "Zuni you talk so Indian."

I let this pass as she was young and stupid; she had become a wife at sixteen and never finished school. On top of that, she had endured two years of being told what to think and do which rendered her an inconsequence.

"Which spot did they go to?" I asked, letting a smooth smile over my lips.

"Oh, you know, the alien rocks with the vortex," she said singsong like.

It was all I could do not to laugh. The alien rocks were known as a spot for orgies and plant-based drugs, supposedly sacred due to aliens visiting a townie almost twenty years ago. The vortex allusion was their childlike way to explain the mountain. This information could not make me happier as it seemed my baker was ready for me at the entrance of the oven.

"Ya wanna come in for some kombucha?" she asked in the most innocent tone she dared.

I looked at her still smiling. I had gone in for kombucha before, it was like entering the most tapestry-laden harem in the country. Where the women lived could be described as one never-ending bed, and since Thomas was gone a lot, they took advantage of those who visited. It was mostly out of boredom, but also the freewheeling culture of the place. I could attest that the kombucha was more than that, and enough to make any man or woman forget where they were for hours. I was initially surprised that Thomas didn't get upset, maybe he did, I was never sure, nor did I care.

"Why thank you, Willow, but no, Ogma and I have an appointment around sunset." Disappointment crossed her face before being replaced by a robotic smile.

"Alright, promise you will come over soon. We gotta catch up," she said taking the cigarette with her, walking away. She paused about halfway to the door, turned and waved, then went inside.

I shook my head and got back in the truck. The women here were strange contradictions, on the one hand all about female power which they referred to as juiciness. The other side was an acceptance of the patriarchy in as much as they saw themselves as goddesses, they worshiped the men as gods. They were in opposition of the goddess I worshiped.

I drove to the trailhead, not bothering to hide my truck, most townies expected to see it parked up here. I checked my pack and let Ogma out, who proceeded to dive into the pinyon. I rolled a smoke, lit it, and let my eyes rove the mountainside. Most people would look and see nothing out of the ordinary, but I was not ordinary.

The thinnest trail of smoke, about four miles tall, spooled upward, right where I expected it. I thought about the others that were on some sort of Anglo vision quest. At least they would be out of their minds from fasting. I hoped that they would be fucked up on peyote or something by the time I got to a visual location.

I began the hike just off the trail, the mosquitos were thick clouds but didn't seem to notice me. Ogma joined me from time to time, and if there were others on the trail, her wolf-like features would send them back down to the parking lot. I think she kinda enjoyed scaring the Denverites on the path; I guess I took pleasure in it too. The sun was hot, blazing beams upon my head as I walked at a slow, leisurely pace. I was not in a hurry as my work would not start until after sundown. I felt almost joyful with the mountain heartbeat thumping below my boots.

I thought about the coming moments wishing I had baked a cake for the occasion. I would have liked serving it to Thomas, but it wouldn't be enough…she wanted blood.

The mountain watched everything. Some could have said that I was born of her watchful eye. My parents disappeared here. Her thighs contained the mine shafts in which bodies were thrown, almost all women and children and I suspected my father as well. The decade didn't matter, men were sinning just the same for uncountable years. When it was only a mining town a century ago, they used up the women and then they just disappeared, the same happens now, and the local Sheriff's department is cockblocked by the transient nature and secretive culture of the town.

I had many conversations with Sheriff Blackwood and Deputy Lawson on the subject. That is until Lawson went crazy and fell down a mine shaft. I rarely saw Blackwood now and when I did, he just looked broken.

I kept a low profile. I figured that this is how no one ever suspected me. Others before had been caught and hanged or imprisoned, but I was a shadow here blending in until I had no desire to do so. I wasn't an avenging angel. I was her son doing the only thing I felt compelled to do.

I took the trail slow following the arc of the sun. The creek was swollen with snowmelt, loud and angry. Since I had the benefit of knowing where they would be, I took a path that switchbacked to a cliff overlook. This jutted-out rock afforded me a view down to the alien rocks, as the Anglos called it.

I would like to say I was surprised by what I observed, but I wasn't.

Below were rocks that had been tumbled then moved by men like Thomas. They stood in triangles of three, about seven in number, and within each was a naked person reclined. It was evident that they were, as I expected, tripping, some reaching out to things only they could see. A vat of something, probably ayahuasca, bubbled over a small fire. Thomas moved from one to the other, especially paying attention to the two women of the group. I'm not sure if they had been sober that they would have allowed the ways he was touching them. He was almost naked except for a loin cloth making his white skin contrast in an almost embarrassing way with the dark greens around him. I could hear him chanting gibberish. I supposed it was his rendition of Indian speak. If he didn't look so stupid, I might have been more upset.

Ogma appeared at my side a little bloody around her snout, I figured she had made a kill or two.

"Well, friend, how shall we do it?" I asked her.

She just tilted her head looking up at me, then turned around three times and curled up to rest. I think she sensed the hunt was coming, and she wanted to be ready.

I didn't want all of them, and neither did the mountain. The mountain wanted the sinners guilty of acts against nature, against women, children, and those who, under the guise of spirituality, preyed upon others.

Patience was a virtue given by the mountain so I figured I would just wait. The perfect moment would come—it always did.

I laid down beside my dog and drifted off for a bit while the sun sailed west in the sky.

When my eyes opened it was dark, the dancing light of flames from a considerable fire below illuminated the clearing. They were engaged in serpentine movement now, still naked, some were beating bongos, and others were playing the flute. A few chanted loudly in their new possession of a fake native tongue. Apparently, on nature drugs, you could crawl into the skin you wanted…fuckers.

I didn't see Thomas, so I dug out my binoculars and took a closer look, counting, and finding one of the women was missing. My best guess was that he was out beyond the perimeter fucking her. I reset my pack and moved slow and silent down the cliff. The thing about fire is that you can see within the circle of its light but not so good beyond, this rendered the dancers blind. Add to that my particular features and dark hair, well I figured if they did see me, they would probably think I was the long-lost ancestor the genetic test said there was a 0.1 percent chance of there being. They didn't see me though and just went on with their soul seeking madness.

I knew the area well, having hunted here a time or two. I knew that the trail led to a smaller, more private clearing and it would be there I would find Thomas. The moon rose over the mountain illuminating the area. And I could see two white bodies in the distance. I stopped when the light glinted off the cold steel of a dagger held aloft in Thomas's hand. It was then that I realized the woman was not moving. The mountain must have already invaded his mind.

Thomas was moving his arms up and down over the woman. I wasn't afraid and deep inside I felt the movement of the mountain telling me that it was time. No sound came from my mouth as I took in the singular sight of Thomas cutting off the woman's flesh and eating it raw. He chewed with slurping sounds, swallowed then sunk his hands back into her body.

"So, you're not only a baker, but you're also a butcher too?" I said, evenly cutting the night's silence.

Thomas looked up. His face and body covered in blood. His eyes were crazy as I clicked on my flashlight. I traced the ground and saw the body was in several pieces, but close together, and that is why I hadn't understood sooner.

He threw his arms over his eyes, "Zuni?" He dropped his arms and shoved his bloody hands behind his back.

"It's a sacrifice Zuni!"

I didn't say anything, part of me wanted to kill him right there for that statement.

Thomas started to weave his upper body from the hips closing his eyes and started in with his gibberish chanting.

"What are you sacrificing for?" I decided to play along a bit.

"Uh well, those kids that were hurt."

"Dead you mean."

"Uh right. If they catch me, man, our church will be lost."

Thomas crawled over the body and towards me, his hands pleading.

"Tell me, was it an accident?" I asked.

Thomas pushed himself up rocking on the heels of his feet wrapping his bloodied arms around himself.

"Well yes and no. I mean people were jumping camp, and I needed some control, brother."

"I see."

"Not dead…I mean they weren't supposed to die."

"Well, friend, they are dead," I said, smiling.

He nodded and began chanting again. I had wanted a more complex interaction, but have you ever tried to talk to someone on ayahuasca? I mean his eyes were crazy I'm pretty sure he thought I was a spirit guide or something.

I looked down at the carved-up body. I recognized the woman. She was a tribal dancer in town. I knew her cause I had hooked up with her a time or two. She had partaken of the ritual many times, seeking clarity on her life drama. I am pretty sure she never pictured this in her drug-addled mind. Her tongue hung grotesquely from her mouth; her neck half hacked away. I knew they sacrificed dogs and such but hadn't thought anyone had the balls for this. I was almost impressed and wondered if the mountain had permeated his mind like my own.

Ogma bounded into the clearing muscles taut, hair spiky. This was the final ascent to my purpose here. I began to feel the change overcoming me, though I had no way to see the fullness of the change. My nails lengthened and fresh teeth erupted from my gums. I felt ligaments exploding and my form elongating. I shucked my boots off in a hurry as my feet began to painfully enlarge in stiff leather. Thomas's face shifted as I watched the blood lust drain out, replaced by the desired result of fear. I could smell that fear like pungent rotten meat, and I wanted that meat with a hunger that tore through my body in excruciating need.

"Run!" I said in a half growl.

I held back with all my might, moving just enough so he could not run to the fire, only higher up the mountain. Thomas hesitated, and his bladder let loose, he was shaking.

"Run!" This time I shouted, and Thomas took off up the trail.

I waited as my body continued its metamorphosis. My goddess changed me with her power and bloodlust. This was not to say I was suddenly a freak animal or a werewolf. No, I was still me only better, faster and with ungodly strength and a damn overwhelming hunger. They say we are immortal; I have my doubts about that, but I enjoyed the feeling of letting go.

Ogma bounded off ahead of me.

I howled, the sound reverberating along the side of the mountain. I wondered if the dancers heard it, then I laughed with my maniacal, enlarged mouth. They were so drugged up, that in the morning each of them would think they had butchered the woman and done God knows what to their shaman.

I threw vocalizations against the mountain in the voice of his wife, "Thomas, oh Thomas, where are you?"

I took off on the hunt. Thomas might be an idiot according to my reckoning, but he was at home in the woods, and in this particular area he was king. Ogma stopped, sniffing the ground then bounded to the left near to the creek. Thomas thought to hide within the sound of the stream and the smells it threw, to hide his trail. A mistake—Thomas did not know what I was. I was driven to madness with the savory odor of blood and piss. I moved with unequivocal speed.

He crouched somewhere nearby and again with the voice of Willow I cried out for help. I could feel his hesitation and finally caught sight of his head twisting around trying to figure out where the voice of his wife was coming from.

"Oh my god Thomas it's hurting me, it's trying to take the baby! Oh my god help me! Help me!"

Thomas turned his head still trying to determine the direction of her voice.

"Hold on baby, I'm coming, Papa is coming!" He finally yelled but took off in the opposite direction.

He had no intention of saving anyone but himself.

Behind him, Ogma growled then struck savagely. Thomas screamed and pushed on the snapping animal. He kicked out and Ogma spun ripping flesh off Thomas's arm. He continued to scream and took off. I jogged behind letting his terror build as he dripped a trail of blood for me to follow. This is where the sport ends in the hunt, and I was somewhat disappointed it was ending so soon.

I followed a bit longer then decided to end it. I slipped behind him and dashed his head once upon the rocks. Not to kill yet, just to make it easier to drag his body to my preferred place for enjoyment—the mines.

There I suspended him, first cutting slits in his hands and then looping the rope through. The slicing of my nails revived him. He looked around the cavern and then to me before twisting in his ropes and screaming.

I continued to assault him in Willow's voice as I tied off the knots. "Thomas why did you kill those kids? Why did you let it eat us? Why? Why?"

Thomas, still drug-addled, just screamed and cried. I don't think he always registered it was me in my current form. He shit himself hanging there, sometimes begging incoherently, sometimes trying to reason with me.

"What are you Zuni?" he asked, his voice ragged like scissors had been taken to his neck.

"I think I can help you, heal you." he begged weakly.

"I think she made me a Wendigo, not entirely sure, but for you I am punishment," I answered in my strange growl. He looked at me more clearly this time, his eyes desperate.

"By the way, I never tell anyone, but my name isn't Zuni, its William," I said with a voice full of gravel.

With my long talon-like nails I began to cut off strips, some of which I gave to Ogma, some I ingested myself. I could feel the rapturous movement of the goddess of the mountain all around me as the blood pooled below and soaked into the dirt. I kept him alive for hours, reviving him from time to time, feasting until he finally bled out.

I slept in her womb enclosed in the blood and flesh.

The next morning the sun glittered on the dew, and I washed in the creek. I dragged the body out of the mine and buried it, creating my best medicine wheel yet. I would love to see the face of the first hippy to find it, the awe and tiptoeing around it in a moment imbued with imaginative magic. They would never know they worshipped at the burial site of a child-killing cocksucker.

Ogma and I took a longer route down, first checking the alien rocks to see if the soul seekers were still sleeping. They were, as I expected, in a pile of peaceful limbs in deep slumber. I suspected they would stay that way till noon, waking up sunburnt and severely dehydrated. I smiled knowing that today would be their worst day ever.

I continued down, but not in a rush. Instead, I found myself enjoying the feeling of her inside like a tongue of fire burning and licking my ribs. Hikers that met me on the trail couldn't help but smile and later tell a tale of meeting the most majestic Indian they had ever seen. They will say they thought I might have been a spirit of the mountain and I would disagree…I was its servant. I was William.

[10]

You were an alcoholic for a time. You like to call it problem drinking, but Sandy calls it different. You changed into one of the monsters you chased out on the highways. Sometimes you were drunk when you pulled them over, a flask of Jack hidden in your boot. You were what people call a functional drunk; the only real sign was your quick temper. You never hit Sandy, but you put holes in the walls a time or two.

When you got called out on a domestic, you always felt like a hypocrite. You slammed a drunk who blackened his wife's eye in the back of your car, chewing on mints to cover your breath. Sandy left you twice during that time, insisting you go to A.A., but you refused. You reasoned that the community was too small, and someone would break the laws of Anonymous, and you would be as jaded in public as you were at home. It wasn't that you were alone in your drinking, it was a problem from the valley to the small pubs that sat halfway up the mountain. Most blamed hopelessness and boredom.

You finally got sober over a long year of starts and stops. But what the alcohol numbed was fully awakened. That's when thoughts of suicide entered your brain. The things you have seen, the bodies, the unexplainable terrors gnashing their teeth now beyond the dreaming hour.

THE TURNING OF TSÉTAH DIBÉ

Samuel pushed aside the shot of whisky, his rough hand catching the splintering wood of the bar. A barely noticeable exchange taking place between the barman and himself. The two men had perfected the drug dealing sleight of hand over the years. It was a co-dependent relationship between them, almost a friendship, but not quite.

He closed his fingers over the tiny bag of blow, slipping it into a pocket. Samuel palmed the shot and drew it to dry lips, the firewater slipping down his throat. The burn was good, like a line drawn in the snow. No matter how he might try to unravel the problems in his life, it just came up in knots.

The door behind him slammed open. Howling winter wind screamed into the bar, setting the overhead lamp swinging. The newcomers cursed, fighting the wind to close the door. The winter had arrived early this year. Temperatures plummeted, and even when the snow stopped falling, the remaining air under the clear sky would freeze in dazzling hoarfrost. The weather brought out the worst in men, as they clamored to the scant warm places to drink, smoke, and gamble. Samuel knew the game—nothing to do, they partied until someone toed the line into an argument, leading to fights that started in the bar and ended outside. Sometimes the violence cooled there, but too often it was taken home.

Samuel didn't look back. He didn't care about anything tonight.

The frigid walk home might clear his head, even if it ended, in his case, at his cabin filled with broken things. There was only silence there waiting; broken chairs, glass, and tossed belongings.

Samuel ordered a case of cheap beer. The barman headed to the back and returned with a brown crinkled sack under his arm.

"Never gonna buy a solid IPA, huh?" the barman said as he hefted it on the counter and slid it Samuel's way.

"I don't drink for the flavor," Samuel said as he tossed some cash on the bar. "Besides, IPA tastes like hipsters' tears."

The barman laughed and took the cash without counting.

Samuel nodded at the package, "Watch this, will you? Be right back."

The barman gave him a thumbs-up as Samuel headed to the bathroom. He pushed open the door and locked it behind him. His reflection in the mirror was rough—depression rough. His shoulder-length hair hung lank and unwashed under the Carhartt stocking cap; three days' or more of scruff showed gray. A red puckered scar meandered down from his eye to his jaw, still smarting if he smiled. He didn't smile very often.

Samuel leaned into the mirror, frowning; he looked like hell. He turned to reach for the paper towel roll off the back of the toilet and pulled off a few. Hitting the sink with a squirt of the half-empty Dial soap, he scrubbed furiously until the surface was a more apparent shade of lime green. The yellow, fluorescent light buzzed above.

When he was satisfied, he pulled the baggy, tapping out a bit of the white stuff. Next, he fished out his driver's license cutting a line with expert precision. He held one side of his nose and snorted the line up without a straw. Samuel raised his head, pinching off his nose, and snorted deeper. It burned, causing him to cough and stumble back a step. An anxious twinge of guilt throbbed in his chest—his wife and daughters somewhere on the rez by now.

Samuel wasn't the first to marry a Navajo woman. And it was a truth that women never seemed to last on the mountain, unable to cope with the environment and loneliness. Samantha lived here before he moved from the east. She refused to call the mountain Blanca, calling it Sisnaajini and talking about it as a living woman. Samuel never questioned her, preferring to ignore her culture altogether. Now she and the girls were with her parents, and he was alone on her mountain.

He looked in the mirror again, feeling the hot fingers of artificial euphoria clinch his heart. He stuffed the bag in his jeans pocket, then pulled down his hat. His walk home a bit more pleasant than the walk in.

He washed his hands and exited the bathroom. Glancing over the hushed crowd, Samuel nodded to those he knew. He pulled on his gloves and double-checked the zipper of his coat, wrapping his arms around the packaged beer.

The door whipped open hard, slamming against him with the strength of two men. He bent his head into the wind as he stepped out into the swirling snow, kicking the door shut behind him.

The storm blocked the heavenly lights, so Samuel headed to the only lamplight in the one-street town. Thick snow scintillated in the air below the lamp's pooled yellow light. He dropped his package into the snow and dug out his headlamp, strapping it around his head. He looked down at his boots, wishing he hadn't forgotten his snowshoes. The house was a mess since his wife had cleared out. There was no telling where the snowshoes might have landed.

He took up the package again, reaching in and popping the tab off one of the cans, quickly downing it before heading out into the wall of white. He couldn't see his tracks from thirty minutes ago, but this didn't worry him. Samuel knew the way between his house and the bar, no matter the weather. His wife, Samantha, laughed about it, saying his compass on the mountain was relative to the bar's location.

He struggled through the snow, sometimes having to lift his legs high to get through. The wind screamed through the pinyon, and he swore he could hear his wife's voice calling his name. Samuel shivered, despite the thickness of his coat and peered through the beam of his headlamp. The snow swirled with increased violence, stinging his cheeks.

He turned his head, letting the beam flash down the tunnels of pinyon pines coated with snow. Both directions looked the same, and the burnt cottonwood was somehow missing. Samuel was not overly concerned; he reasoned that he could backtrack to the bar and catch a ride home if nothing else. He hitched the package in his arms and took more steps into the snowy dark.

An oppressive feeling sat heavily on Samuel's shoulders and gnawed at the reptile part of his brain. Samuel at first ignored it. The snowy environment's otherworldliness would worry any man stupid enough to keep on a path with no clear, recognizable landmarks. He continued his march through the snow as the feeling grew, a sense of doom stronger than the euphoria of the drug. He started turning his head back and forth, knowing that even in the swirling snow, the light would catch the glow of eyes. Most of the dangerous animals were in hibernation—but not all. He paused, peering into the shimmering snow, down through the clawing limbs of ghostly trees. Nothing moved within the beam of his headlamp. Samuel laughed, feeling his frozen face and beard cracking.

Behind Samuel, a limb snapped. He froze mid-step, whipping his body towards the noise so fast that he lost his grip on the beer that fell with a thud at his feet. Red glowing eyes blinked at him from the dark. His mouth went dry as he reached reflexively for this gun. His guts sank, realizing that he had left it at the cabin. The eyes blazed with fire from a head he could not see that rose to a good two feet higher than his tall frame. The eyes hovered in the inky black; Samuel tried not to move, his heart pounding. If it was a big cat, any movement could set it off. Samuel flinched as his imagination went haywire with visions of claws and teeth slicing out of the dark. The eyes moved, blinking through the trees and swirling snow. Something big hit the limbs, disturbing the heavy snow that clung to the pine boughs. Samuel forced his tense body to remain still.

The eyes closed, absorbed by the dark, and Samuel waited for the thing to charge. Farther in the dark, where his headlamp couldn't reach, frozen limbs cracked like explosions.

He counted under his breath, and each number seemed to calm the rising terror in his guts. The sound of breaking wood stopped suddenly. Samuel swept his head left and right, illuminating any large shape he couldn't explain. Mule deer and elk often bedded down under the trees, but the headlamp revealed only empty pockets beneath, mixed in with the tangled roots. He knew some animals on the mountain were infected with a wasting disease. The terrible illness caused them to act strangely, losing the fear of humans, their sickly forms mistaken for misshapen monsters. Samuel glanced one more time then gave up—the animal must have run off.

Samuel reached down, carefully picking up the package of beer at his booted feet. He made a full turn squinting into the beam of light, still unable to see anything moving and certainly not a pair of glowing red eyes. He doubted his vision but decided at that moment that heading back the way he came might be the best decision considering the storm.

He lumbered through the snow. The direction was hard to tell with the moon and stars blanked out by the static of large flakes. The wind died down, replaced by the strange silence, and crunching of snow beneath his boots. Samuel followed his footprints as best he could, but his path quickly disappeared under the blanketing snow. Nothing was recognizable in the alien landscape.

Samuel stumbled, the deep snow hiding a fallen limb. He landed hard on his face, the package slamming into his ribs. Stunned, he rolled over; the curling trees above curved like the legs of a tarantula. Quickly melting snow trickled down into his boots, followed by the first twinge of frostbite.

Exhausted he laid still, pushing air through his lungs in great gasps. A part of him didn't want to get up. The thoughts that he had pushed away came rushing back; his daughters Jess and Jenny smiling and laughing, Samantha dressed in big socks and his blue sweater dancing in the kitchen. Then the rage that had driven them running from the house, their faces fixed in fear—fear of him. His wife ran to her family on the Navajo Nation, where he was not welcome.

Pain welled up in his chest and flowed out of him in body-shuddering cries. Nothing in his pocket or the damn package would erase what he had done, or what he had chosen.

Tree limbs cracked like gunfire beyond his head. Samuel struggled to get up. The deep cold had taken over his extremities as he gracelessly flipped his body over in the snow. There, in the dark, red eyes, hovered as if they floated in the sky.

Samuel, frozen in place, could not make his limbs move.

The glowing eyes were set in a gruesome face that resembled the head of a bighorn ram. Massive curling horns erupted out of the overly large head striped in black and white. Steam flowed out of the tapered snout, and saliva dripped out of its mouth. It stood upright like it didn't know that its behavior was wrong. Samuel read somewhere that the sickened animals showed tell-tale signs, like an overproduction of saliva and mangy coats.

Unafraid of humans.

A sickened bighorn ram was as dangerous as a healthy one.

It let out a bleating sort of moan; a long pointy tongue rolled out over yellowed teeth.

Samuel wanted to scream, but all sound caught in his throat. It felt like he had swallowed razor blades, and he choked there in the snow.

The ram was powerful, standing at least eight feet tall and rippling with strength under its shaggy coat. It bleated again, its chest heaving.

The creature tensed, lowering its head and enormous curling horns.

Samuel focused on those terrible horns. The smudged black and white stripes of them hypnotic under his lamplight. He felt liquid warmth soaking the front of his pants. Pushing off with his feet, Samuel crouched, feeling his ankle twist painfully. He bit his lip hard to prevent himself from crying out, launching his body away from the animal, diving headfirst into a tangle of low pinyon.

A deep guttural moan followed him. Samuel struggled, pushing away snow and tree limbs until the way cleared before him. He ran, limping and sliding in the snow. Why didn't it attack? This question led to a more troubling thought; the creature was in no hurry to catch him.

Samuel glanced back—home or the bar; at this point, he would take either. He kept moving, sliding through the snow that grasped at his boots, growing deeper with each stride. His chest and ribs ached with cold and bruising, but the sound behind him seemed to be getting closer. A few times, he caught the gleam of burning eyes, and he yelled over his shoulder, hoping to frighten the creature away.

No lights of home or town materialized beyond the trees choked in swirling snow. He felt the terrain growing steeper and the oxygen stripped from the air. The creature was forcing him up the side of the mountain.

Samuel scrambled up loose rock and slippery ice, falling and then standing. His hands slipped on the rock above before he finally got a handhold. He swept the beam of his headlamp back and forth, looking for somewhere to hide, somewhere to find his bearings. Below, the cloven hooves cracked rock.

Samuel looked down, his chest pounding. Only crimson eyes discernable in the darkness below. Samuel's foot slipped, sending an avalanche of snow and rock tumbling, but still, it came. The thing bellowed, the guttural sound amplified off the mountain, rattling his teeth.

An alcove opened with only a dusting of snow, and he shoved his body into the small space. Samuel crouched, desperately pulling the baggy out of his pants, and pushing a white wad of powder into his nose. The drug slammed into him, an uncoiling euphoria of warmth cascading through his body.

Below a throaty scream shredded the night sky. Samuel peered down into the darkness; his headlamp caught the menacing flicker of the creature's eyes, its pallid face framed in the curling horns.

Samuel forced himself up, standing on cramping legs. He jumped blindly against the rock face catching, then pulling himself up the lip. The narrow perch started to crumble below his feet and hands. He scrambled for another hold on the mountain face before he felt gravity jerk him into an unknown dark.

His body smashed into rock, hitting a narrow spot that sliced up his sides.

His head whipped back, cracking; blood poured down his neck, causing the headlamp to slide past his ears.

He landed hard on his feet, jarring pain stabbed into his knees and spine. Dizzy, Samuel grabbed at the lamp around his neck and pointed it downward. Below him was red sand that glittered, crunching like glass. The dizziness hit his gut fast, leaving him nauseous, reaching out to steady himself with his other hand. He closed his eyes for a moment before forcing them open, his hand resting on warm rock.

He swung the light and found he was in a small cavern with an hourglass curvature. Above him was the bottleneck he had fallen through. The light failed at a certain point, and snowmelt dripped down on his head. Samuel couldn't guess how far he had dropped through the mouth of the mountain.

The crazed ram above seemed more like a dream than a danger. Samuel didn't hear the hideous guttural moan anymore. It was warm, almost hot in the small space as he sat down hard in the sand. The fear of the creature was lessening as a new sensation of pressing walls closed upon him.

Samuel ran his hand over the back of his head. The blood was dripping freely down his neck, and his fingers probed a deep gash. Samuel felt lightheaded from the combo effect of falling and the drugs racing in his blood.

He dropped to his knees and slowly crawled around the space. He guessed it was six feet across with no apparent openings. The solid mountain rock walls felt like they pulsed inward, and he settled himself in the center, unsure of what to do. He pushed down panic. When the sun came up, he would try to climb out, the neck above was narrow, and he figured he could use his feet and back to scoot his way up.

He rested, reasoning once again that the thing above was not a monster but a diseased bighorn. Samuel figured the sheep suffered from the wasting disease that the Colorado deer were sharing in their population. This could explain its strangeness. The thing didn't attack him, and if its mind was diseased, that might explain why it followed him.

Samuel dug with his fingers into the sand that radiated warmth. Perhaps there was a thermal vent below; hot springs weren't uncommon around the mountain. His fingers stopped, resting on something smooth. He pushed his fingers down deeper, wiggling, tracing a curved smooth surface with hollowed round spaces.

Samuel paused, afraid of what else might be down in the dark with him. He figured he wasn't the first unlucky animal to fall here. Most animals would not be able to climb back up, leaving this cavern as a gathering grave. Looking up, Samuel wondered if he would be able to climb back out with his foot messed up.

He pushed his finger deeper, still looking up.

It was a skull; he felt sure of it now—a small one, like that of a marmot. For the bones to rest in such a place, the sand must have quickened, sucking down the doomed animals. In the darkness, Samuel wondered if this cavern might act like the stomach of the mountain.

He lifted his cupped hand, sand the color of dried marrow glittered under his headlamp. Below his knees, he felt a small tremor. He froze, unsure of what to do. Nothing but the sides were solid rock. He slowly crawled back to the wall, the light bouncing with the action.

The sand moved again in a strange circular swirl.

He wiped his face with his sleeve, trying to get his breathing under control. He couldn't say why, but he needed to know what was under the sand.

He crawled carefully back to the center.

Samuel began to dig, hesitantly like an archaeologist. A forehead began to show, and small bits of dark hair. Samuel continued revealing a small skull with parchment skin still clinging below the hollow eye sockets. The nose was tiny and human, the little shriveled mouth gaped open, cracked, and flecked in dried blood.

He stared at it; the features though decomposed, looked familiar somehow. He brushed away more of the sand.

Samuel recoiled, scrambling backward, howling.

He couldn't catch his breath; little animal cries, escaping his mouth. He pushed his palm into his teeth, trying to silence the growing terror.

It was the head of his youngest daughter.

He had just spoken to Jenny and her sister on the phone—they were south on Nation land.

He pawed at the lamp around his neck, switching it off. In the opaque darkness, he only heard his breath.

A sound of swishing in the sand arose before him. He counted again, one, two, three, and then switched on the light.

The dead child was sitting up.

The head turned with a sickening crunch of bone. Empty sockets pointed in his direction. Air hissed out of its chest and mouth. It raised its skeletal hands, moving finger bones as if testing to see if they still worked.

Samuel pressed tight against the wall, one hand reaching out and then pulling back. He closed his eyes.

"Just a dream, it's just a dream," he whispered.

Samuel snapped his eyes open. The child was bent over digging, and Samuel watched, unable to move.

The child's boney hands scooted the sand away, revealing another rounded skull. No flesh remained on this one, but Samuel somehow knew it was Jess.

No, no, no…

Samuel shoved his knuckles into his teeth, rocking back and forth.

The skeleton began moving as its limbs released from the sand. It wiggled out of the hole crawling in a full circle before butting its head against that of its sister. They began spewing out sounds, their dried-up lips and tongues clicking rapidly. Samuel's daughters' skulls nodded, continuing their metallic grunting as they pressed their dry rotted hands into the sand. Together the hideous remains of his children worked in tandem, digging deeper into the place of resurrection.

There was nowhere to run. Samuel's mind fractured as he watched the macabre working of his children. Their flesh was peeling in places and nonexistent in others. Little bits of dark brown hair clung in patches to the exposed skulls. Together they bent to the work below, ignoring their father weeping against the wall.

They dug, making the strange clicking noises to each other; the sound reverberated in the small space. They continued to ignore him, moving sand in a steady rhythm.

Samuel knew what they were digging for.

He reached into his pocket, fishing out the baggy. He untwisted the top and buried his nose, repeatedly sniffing, hoping for a heart attack.

Time was fuzzy in his brain, even the time Samantha and the girls had left. But the things before Samuel now looked three months dead.

Everything slammed into place, and the lie he'd told until he believed crumbled into a grotesque truth.

He had stumbled home drunk and drugged, at three in the morning. Samantha was screaming at him, her long dark hair flying, before he grabbed a handful, twisting. He jerked hard, pulling her flailing body into his arms. She scratched at his face, drawing blood, releasing a murderous rage within his body.

Samuel had swung his fist, the impact exploding the bone of her jaw. She dropped, her body going limp, blood flowing from her mouth—Samuel remembered. She hit the floor; long strands of her hair dangled with bits of skin in his hand. He hadn't wanted to hurt her; he'd only wanted silence.

The girls, sleepy-eyed, stumbled from their bedroom. They both had white flannel nightgowns on, their hair messy from sleep. Their faces transformed from confusion to horror when they saw their mother crumpled on the floor. With a cry, they ran, throwing themselves over Samantha's body, their eyes flashing up at him with something like hate.

Their small necks, like those of sparrows—snapping.

The dead children reached into the sand up to their bony elbows. They pulled on their mother who was stiff in the sand. Samuel pressed himself to the wall, not wanting to see into the hole. The daughters clicked rapidly, a hideous sound like insects, as they tugged at the sandy rotting arms.

Like a dark curtain pulled away, Samuel recalled the action of pushing their bodies down a dark hole.

His eyes trailed upward to the hole he could not see; the dead ones turned in his direction like they read his mind.

In unison, his daughters crawled towards him in spider-like movements. Their bodies brittle from decomposition.

The smell of rotting meat wafted to his nose. Samuel stared, unable to move. Things crawled in the empty eye sockets; their mouths open, and the clicking continued from the black stubs at the back of their necks. He bit his lip, trying not to scream as his headlamp illuminated through their naked bodies.

He sunk into the sand pulling his limbs tight. Beyond them, he could see his wife's fingers making small movements. They dug into the sand, flattened as she pulled her arms and head loose. She pulled herself up, gasping, her skin clinging to half of her skull. One remaining milky eye rested on him. Her mouth stretched in a grimace, bone protruding near the ear.

"Tsétah Dibé, you chase yourself here," she whispered with a rattle.

He touched the long scar on his face, tears welling up in his eyes.

"Tsétah Dibé, baby, help me," she said, reaching out her arm from the sand.

Samuel kept his hands clutched tight to his body.

The clicking slowed as the skeletal children crawled backward and rested on either side of their mother. They began digging their boney hands into the sand, uncovering more of their mother's torso and legs.

The daughters' clicking grew louder and faster. They pulled their mother's wrists as she dug herself free on boney elbows.

The three of them hummed together like locusts as the mother pulled her children close. Abruptly they stopped. The remains of Samantha eased onto her knees as the daughters pushed into her, their arm bones resting inside her gaping ribs. Their empty skulls faced his direction, watching.

Like a bolt, they crawled across the few feet, wrapping themselves around him, their bones snapping and cracking. They seem to fuse their bodies, locking together, the maddening clicking coming from every direction. Samuel pushed outward, but they just encircled tighter, squeezing as their bones fused into a kind of cage around him.

Samuel screamed, their bones jamming into his chest. The daughters and mother clench tighter, pushing the broken ends of bones into his organs. Desperate, he pushed his elbows out through the cage of bone.

The sand below began to shift, falling away, sucking at his feet and legs—hard knobs of something undulated underneath in a swallowing motion, jerking him deeper into the mountain. Searing pain exploded as his legs and torso were sucked into the unseen meat grinder. The cage of bone morphed around him closer until he could not sense a beginning or end to his daughters and wife. Their heads pressed into his as their hideous clicking joins his screaming. Sand filled Samuel's open mouth, ears, nose until crushing blackness remained. Unseen teeth continued the mastication until there is nothing.

Startled awake Samuel opened his eyes to the last notes of his screaming. His body is electric with unspeakable pain that slowly decreased like a retreating nightmare. His face was cold and wet. He blinked and took in the snow and trees in augmented peripheral panorama. Confused, he tried to sit up but his body responded strangely, like the joints were locked-up, fixed in the wrong places. His head ached and felt heavy. Samuel couldn't move his arms to wipe the snow from his face, his fingers felt fused together in hard knobs.

He forced the phantom-like limbs to move, struggling to stand in the snow but only managed a strange locomotion forward. He tilted his head to the side brushing against course fur where the smoothness of his coat should be. Confused he glanced down to where his arms and hands were planted in the snow. Instead of human limbs he was confronted with forelegs that ended in cloven hooves. Samuel cried out in confusion, but the sound was guttural. Dizzy and fighting a sick feeling in his guts, he took a shaky step. He tried to stand up on his back legs but could only manage it for a minute or two. His massive body propelled him forward through the swirl of night.

Like a ghost, a man stumbled out of the trees before him a beam of light emitting from his head. In the man's hands was a crumpled brown package.

[11]

A year ago, when the plague still raged, when you couldn't stop them from burning the bodies, when you mostly stayed in your car or the office, a call came in. The call was so crazy you knew it was real. People weren't acting right and most in the town where the call came from weren't right to start with.

You took a team to the mountain location, whispered into the phone. You found a crime scene awash in blood. There were no bodies, but the blood was everywhere—at the base of trees, around a still-warm fire pit, you found red fabric and rope but nothing else. You couldn't explain it, so you wrote a report that said a mountain lion had made a mess of a kill. You wrote it and filed it, but it never sat well with you.

"Women are dead on the mountain—she is hunting them," the voice on the line said.

You didn't go back; it was risky to be there with the world illness mainly focused on that mountain town. They denied science there or rather any version that didn't align with their new age soup. Sandy had never been there, so she thought you were crazy when you described the scene to her. She begged you to retire, so afraid you would get sick. At home, Sandy acted like the plague didn't exist; hers was the only face you saw unmasked for two years except for the dead. The dead didn't wear masks, their mouths gaping.

WHAT REMAINS

Manet's mother died in the first wave of the plague; her body cracked open from the cough that percolated in her lungs. Manet's father sat despondently in those early few hours beside his wife's corpse until the remaining elders came and took it away. She was not allowed into the room when her mother fell ill, the healer commanding her to shut herself in her bedroom in the preservation of her health and sacred womb.

She watched from her window that day, feeling the sun-warmed adobe below her fingers as they carried the corpse out on a stretcher. The body was tightly wrapped in the shroud her mother had picked in those last days feeling death walking close by. She thought her mother looked like a blue silk cocoon, and not fully understanding death, wondered if she would peel back the shroud and sit up renewed. She couldn't help but feel relief that her mother was released from this place. Deep down, she wanted the same.

Womanhood came on the last day of the world. The beginning was not so different from others; all girls considered the fresh buds of the mountain. Here they were revered as the Elk Girls, those who would bring forth the next generation. Cara, her dad's second wife, took over the training, and Manet was reminded daily that to be inducted into the Red Women was the highest honor the town could bestow on a girl.

The Elk Girls before the virus had been a small group, overseen by the Red Women and the Temple of the Rock. Since the pandemic, the group had taken on new importance in the training and duties of the Red Women. The need for mothers growing critical, overwhelmed by the deaths of the fruitful and those who became barren with the fever. Cara was one of the fever barren and grew more cruel and fanatical because of it.

One morning, two months after her mother's death, the Red Women told Manet's father, Daniel, that it was time. He balked at first but found that he couldn't stand up to Cara's pleading. She reminded him of the mountain sacraments and the mandate pressed upon everyone within the small community. She reminded him his resistance only assured a more deadly presence of the pestilence within the town.

While they argued in hushed whispers in the next room, Manet swept her fingertips over her phone, unaware that their words were unraveling the threads of her childhood. Whatever the argument, Manet knew her father would lose as he always did to this woman. Her mother, the only slice of protection within the house, existed as only ash in the sky. It was Cara's dominion now.

She turned off her phone and crawled into bed, pulling the quilt up over her head. Threading her hands below the pillow, she folded it to the sides of her head, trying to cut the sounds of the house. Since her mother died, there were only two sounds—one of Cara's high-pitched voice and the other loud silence like a tomb. During her mother's last months, the home grew quieter and colder. It was more of an ice palace—the heart beating slowly until it froze mid beat.

The muted sun was buttery over the edges of the mountains when Cara shook Manet awake. She hovered over the girl, red-faced, flushed from being outdoors during the increasingly long rituals of the Red Women. Cara traveled daily to their secret place, returning with the pungent odor of sweat and wood smoke. She wouldn't speak of it but looked more dazed as the months slipped by and more prone to angry fits.

Cara tossed a rumpled dress from the closet across the bed. Manet held it, unsure what was expected of her, half-awake, blinking in the glimmering sunlight. Cara crossed the room and grabbed her arm, dragging her from the bed. Annoyed, Cara indicated Manet should undress and pushed the dress over her head. Cara tugged the dress down. Manet winced, the buttons catching and ripping at her hair. Cara smugly grabbed a fabric belt around Manet's waist—cinching it hard.

Cara stood with hands on her hips, gnawing on her lip before deciding to grab the brush making quick, painful work of the tangles. Manet knew this manic mood and felt the hard ball of hatred rolling in her guts.

"Cara?"

"Mother," Cara corrected.

Manet inwardly seethed. She tried out a few cutting remarks in her mind before willing a generic smile to her face.

"Mother, it's Friday, why the rush?"

"We have to be somewhere, and we're late," Cara said, releasing her hair.

Manet shrugged and stepped away, trying to find her sandals.

"No time. Go barefoot, and you don't need shoes where we are going."

Manet could feel the hard press of hands on her shoulders as she was shepherded through the room and down the stairs. She looked for her dad, but he was long gone down into the valley as an essential worker. Cara grabbed one of the homemade masks off the counter and tightened it over Manet's face making it hard to breathe.

Cara pushed her through the door, locking it quickly.

The air outside was sweet like flowers after an overnight rain mixed with snow. Manet dipped the top of her mask to take in the fresh air in long gulps. Raven and magpie called from the trees. The wind was light as it caressed her skin. She looked out to the mountains tracing the rough edges downward with her eyes.

Thick, pungent smoke rose from the valley where the bodies were burned. Dancers that looked like tiny black ants circled around the ever-churning fiery mouth of the pyre.

She shivered, catching once or twice the sound of singing mixed with drums on the wind. Death felt like a person walking among them, so real that some prayed to it, choosing to worship the intruding force on the mountain.

Cara started the engine of her Subaru, throwing open the passenger side door. Manet got in, knowing it would be a mistake to keep her waiting. They didn't talk; the mutual dislike thick between them. They drove farther up the mountain until the pavement broke into washboard gravel. The road wrapped the mountain, exposing the sheer side of nothing and treetops. A year ago, this road had frightened her, now she only sensed the world and its overwhelming rawness of nature and death.

They passed shrines where someone had stacked rocks one upon another, almost defying gravity. People had left tokens to the gods in desperate bargaining for health. Long ribbons of prayer flags fluttered across the pinyon pine and cottonwood, some Buddhist, others looked Celtic in design.

They passed gated monasteries, with rusted locks now barring entry with the pandemic. They drove past others; gates were thrown open, those who had lived there either abandoning the place or having left it as a tomb. There were worn women on the road, walking, hands pale from months quarantined indoors. Manet leaned forward, trying to figure out who the women were, their faces wrapped in scarves against the virus.

Manet turned, glancing at the woman sideways. Cara had bottle-blond hair that only just touched her shoulders. She was tall, skinny from her raw vegan diet. Her hands were long-fingered, elegant but ended in nails that were more like claws. Since she had already contracted the fever and recovered, she did not cover her face. Cara only moved to change gears; her knuckles white, her forehead wrinkled in concentration.

Manet slid her thumb absentmindedly over the smooth glass face of her phone, switching screens back and forth. She knew there was no number to call for help, the messages and calls having stopped in the onslaught of the virus and its never-ending quarantine.

"Mother, where are we going?" she asked quietly.

Cara's thin lips pressed together. She shifted the gears hard, causing Manet's chin to hit the dash.

"The Red Women have called you to the mountain. As they do all the Elk Girls when it is their time." Cara flashed a wicked smile in Manet's direction.

Manet rubbed at her chin, dropping a hand to the door, sliding it down to the handle, thoughts of opening it and rolling over the side not far behind.

"It's locked, stupid." Cara turned her head, her face twisted and red. "And pull that mask up. Will ya?"

Manet gripped the door tighter and pulled the edge of the mask, a requirement to navigate the outside plague world.

The Red Women frightened her. They were the mountain's silent powerhouse; no decision was made, either by the town board or the community, without their whispered yes or no. If her dad and mom had understood this before coming here, perhaps things would've turned out different.

"It's your time," Cara said in a cryptic half-whisper.

Manet noticed the marks on the calendar keeping time with her period over the last month. Cara had begun asking questions about her "moon," as she called it. Manet just answered her in half-broken sentences, disgusted at having to talk about things that should have only been for her real mother. She caught Cara checking the garbage and looking almost upset each time she found nothing to report to the Red Women. Manet was thin and tall for her age, and doctors had told her parents that she would need birth control to get her cycle to start. Manet was in no hurry to be a woman and refused the doctor's pills and various herbs the Red Woman had sent home. She endured their looks of concern and questions whenever she went into town.

It was a week after her mother died that she first felt the cramping, but still nothing. Only a month ago, she'd found the first spots of blood. Manet tried to hide it from Cara, but the woman methodically went through the garbage. It was over dinner that Cara sat with a pained smile, announcing that Manet was now a woman and could, after introduction, take part in the rituals of the Red Women. Her father kept on eating while Manet squirmed in her chair, feeling sick.

Manet didn't know what the women did up there on the mountain, but she knew it was after her mother had been inducted that Cara had shown up, and her mother had shut down. At first, her father had refused to take an additional wife, but the pressure built to follow the Red Women and Temple of the Rock traditions. Manet saw that Cara was sucking the light from her mother, and when the fever came, death followed.

Cara stopped the car at the bottom of a hill that grew out of the mountain side. A steep path zig-zagged upward, disappearing between two large rust-colored boulders. They both got out, and Cara came around the car, taking Manet's hand in her own. Manet was taller but still felt some fear being so close. Cara held out her other hand.

"Your phone stays in the car."

"No," Manet said, trying to sound more substantial than she felt.

Cara leaned in to take the phone, her hands clawing. They struggled, nails ripping at each other. Manet's phone slipped, hitting the ground. Cara quickly crushed it below her heel. She struck Manet hard across the jaw, her teeth clapping together painfully. Cara continued her assault, kicking out a booted foot in hard contact with Manet's knee, knocking her to the ground.

Manet lay there hot and angry, waiting for the sky to stop warbling. When she finally sat up, Cara was leaning against the car, watching with her arms crossed. There was blood on her dress from the scratches on her arms.

"Get up," Cara said with menace. Her face reddened with flushing rage as she pulled a gnarly looking knife from the belt at her waist.

"Get up!"

She moved behind Manet, grabbing an ear, twisting, and pulling the knife in the other hand, going below her chin. Manet could feel it cold and sharp.

"You're like a porcupine, but even they have soft bellies," Cara spat.

Manet struggled to her feet, the knife trailing across her neck and arm until she felt it on her back as a warning. Cara twisted it there until blood dripped, mixing with the sweat under her dress.

"Where are we going?"

She answered with the knife, driving the point deeper into Manet's back. Manet flinched, biting her lip against the pain. Cara pulled back on the blade and pushed her forward.

The wind changed, pushing the choking smoke from the pyre far below in their direction. Ash from the bodies began to fall like gray snowflakes. Every breath was a mix of mountain air and the burnt remains of virus victims. Manet could taste them on her tongue, a combination of juniper and alkaline ash. She imagined it was her mother that she was swallowing. Hot tears burned her eyes, and she bit her lip hard, not wanting to give Cara the satisfaction.

The smoke-laden wind rushed into the space between the boulders—a hollow moaning spilled from them, sending a chill down her spine. Cara slowed, releasing the pressure at her back. Manet stood still, not sure what her insane stepmother wanted.

"We go through there."

The smoke continued its swirling dance between the immense boulders as if the rocks themselves were inhaling. The place felt different like the air had an oppressive weight, and every part of Manet's body shuddered in its refusal to go forward.

"Go!"

Manet's joints were suddenly awakened with the tip of the blade biting into her back. Cara took hard breaths, putting pressure on the edge propelling Manet forward. The weight of the wind increased between the boulders, pulling at their dresses and hair. Strange writing and runes covered the otherwise slick sides of the gigantic rocks. She reached out a hand feeling the sharpness of the strange etched lettering, her fingers fitting perfectly in the grooves.

As they stepped over the threshold beyond the rock gateway, the environment changed, becoming darker, almost twilight. The air was colder and swelling with dampness.

Two naked women met them standing on either side of the path. Their heads and faces were covered in the smooth skulls of elk, black raven feathers with long strands of ribbons hung from the sides of the skulls to their waists, blowing in the breeze. They were like statues, standing motionless with their long arms at their thighs. Manet took tentative steps past them as their heads moved in unison on either side, creaking like plastic.

Manet swallowed, willing her body forward, careful of the knife in her back. Sunlight penetrated in weak beams through the trees filtering between the peeling white bark. The rocky path had become soft with dark loam and moss below her bare feet. Off the main trail were narrow ruts leading into circular clearings populated by fern and wildflowers. Within the enclosures, more of the elk-skulled women stood without movement. Only their freakish skulled heads moved with the same crunching sound as they passed.

"Stop," Cara whispered.

Manet felt the blade trail down her back and then disappear.

Wind in the pines just beyond the aspen whistled as disembodied voices. It arced up in tone and then dropped quietly. Manet heard the rushing of rapids nearby, translating the thick moisture in the air.

One of the skulled women sprang to action, her long limbs jolting in strange locomotion, knees and feet lifting high over the foliage. Cara wrapped biting nails around her arm, holding her in place.

The woman came closer, head tilted forward, back bent, suggesting an advanced age. Mixed in with the feathers and ribbon were long gray dreads that fell limp to the waist. Manet felt a whisper of familiarity. The woman's breasts sagged heavily against a still-muscular body. Manet felt fear in the pit of her stomach building as she recognized one of the Red Women elders.

She tried to imagine her mother coming up here parading with an elk skull on her head. She pushed this thought out; her mother hadn't been given a choice. Women on the mountain were stripped of choice. Some, like Cara, thrived under the tight rules and others withered and died.

The elk skull woman stopped in front of her, eyes blinking beyond the scooped-out hollows.

"This is the one?"

Cara nodded, pushing Manet. The woman reached out, taking hold of her wrists; another woman approached, quickly passing a loop of rope. The older woman held Manet's wrists as the other tied them. She struggled with the woman, attempting to take a step back and pushing downward with her fingers interlaced. Cara brought the handle of the knife down hard on

Manet's skull. Dizzy with pain, Manet folded, dropping to her knees. Her arms painfully wrenched back and cinched with loops of rope, her head shoved downward until her forehead pressed hard into the dirt.

She twisted her head to see the feet of Cara walk off towards one of the clearings. Cara shook out of her dress. Two of the skull women placed an elk skull upon Cara's head, and she was transformed into one of the Red Women, indistinguishable from the rest except for the blond hair that peeked out from beneath.

Suddenly jerked upward, the older woman pulled Manet close to her thigh. The woman smelled ripe and earthy like mud. The woman reached out a hand, and another of the elk-headed women passed an upturned horn sloshing with liquid. Manet's mouth was forced open, and the drink tipped past her lips.

She choked on the warm liquid, trying to spit it out, coughing, ending up swallowing some of the bitter drink. As the liquid went down, fire rushed into her veins. Her body flushed with sudden drenching sweat. Manet's stomach lurched hard, and the world started a strange movement, the ground becoming unsteady. She was lowered to the ground as the early morning morphed through drug dreaming hours.

When her eyes opened again, she was surrounded by elk skull women who were all in some form of movement, the black feathers and ribbons floating around them. Long white limbs glitched in angular jolts of dance and tracing lights. Manet attempted to raise her head and then her upper body, finding her arms heavily wrapped in rope. One of the elk women took a handful of hair, hoisting her upright. She stood, barely able to keep balance. The woman pulled her head farther until her neck was laid back over a boney shoulder. Above, the aspens shuddered, the white gold leaves shimmered and whispered.

"Help me," Manet droned over and over.

The woman who held her laughed, and the other elk women answered with their musical laughter. Drool trickled out of her numb lips. She stumbled, trying to mimic the laughing woman's stride.

The woman pushed her to the center of the dancing. The elk skulls swirled, coming close then drifting away. Manet watched the terrible branches above her head, bouncing on the boney shoulder.

Sometimes Manet felt the bodies press into hers. The leaves above her head seemed to melt, dripping liquid gold. Hot drops fell on her skin, burning and then mutating into a wet coldness. She shivered, struggling with the uneven footing.

Abruptly the procession stopped. Manet's head snapped forward. Nausea clenched her belly. Manet swallowed hard to keep from vomiting.

"By the Goddess, may she bless this one!" a voice called out, followed by a mirrored vocalization from the other skull-headed women.

The women had donned red cloaks that hung from their shoulders, their heads still shrouded in bone skulls. Manet tried to focus, attempting to see if any of the women were recognizable. The skulls shimmered in her drugged state, morphing together.

"Who brings the girl to us?" the old woman asked, thrusting Manet's body outward.

Cara answered, her voice pitched high, "I have. I have brought my daughter here to you."

The woman relaxed her hold, allowing Manet's head to tip forward. They walked then for what felt like hours, the sky changing, the clouds that she could see all taking on faces that spoke without voices. The fire in her veins tilted the world in strange angles and fantastic colors. The creek's rush grew louder, and she could smell the wet mossy rocks that made its natural chute down the mountain. The Red Women pressed hard behind, an oppressive wall without escape. The shadows of the women danced and moved like serpent shadows.

She was pulled right up to the three-foot lip of a carefully constructed pool—the pool fed by the creek that thundered a few feet behind. The rim of the water was crusted in blue ice, the middle tranquil and dark. Her head spun, looking down, following its curvature. Her eyes rested upon a thick rusty chain that disappeared into the water.

The Red Women funneled around Manet, closing the six feet to the pool. Cara was the first to reach down, wrapping her long fingers around the chain. She pulled hand over hand; the chain gave up its length. She called on others to help.

They began to pull.

Manet tried to focus on their work even as the world shifted. They worked together, pulling the chain, piling it into a mound of rusty links behind them.

Manet heard a gasp and looked down. A foot had broken through the water, and as they heaved together once more, a pale waterlogged leg and knee followed. The flesh was peeling in shades of purple, exposing white bone.

Horror curled in Manet's guts.

The Red Women pulled harder, and another leg and torso followed. The chest and breasts of the thing were bloated with blue veins. An overpowering smell of wet cheese wafted up from the body.

Cara looked up, then smiled straight into Manet's eyes.

Why was she smiling like that?

Cara turned her head, yelling at the other women to pull harder. They bent their skulled heads, struggling to haul the body over the lip of the pool. They pulled, grunting and yelling in the exertion. The corpse slipped upward over the rocks, the bloated head thumped, and then rested in the wet earth, the long hair still floating in the water it had just been released from.

The face was swollen twice its size from being submerged. Manet focused until her head hurt. Slowly she began to see something familiar about it. She willed her malleable brain to search the features until recognition hit.

Manet's body seized—the muscles of her body contorting, ratcheting downward, hysterical howling exploding out of her chest. The spasm looped through her limbs, twisting her into a tight ball. All she could hear was her inhuman voice combining with the angry rush of the creek spilling down the mountain.

Her nose and mouth burned as she awoke in a blanket of smoke. She opened her crusted eyes slowly; everything was fuzzy at first until the red-cloaked women came into focus silhouetted in flames. They were standing around a massive smoky fire; elk skulled heads inclined in a quiet watching. Manet lowered her eyes into slits and dropped her head, sensing danger. She tried to be smaller, so they would not know that she had regained consciousness.

A burned meat and hair odor permeated the air, reminding her of the pyre at the foot of the mountain. She glanced towards the fire, her stomach wrenching violently. The Red Women had spitted the body of her mother end to end, the pole coming out of the gaping mouth. Her smoldering hair had wrapped around her head in the turning.

Manet vomited.

Heaving in ragged breaths, she wiped her mouth, forcing her eyes to stay locked on the ground. She crawled away from the fire.

"You are wondering how we have her?" a voice said from nearby.

Manet glanced up, another of the elk-skulled women stood near her. The woman smiled before dropping down to her knees.

"When we took her, she was preserved in the deep freezer of an elder until this day. Cara had sensed your time would come and had planned accordingly."

The woman pulled her red robe tighter around her shoulders.

"We settled her in the pool for this," she whispered near Manet's ear, nodding.

Manet looked at her, focusing on the woman's dark eyes set inside the elk skull. She clenched her teeth hard, unintentionally biting her tongue until the taste of blood flooded her mouth.

"Is this what you do to all the Elk Girls?" Manet managed.

The woman smiled, then said, "You will see."

"My mother died of the virus, you are all fucking exposed now." Manet spat the words, looking up. Her mother's blackened body smoked, fat dripped, causing the fire to crackle.

The Red Women turned; the old one stepped forward, waving a hand. The woman beside her nodded, jerking Manet onto her feet and pushing her forward. Manet resisted, locking her knees. The woman holding her kneed her in the back, sending her sprawling.

A man came through the line of Red Women masked in a leather-strapped bear skull. He walked towards her then dropped to his knees. The man heaved with sweat dripping down his chest. She struggled to get up, digging her elbows into the dirt. He crawled around her, and when she started to rise, he roughly pushed her flat, holding her down.

His masked head lowered until it was parallel with hers. His eyes were wrong with huge blown pupils. His breath hot and sour on her face.

"Maiden of the Mountain," he whispered.

Manet tried to roll away, but his hand held her in place. The man pushed down on her back, crushing her chest.

"Our daughter will eat of the mother, taking that sacredness into herself," he said, almost shouting. Manet's eyes shot to the flames and roasting corpse.

The Red Women all let out keening calls, their elk skulls wobbling on their shoulders.

Manet dug her hands into the dirt, twisting her body away. The man reciprocated her movement by digging his fingers into the flesh of her hip.

"She will eat!" he yelled.

"She will eat!" The women shouted the refrain.

He started to howl, filling the air in reverberating echo as Manet kicked her legs.

The Red Women started to wail and undulate their bodies.

Manet kicked hard, rolling just enough to get an arm from beneath her chest. She curled her fingers, raking her nails across the man's belly. He looked down, locking eyes with her smiling before striking her hard across the face. Manet grunted in pain as a wet trickle oozed out of her nose and mouth. His hand fell upon her head, and his fingers threaded through her hair before jerking her face up.

She watched as the older woman approached her mother's body, bending to pull a knife out of the ground. Manet watched in horror as the older woman effortlessly sliced off a piece of her mother's belly. The woman then bent closer to the fire, holding the sizzling flesh on the tip of the knife over the flames as if to cook it a bit more.

Manet shifted her knees back and forth, gaining only painful inches. His nails dug into her scalp and wrenched her head farther back. She could feel the hair pulling from the roots as her eyes were forced upward into the sky, bleeding into darkness and stars.

Manet could hear the leather and bone of the mask creaking closer until he pressed into her cheek.

"You will eat," he said, his voice familiar but still unplaceable.

Manet squeezed her eyes and mouth shut, trying to pull her head away. Suddenly she could feel the heat of the knife near her face. She bit down on her closed lips. He yanked hard on her hair, causing her eyes to open. The blade glowed red hot, inches from her face. Her mother's meat sizzled on its tip.

"Eat this flesh and become the mother."

Manet clenched teeth together, sealing lips, shaking her head violently. Her hair was pulled tighter, and a knife was thrust into the nubs of her vertebrae. She screamed, mouth opening wide as he shoved the meat into her mouth, the edges of the blade burning her lip. The flesh was juicy and tender, practically melting in her mouth. She tried not to chew, pushing it around with her tongue. It was burning her mouth before her saliva cooled it filling her mouth with smoked flavor. For a moment, it was enjoyable, and her stomach growled in anticipation. Her brain, however, began to scream in confusion.

Manet choked, retching as he clamped a large hand over her mouth. Tears streamed down her face as she violently twisted her body, trying to get him off.

Reflexes took over, her body trying to save itself—swallowing.

The man held her like a dog refusing a pill, running his rough hand up and down her neck as she bucked, shaking. When satisfied she had taken the meat into her body, he released his hold, letting her face fall into the dirt. She sobbed, rubbing her lips in the earth, then opening, letting her teeth sink into the soil until her mouth was full. Manet tongued the dirt in her mouth and swallowed.

She felt the meat of her mother in her belly. Reanimation of dead cells as they sparked within, reaching out tangled arms, intertwining with her own. They spoke, and through the connected neurons and blood, a simple message was communicated, differing from the gathered red flock's intentions.

"Vengeance," the voice of the mother said inside her.

Something deep shook itself free, crawling up through her belly and crawling its way up her ribs into her brain.

The moon broke the clouds, and suddenly Manet heard sounds beyond the circle of Red Women. She listened to the mastication of insect mandibles and the breathing of the elk and mule deer. Within her bones, she sensed the mountain in its mighty rumbling. She shook her head and felt as if it were growing tiny for her frame, stretching, cartilage popping; her bones and muscles rolled and cracked.

The man above was removing his clothing. Manet looked up at him with new wild eyes; she knew what his next move would be. Manet also clearly understood what the Red Women required of the young Elk Girls in the forward moment from maiden to mother.

She felt a change going on inside, but it differed from their expectations.

Her bones began breaking, the pain ricocheting through her body in anguished twisting. She sensed the marrow as it sent a flush of cells out, percolating into the spaces.

She screamed, thrashing in the dirt as feet curled, broke, and then lengthened. Her hands snapped and popped as claws sliced through the tips of her fingers. Manet heard her mother's voice still echoing off the walls of her brain.

The pain was terrible; the pain was exquisite.

Most of the Red Women backed up, not knowing what had brought on the seizure. The man, however, disregarded the storm of Manet's body and flipped her over. He yelled at the Red Women to tend the fire and turn their backs.

"Do not look upon us till the act is done. It is only for the mountain to witness." Manet heard nothing but the rush of her mother's voice and the fire in her veins.

Pain pulsed in her gums, her teeth loosened; with her tongue, she wiggled each tooth free spitting them out on the ground. Her torn-open gums were raw beds. She ran her tongue over them, smiling as the first stabs of jagged points pushed their way up.

The man took hold of her on either side of her hips. Manet let him, willing the body quiet in its curious storm. As he pulled her close to his chest, she no longer smelled the smoke nor the forest air. All that her senses screamed for was his blood coursing through the veins of his neck and chest. The hot coppery smell was overwhelming; it supplanted the drugs in her veins, intoxicating her in delirious hunger.

She leaned into his neck, reveling in the fragrance of the blood, his breath coming hard in his arousal. The Red Women chanted louder by the fire, sensing something they could not quite grasp, wondering if their dark rituals had a more significant effect than they could have imagined.

Manet licked his neck and could feel his conquering smile in his jaw above.

"I will make you a mother," he whispered, repeating the phrase over and over.

"I will give you to the mountain," she whispered back through her fangs. Her body rolled with hunger.

She felt his body shaking with excitement, the thrill of taking the flower of the Elk Child. In the small part of her brain not ravaged by blood hunger, she knew suddenly what always happened to the Elk Girls. The haunted look in their eyes and unexplained pregnancy. The children all looked the same.

She allowed him to lower her to the ground, taking his weight and sweat upon her body. She pushed her face deeper into his neck, licking and then lightly nibbling. He moaned, and so too did the Red Women.

Manet drew back and felt a faint pop as her jaw unhinged in the exact moment his penis entered her. Her teeth sliced deep into the flesh of his neck. Something opened within her, and a similar sensation of opening was felt between her legs—teeth deep within locked onto his hard organ, sliding like razor blades. The man screamed as the fountain of blood rushed into her greedy mouth. He howled, trying to push away as her teeth hit the bones of his vertebrae and windpipe, silencing him. Between her legs, the teeth met as blood flowed out and down her thighs.

Manet chewed through his neck until the weight of the mask caused it to roll away. His organ was expelled from her body, his corpse jerking one last time.

Manet slurped up blood from the neck stump, the salty rush spilling onto her stinging burnt lips.

Taking her fill, she lay beneath the draining corpse, smiling up at the stars between the tangled branches. The voice of her mother hummed in her head in repeating commands of retribution.

She threw off the body and stood. The backs of the Red Women still turned toward the fire. They chanted, but Manet knew the mountain was only listening to her.

She approached the women silently. She could smell their sweat mixed with the smoke from her mother wafting into her nostrils. One woman still turned the body over the coals.

Manet laid a clawed hand over the nearest elk skull, resting it there for a moment. The woman underneath didn't notice the slight pressure. With sudden force, she pushed down, clinching elongated claws together until she felt a satisfying crack. The woman jerked her head, and Manet grasped harder until the human skull below popped, spewing the woman's eyeballs and brain matter outward. Her heavy claw uncurled from the broken skull allowing the body to fall forward.

The women all turned, not fully understanding.

Someone screamed, then all the Red Women added to the commotion. Some gathered their senses enough to run; others stood in shock, unable to do anything as Manet ripped through their bodies, the hunger insatiable. The women who ran—she would hunt down in time. They were not lost but distinctive; their smells separate threads that ran in different directions on the mountain. Her new heightened senses assured that everything was in its proper place.

Her nostrils flared, her body shedding rivulets of blood as she sniffed the air for Cara. Her life thread diverged in the direction of the pool. Manet crouched naked and powerful. Her uplifted head moved from side to side, the ribbon of smell almost rendering her delirious.

She moved like a panther, diving into the woods in smooth strides. It didn't take long to catch Cara, who stumbled in the dark. The woman was sobbing beside the pool that had contained the body. She couldn't see in the dark like Manet, so Cara didn't feel Manet beside her, flexing her jaws, staying the urge to swallow Cara's head whole.

Cara backed up, barely keeping her footing on the slippery rounded stones. Snot ran out of her nose as she reached shaking hands out into the dark.

"I know you are here. You were always an abomination."

Manet reached out, taking her outstretched hand. Cara didn't stop her, sobbing harder. She pulled Cara tight in her arms, resting her massive jaws on the top of her bare head.

"You took from me," the mouth of the mountain mother said.

"You took from me," the voice of the Elk Girl said.

Cara opened her mouth, a rigid mix of hopeless crying and howling flowing out.

Manet placed a bloody finger over the woman's lips. She did not want the flesh of this one in her belly. Cara tried to stop crying and began pitifully begging.

Manet lifted her with the tenderness of a mother and carried her to the pool.

"I want you to watch me," she said to the woman in her arms. "You like to watch, don't you?"

Cara thrashed, screaming.

She fought hard as Manet gripped her shoulders, pulling her close before tearing out the veins at her throat, spitting the flesh to the side. Cara did not die right away, her eyes wide, absorbing the moonlight. Manet watched her wishing the moment could last longer.

She slowly wrapped the chain around the woman's body, dropping it into the water. She watched, fascinated as the limbs thrashed either from the last signals of the nervous system or the final moments of Cara's life. Manet hoped it had been the latter.

Manet watched the pool swallow the pretender until the scent of the ones that ran tickled her nose. She took off on bare feet, reborn the mountain's huntress, guardian of the remains.

[12]

Your job is different than what folks face back east. You must answer to the citizens, tribes, government officials, including your father who is older than the hills and set in his ways. They don't tell you that you will respond in some communities to a shadow body that operates in the background. The Red Women whispered about; you've never seen in any official capacity. But you have seen the same women appear at the edges of crowds when you respond to a disappearance or murder in the mountain town. You are always an hour out when the call comes in. It gives you an hour to settle your mind, or that is reaffirm the lie you tell yourself.

Nothing ever prepares you for the strangeness on the mountain. You spend the following few hours questioning folks who are stoned, none of which have a real name, nor will they give you one. Asking for ID becomes a shouting match that settles into you and your deputy standing quiet as they rail against "the man." You know the law, in theory, reaches here, but that too is a lie.

You never know what new guru moved into town brainwashing and directing their followers to throw off your investigation. Sometimes you recover women so severely damaged they are detached from the living, whispering gibberish, clinging to you with digging fingers and wild eyes. If you're lucky, they have family outside of Colorado who can take them in and start the long deprogramming process, but you never get a proper testimony. Most of the cases go unanswered, get buried, and never see a day in court. Some do, but the judges are either paid off or give judgment in fear, letting the guilty walk, take up new names and faces. The women standing at the edge of the crowd smile at you. They know your powers ended as soon as you turned on road E with your lights on.

The recovered women never leave the state entirely; they take up a strange residence in your brain. You hear them begging you to make it stop.

SERAPHIM

Each time someone extended the hand of condolence, I squirmed, an unwanted hug, a kiss on the cheek, the heavy aroma of flowers and herbs used to mask the smell of death. My mind raced back to my childhood, butchering day, the pitiful bleating of the sheep and goats, their cries childlike until the ax fell. My finger stuck in a warm goat aorta.

I hooked the heels of my boots into the folded kneeler of the pew, letting my hair fall like a curtain over my face, trying to be small—a habit of childhood in a community that punished the lively and the beautiful.

Only the nose of my brother peeked out over the velvet covering. His still body is framed in the coffin's wooden encasement. My family shuffled about in murmuring packs of reds, greens, and Father John in black vestments. Each color a statement of stature within the familial community.

I wanted to be anywhere but here, but mostly I craved solitude to be alone with him. Half of myself, my twin, was to be burned or buried as the Father decided. I caught Father John's eye both in the past and now in the sanctuary. My brother and I thought he had died, that we had killed him. But the man stood frowning, the dark secret of that night shared between us.

"They said it was terrible; they found him in the creek, you know—" Aunt Marjory enunciated details she couldn't possibly know.

"I heard it was heroin," another aunt added in a correction. Her face stern, a look she wore all her life. Their faces were misshapen, a side effect experienced by many here. It was strange to think that we were not only twins but cousins, our family choosing only to marry amongst their own.

I chewed gum, my jaw clenched and unclenched, the action doing nothing for my cigarette craving. Most in the small church did not speak to me; only the elderly family members with fuzzy memory paused to hug or talk to me. I hated a good number of these people, yet there were rules to follow. I already pressed the line when I drove up the mountain road unannounced. No one here knew that a cousin was thoughtful enough to go to town and had Undersheriff Blackwood send word that my twin brother was dead. I scanned the room, gathering the uncomfortable looks launched my way from the incestuous lot. They didn't want me here, and the hushed whispers suggested that they wanted to eject the disloyal member. My brother and I represented sin most viscerally, the secular and bringers of fire.

I stood up, and it was like leathery wings unfolded, expanding the space around me, pushing the crowd back. My feral aunts and cousins snarled on about the tragedy of it all, freezing mid-sentence under the edge of my rigid-eyed scrutiny. I used to cringe under their judgments, and now I reveled in them. I imagined that this was how Lucifer felt in the presence of angels. The Morning Star would not feel low but proud in his ability to disrupt; after all, according to the Book of Aaron, he was the highest angel.

My mother sat alone; her face creased in sorrow. She had to remain stoic; it was the way and had been the way for generations. She did not look at me from under her woven hat, nor did she speak. I was shunned here, like a ghost, but she could see me. I felt her eyes watching.

I pulled at my black skirt and tattered sweater, a cast-off from my brother. I kept the sweater and wore it today in a small gesture in homage to him. I wiped my nose with the frayed sleeve fighting back the tears. Refusing to cry in front of these people, I forced my feet into movement. My family parted around me as I walked up to the coffin, curling trembling fingers to catch the edge.

I hovered above my brother's white face. His lips were so blue, as if he had died in the cold. Mattathias didn't appear bloated from submersion under water, nor was his face burnt or gaunt from drugs. Sound and grief tangled in a large ball in my chest. I bit my lips, refusing to let any of it out.

His body lay in repose wrapped in a yellow quilt, hand-stitched by my mother. My brother and I had slept beneath its heavy folds so long ago. I turned and glanced at her, almost invisible in the corner; tears flowed freely now from her dark eyes. She returned my glance, smiled weakly, and then shook her head—no. My mother could read us like a book, sensing our mischief before we had raised a finger. In her own way, she understood that we were different. A gift of future-gazing, though I could not imagine what she thought now, her only son gone and a barrier of tradition between us.

I leaned over him, the family taking a cue to stand back, some practically climbing the walls. He smelled of juniper and cedar. I drew in deep breaths and could taste the turning flesh of his corpse in my mouth. No matter what you tried, death had a taste and smell that lingered, like the forest floor: dry, rich, and moist.

"These people are mad," I whisper near his ear.

The room suddenly went quiet behind me. I suspected that my family thought I planned something nefarious, and I smiled, wishing I'd brought some blood from a chicken or at least a claw. They suspected me of witchcraft, but my sin was rebellion. My twin and I were large spirits; mother said we were too big for this small world. Our family had tried through the years to pray it away, and when that failed, they resorted to harsh discipline. We endured the beatings and wrapped our bodies around each other; tears, blood, skin, and scabs. If we had been hopeless in those days, we might have stayed. Instead, we ran away from the family compound with flames in our wake.

I looked over my shoulder once more, noticing various members crossing themselves. Father John watched me, his large frame stiff in his preacher collar. He was not family but rose through the ranks after his mysterious arrival twenty years ago. His words were a fire in the community. Father John often experienced seizures, falling under the righteous hand, slain in the spirit. Throughout his recovery, Father John recounted visions sent from angels or the prophet Aaron. After my fifteenth birthday, he dropped with one of his seizures. He awoke with the prophecy that God had chosen me as his bride.

"Children of Eris, we always will be," I say, mimicking a prayer, but in my heart, it was a truth.

My brother looked asleep, his face hollowed, skeletal already. My family did not dress the dead in makeup or a suit. The Book of Aaron deemed that we went into the ground as we arrived, naked and vulnerable. I wondered why my brother returned to these people we had worked so hard to escape. I knew he struggled in the real world, away from the mountain, but to return seemed impossible. I was resilient, but he suffered. The terrors of the mountain followed him no matter how far we ran. A month ago, he left only a cryptic note of goodbye and disappeared.

I caressed the cold, stiffened jaw dipping my face closer. His dry lips were slightly open, revealing his teeth. A gash above his brow seemed to be glued but not scabbed over, hinting that the wound happened recently. I prodded at it feeling the hard edges that held the wound shut. Anger built in my chest as I pushed the emotions down. I traced my fingertips over his gaunt cheekbone. At first, I thought it was blood between his teeth, but it didn't wipe away. The red was fibrous, revealing the tiniest bit of red thread between the lips.

Without hesitation, I probed deeper into his mouth, catching the thin cord on my fingernail, and pulled. The string caught on something then released. A thin braid of red, green, and black joined the first string. The braid, at first dry, quickly turned wet in my fingers. I coiled it on the white pillow beside his neck.

"What's this? Mattathias, were they trying to keep you quiet?" I whispered

The braid caught again, and I hoped that it only looks like I caress his face bent in sorrow. I pulled hard once more, and a small copper key slips out, tied to the last bit of braided string. Quickly I shoved it into my sleeve, feeling the blood smearing on my forearm. I grabbed a tissue from a pocket and wiped my brother's face where the blood had smeared.

"You have had enough time, Anais," Father John said behind me.

His hand is at my waist, fingers bridged between the skirt's fabric and the skin of my abdomen. His finger sweeps up and down, and I imagine the fucker with a hard-on as his breathing grows heavy.

"Yes, Father."

I started to walk before he pulled, his fingers digging suddenly into the soft flesh of my belly.

"We are not pleased that you came. Our call was but a formality," he whispers near my ear.

Ah, I thought, so he knew someone had called.

"But you are here now and will abide by the rules. Like your brother." He looked at the corpse, and my eyes followed. His arm slid around my waist holding me firmly.

I stiffened, remembering the fall of the belt on bare skin and long nights in the redemption cabin, Father John's hands on my body, unwanted. I looked now into Father John's face, his penetrating eyes, remembering what he had done to me and what my brother had done to save me in the burning barn. I realized at that moment that I had lived in relative peace because I thought he was dead.

"Yes, Father," I said, hating myself.

I walked the aisle between the wooden pews full of the faithful family. None of the assembled spoke to me as I pushed through the doors and take the steps down into the sandy yard. I took the old trail that cuts through cottonwood and juniper down to the creek. I wandered a while until I found our tree and traced the place where my brother and I had carved our names into its hard flesh.

My fingers searched the sleeve pulling on the braid, the teeth of the key catching at the sweater. Dried flecks of blood clung to the metal in my hand, and I wondered if Mattathias swallowed it or if someone hid it deep in his mouth. The thought made my stomach lurch. If it was placed after he died, then someone wanted a secret buried with him. If Mattathias had done it, then my brother had a secret waiting for me.

My family had many secrets.

A branch snapped behind in the trees. I closed my hand over the key and turned. At first, I didn't see anything beyond the stand of cottonwood. I heard more crunching and saw my cousin's bare knees; her skirt hiked up to avoid catching the hem on the grabbing underbrush. She was close in age and mousy, not the golden hue of most of the family. She made her way to where I sat, then moved closer to the creek folding her frame with her back to me.

"Anna?" I said her name with the lilt of a question.

"I saw you leave. I saw what you took from his mouth."

Startled, I clutched the key tighter. I didn't remember Anna in the church and wondered at her absence.

"You were there?"

"Yes," she said, slightly turning her head, the sun outlining her profile.

She spun around, pulling her legs up under her green skirt, the color of all the married in the family.

"You weren't supposed to find that—the key, I mean," she said, her voice almost singsong.

I opened my hand, holding the key under the sunlight.

"What's it for?" I pointedly asked. "How did Mattathias die?"

Anna squirmed a bit, turning her head away from me. Around us, raven and magpie called out, landing closer and closer, looking for food. The trees moved with the wind causing showers of golden leaves to fall. It would have been beautiful, but now it only reminded me of death and the process of dying.

"I don't know really, he broke a rule, and they took him away. Then I heard Mama weeping in her bedroom before she told me he died."

"Mama?" I was confused. Her mother passed when we were children.

"We took your mother in when you left."

"We?" I asked looking up at Anna.

"You left, so I offered myself to Father John."

Vomit rose in my mouth. Anna would have been thirteen at the time.

"They took him away?" I pressed, my voice wavering, my mind trying to untangle the new information.

I closed my fist tight until the teeth of the key bit into my flesh.

"He came to the meeting messed up on something. He wasn't acting right. He couldn't stand still for the exit ceremony."

"What?" I nearly screamed.

I wanted to grab her, shake her until she couldn't breathe.

An exit ceremony was pretty much an exorcism. I only watched one as a child and still had nightmares of the screaming woman who suffered through it.

"No one can stand still for that; it's hours long," I said, my body still with tension.

"They are watching you."

"Are you?" I asked

"No, not really. But the Father John is." She smiled, her dirty blond hair escaping the family standard bun. "But you know that."

"The key?" I asked once more.

Anna stood up suddenly and stretched like a cat.

"Mattathias came here looking for something; maybe he found it. In any case, he died for it," Anna said.

I thought hard about our childhood but couldn't think of anything but the redemption cabin. If they took him somewhere, it would have been there. The abandoned cabin, always so cold as we knelt on naked knees starving and praying away our sin, the cold stone floor biting into my back and the weight of Father John upon me. The imprint of that night forever tattooed on my body. A secret my brother and I kept locked away.

I wondered if the old place still stood. Memories of beatings and reciting the word zig-zagged down my spine. My hand tightened on the key, and I could feel blood in my palm.

Anna twirled her long skirt around her legs.

"The community waits for you. They have waited a long time." She smiled dangerously at me. "You are his first flower, right?"

A chill stabbed my body, remembering the barn before it burned.

"It is doubtful that I was his first flower," I answered coldly.

Anna pressed her lips together, a look of disapproval crossing her face until it dissolved in a faint, knowing smile.

"I was sent to fetch you home," she said, reaching out her hand.

"What?" I shook my head. "No way, I'm driving home tonight."

"Don't be silly; Father John will not hear of it."

I stood up and brushed the dried leaves from my skirt. The sun reflected off the water in glittering veins of gold. I took a few steps to the water's edge, weighing my curiosity about the key. I knew it held a secret, but I felt sure staying on the mountain would be dangerous. I turned to Anna; her hand still held out.

"I'm going home," I said firmly. "You can tell Father John and the family I will not bother them any longer."

Anna lowered her hand as I passed her walking up the trail. I paused, turning, "Tell my mother that I heard her."

I left Anna standing there by the creek and took the long way around the buildings.

I pulled myself into my truck, feeling old behind the wheel. The key added to the necklace around my neck felt heavy. I would always be the holder of our secrets.

My truck spun gravel under my heavy foot. I drove through the wrought iron gate that read Pastures of Promise, heading down the rocky road that exited the compound. The road was unkempt, full of debris and potholes. Overhead, aspen reached long spindly fingers across the narrow road, shedding leaves golden and twirling on the wind. The sun slipped into the San Juans' rounded edges to the west, and dark shadows mingled with the blood-red of sunset. Soon the stars blinked, draped across the sky. The road was dangerous in daylight and terrifying at night. I slowed the truck until it was only creeping down the mountain. Finally, I could let the tears go. I howled until I felt light-headed.

Ahead something moved across the road. I blinked, trying to discern what it was. It happened again, and my foot unintentionally slammed on the brake. Rolling down the window, I listened but couldn't hear anything that didn't belong in the mountain's darkness.

Something hit the truck hard, rocking the frame.

I grasped the wheel tightly.

It hit again. The truck rocking violently back and forth.

I peered through the windows seeing nothing in the dark. I still heard nothing, no slide of rock, no screaming elk or goat.

It hit this time with such force that the truck groaned in slow tipping. I braced myself with shaking hands that slipped along the door as the truck rolled.

The sound of crunching gravel and screaming metal exploded in a cacophony. My seatbelt hitched hard, knocking the wind out of my chest. My head smashed into the driver's side window, making the tiny world go monochrome.

When the truck rested, I found that I was sideways, looking up through the passenger's window only to see stars. It was quiet outside except for the humming engine of the truck. A boulder must have come loose, rolling down the mountain. Posted signs hinted at the danger every five miles or so, but I had never actually heard of it happening.

I took a few deep breaths reaching for the seatbelt; I would have to climb up to get out. I killed the engine, pulling the key with trembling fingers. I sensed the sheer drop that the truck was balanced on and tried to move quickly. I pulled my legs out and clamored up towards the skyward door. I popped the handle and pushed.

A shadow passed over me, blocking out the stars. A colossal force hit the truck sending it aloft. Violently the truck hit the ground, continuing down the mountain side. I smashed into the frame and windshield, metal crunching around me. The steering wheel broke into my body as it bent, pushing into my legs. Pain erupted across my body; the windshield exploded; glass injected deep into my flesh. The smell of gasoline and thick smoke, and burning plastic filled the small compartment. My arms were jerked, and hard steel slid along my legs as the world slipped into thick darkness.

Smoke entered my nose; I rose through the grayness of consciousness. This smell was different; the scent of wood-burning, a pleasant memory of childhood. I opened my eyes slowly, unable to move, feeling cold stone below me. My body remembered before I did the redemption cabin.

I blinked, unable to keep my eyes open. My first vision was the roof's timber, followed by the play of firelight on the walls. The black-robed form of Father John stood, his arm on the fireplace mantel, watching.

My body felt bruised, but I could move it in small ways. I felt the cold metal of the key between my breasts as I exhaled. With effort, I sat up, every muscle screaming.

"The rules are in place for a reason," Father John said.

Dumbly I looked at him.

He lowered his arm to his side and walked towards me, his boots heavy on the stone. Squatting down, Father John reached out, touching my tangled hair.

"My first flower," he whispered.

Suddenly behind him, shimmered a dark shadow. The form did not touch the stone floor; instead, it hovered in the air. I stared beyond Father John's shoulder, my mouth dropping open. The form swirled and then lightened into gray and white. It was the horrible naked corpse of my brother. I couldn't speak and tried to scoot away. Father John grinned, assuming he was the cause of my sudden terror.

My brother moved his long white arm, placing a finger to his lips, and shook his head—no, just as my mother had done. Behind him, substantial black wings began to take shape gracefully, moving back and forth. I pointed, and as Father John turned his head, the thing that was my brother moved back into the shadows of the room, disappearing.

Father John continued to look but did not see what had filled my vision. He turned back to me.

"You will participate in the exit ceremony, returning to the flock. Your little games end here tonight."

I didn't speak; instead, I watched as he stood, walking across the room, leaving me alone behind a locked door. I crawled to the place where I had seen the ghost of my brother. Nothing floated there now. When Mattathias and I experienced banishment here, it was unkempt, dirty, and cold. No fire lit to keep us warm.

The Book of Aaron was in its usual place on the mantel. A table and chair stood against the windowless wall. I examined my body; there were cuts and bruises, but nothing seemed broken. I limped the perimeter of the small cabin, cursing my decision to return. I knew better. My brother knew better.

I sat on the floor again before the fire, noting the wooden kindling box beside the fireplace. There were no locked drawers or doors that took a key. The lock in the door Father John had exited was too large for the key around my neck. I looked harder at the kindling box, noting it stood with a gap between it and the wall. I moved towards it and pulled the box away from the wall. I found another small narrow box only as wide as my hand. Its lock was small and old-fashioned, just like the key. Quickly I removed the key from my neck, fitting it into the mouth of the keyhole, and turned. I heard the teeth catch, and the top opened. Inside was a letter.

They brought me here. I did not leave you. I would never leave you. If you came, then I am dead. They know it is the only reason you would come. He knows it is the only reason you would come. They are dying here. nothing lives. The mountain does not want them here. She is coming. He told me that you would be the sacr—

The letter abruptly ends with the smearing of blood. I glance into the box and see that I missed something hidden below the paper. Resting on its side is a vial; its smoky glass shows an amber liquid inside. A tag is attached to the top, and in my brother's handwriting, it read:

Drink me...

I set it on the floor, wondering what the liquid was. A last gift?

I imagined Mattathias discovered, swallowing the key, letting the thread catch between tight teeth. Moving away, I threw the note in the fire. It caught quickly and flamed up, consumed. A whisper of a breeze brushed the hair on my back, the lightest touch of fingers on my neck. I turn sharply, but the room was empty. I knew he was there, though; the open places in my chest suddenly filled with him.

As children, we drew wings in black marker on our backs. Not the fluffy white of angels, but powerful like those of the raven. It was a way to feel strong during the horror of this place. I thought of them now growing out of my back just below my shoulder blades, unfurling, gigantic.

I glanced at the box and began to crawl to it. Father John would come. I knew what was outside the door—a bonfire and the white-clad, humming community gathering for the exit ceremony. I looked up to the Book of Aaron. The words slipped across my brain: *Exit my mortal frame, purge the rotten blood, I am dead, to self, and the flesh. I am doomed to madness; I am a reborn child of the mountain. I am no more; I am, I am.*

Did the woman die? I couldn't remember it was so long ago, wrapped in mystery and terror. I remembered her tied up on a long tether pulled taut from the top of a pole. Her screams. Why did she scream?

I heard a key in the lock. I grabbed the bottle, wrenching the top, and put it to my lips. The amber liquid was like fire. I swung my legs back around, dipping my head as if in prayer.

Father John entered the room with two men following; I didn't fight them.

Outside, the community gathered as remembered so long ago. They dressed in the robes of the sainted, white—like lambs. They held torches that lit up the woods around the redemption cabin casting strange shadows on the ground.

Some of my aunts came to me, the men giving up control as the women stripped and scrubbed my body raw before dressing me in a simple white shift. They led me to a large dead tree, not the pole from memory. One of the men pulled a long tether affixing it to my wrists. My body faded from warmth to a stiffening cold, my limbs not feeling like my own. Father John began a prayer as the family circled the tree.

They chanted prayers of adoration and gently pulled me along by the rope. Suddenly, my cousin, Anna, was at my side placing her hands on my arms, dreamy and magical. I laughed but did not know why. Three or more times, we walked until the rope pinned me to the tree. I felt relief, my body growing more and more tired. The knotted bark of the dead cottonwood dug into my back.

Father John and the others curved around, their torches brilliantly blazing. He stepped up to me, resting his hands on either side of my face. Our eyes locked; he leaned in, his lips on mine, his tongue in my mouth.

I bit until my teeth met, the rush of blood hot on my lips. It felt natural, like the next step in the ceremony. His tongue in my mouth thick and unchewable, the blood salty. I swallowed.

Father John stumbled, attempting to scream but constrained with only the root of his tongue left. His face a mask of disbelief and blood as the community gasped behind him.

Father John mouthed words, coughing, blood pumping from between his lips. He swallowed and spit, raising a hand to point at me. The assembled community walked to the tree and its low-hanging branches, lifting their torches high and low. The cottonwood's dry body drank the fire, and the flames licked hungrily at the bark. Above me, I watched the fire as it cycloned and spread.

"Say the words of exit Anais!" a voice I knew all my life shouted from the shadows—my mother acting as the precursor.

"Exit my mortal frame, purge the rotten blood, I am dead, to self, to the flesh," I screamed, the words coming easily from my memory. "I am dead to madness; I am a reborn child of the mountain. I am no more; I am, I am."

The rope tightened, a mass filled the gap between my body and the bark. Around me, sparks floated, and blazing limbs fell. The rope grew tighter, cutting off my breath. My skin grew dry and tight like the teeth of a zipper ripping apart.

"Shake out of your flesh," my mother screamed.

I shook my body as the skin blackened and shrunk, catching fire now, the flaming tree coming down around me.

Father John stood stunned as the family cowered. I could not see her, but I felt my mother watching. I shook harder, and the skin fell away like charred clothing. I knew then that the gaping hole in my back was widening and filling up with the enormous wings that I pretended to have all my life. I could move them with only thought as the fire began to eat at the tether.

I fell forward, catching myself as I beat the great wings, lifting into the air, my hair on fire. Every part of me was hot and burning. I hovered there as flames wept from my body. Other trees caught fire around us, the flames eating the drought-dried timbers.

People screamed, running into the woods, leaving Father John standing, his mouth and chin bloody. I swept lower, my fiery reflection dancing in his eyes. I could feel my brother's pulsing soul and knew he was coming.

Mattathias appeared on the other side of Father John in flame and wing. We surrounded the man like the angels that graced the Ark of the Covenant. I looked at Mattathias, recognizing a similar change in my flesh; our wings outstretched were like fiery mirrors with stars reflected. Our bodies were made of the same dark matter. We understood death better than most; we understood at a subatomic level that it was a metamorphosis.

Mattathias grinned with gleaming teeth that were long and sharp. I touched my own with my tongue feeling a deep hunger. We each raced down, grabbing an arm of the man who had escaped us once. Lifting him, we beat our great wings in the heated night air until Earth was small below us. Father John screamed and prayed for God to save him, but his God was dead, an old myth used as a weapon.

We dropped the body, letting it fall to the Earth.

My brother and I regarded each other. No words exchanged; our minds entangled now into one. We lazily dropped through the heavens. Mattathias took my blazing hand, gesturing with his other towards the mountain we called home so long ago. I mirrored his action, hand upward facing and extended in front of me. Tongues of fire push through my fingertips, hovering like small pillars. We turn our hands over dripping flames. Together we lit the mountains on fire, and this time nothing remained.

[13]

The stars blanket the sky. Out the windshield, the open gash of the Milky Way looks so close you could touch it. You pick up the Glock and place its muzzle to your temple, the cold circle of metal flush with your skin. A vein twitches there and within it you feel your heartbeat.

You aren't scared. There is a strange silence in action; all those voices go silent like they are holding their breath waiting for you to do it. You wonder if they go silent because they wait for you just beyond the thin dimensional membrane.

The radio crackles and pops.

"Blackwood, can you call in? Sandy sounds like she might kill you if you don't get on home."

You look down at the radio, the barrel still against your temple. You come to this decisive moment so often—drop the gun, pick up the radio or pull.

You can hear your grandfather's voice in warning; you recall Sandy talking about the church service you missed when you were out on an investigation. You hear the Red Women's silence and the strange nonsense coming from the mouths of the recovered, the ones that lived, but would never tell.

Jeff's voice comes over the AM, "Well, friends, it has been real! I'm signing off but will throw two more tunes at ya from Colter Wall."

"Snake Mountain Blues," starts with a slow-picked acoustic. Your eyes flick up as your pointer finger eases into the trigger. Light glimmers brighter on the mountain. At first, you can't make it out. The lights spark in other spots and seem to be falling from the sky, but not like lightning. You watch as the lights grow into the triangular shapes of trees engulfed in flame—the unmistakable shimmer of orange and red—feeding like lapping tongues in the higher elevations.

You uncurl your finger from the trigger and slowly lower the gun, dragging it down across your jaw.

Without thinking about it, the Glock 19 gets holstered. You pick up the radio until it touches your lips.

"Dispatch? Mike, you there?"

"Yeah, Blackwood, damn where you been?"

You ignore the question watching as the flames eat the dry pinyon, traveling with ungodly speed.

"There is fire on the mountain."

Static answers, silence then static again.

"Holy shit Dave, I can see it out the window."

"Better alert Fire, call in the hotshot teams," you say, watching the flames spread with unbelievable speed. Minutes tick in slow motion, almost suspended as you watch flames eat the mountain.

"They are suiting up. You going with them?" Mike asked with static in between.

"Naw, I'm coming in," you say, putting the car into drive and making a U, pulling back onto the blacktop heading west. In the rearview mirror flames dance, but you don't look back. You might be done looking back. You sure hope so.

ACKNOWLEDGEMENTS

This book would not be possible without Mario Acevedo, who read every word and took time to teach me the craft in his no-nonsense, no short-cuts expert way. There is truly no instructor like him!

I also want to thank Dr. David Hicks, Lori Ostlund, Hillary Leftwich and their wise mentorship and support. My Regis University family including, Sinjin Jones, Gavin Sell, and Katie Hankinson, for enduring the early cannibal story days.

I thank Mario Acevedo and Stephen Graham Jones for reading at the summer Regis residency in 2018. During their reading, something clicked, and I knew that the story I wanted to tell would be told in the love language of horror.

I want to acknowledge my English professors at Adams State University for refining my definition and ability in the scholarship of writing and literature.

I also want to recognize the Denver Horror Collective and Josh Schlossberg for the community and resources they offer writers.

I also want to thank Gabino Iglesias, Josh Malerman, Stanley Wiater, and Raw Dog Screaming Press for taking time, providing inspiration within their bodies of work, and helping me in my writing journey.

A thank you to my mom for showing me *The Birds* and *The Ghost of Mr. Chicken* with no explanation freaking me out as a child and believing when I started that I could do anything. Thank you to Valerie Roberts and Joy Yehle, one a sister and one who is hereby adopted at as one. Diana and Nina, friends who encouraged the dream early on—you know the mountain as well as I.

I dedicate this book also to the voices of the mountain, the lost, the disappeared, the departed and those healing. I remember and honor you.

And finally, from my heart I thank my Twins—The bravest final girls I know. You faced so much with courage. I am so incredibly proud of you. Together we have done it and continue to slay! I love you.

Thank you to Jennifer Daveler & the House for family, friendship, and courageous support.

PREVIOUSLY PUBLISHED

"Snake Man"—Twisted Pulp Magazine Issue #3, 2021.

"Blood Mountain"—Consumed Tales Inspired By the Wendigo, Denver Horror Collective, 2020.

"Darling Valentine" and "William Zuni"—Haunted MTL.

"Black Gold"—101 Proof Horror, Czykmate Productions, 2021.

ABOUT THE AUTHOR

Brenda S. Tolian writes within the Southwestern horror genre, slipping between gothic, grotesque, folk, ecological, and body horror. In addition, she cultivates an academic and creative interest in the treatment of the female body within horror, expressions of queerness within dark fiction, and oral traditions of the southwest. She also writes poetry, paints, and composes music, all overlaid with dark themes.

Brenda S. Tolian is a member of HWA, HAG, and Denver Horror Collective. She earned her B. A in Secondary English at Adams State University and her MFA from Regis University in Creative Writing and is currently earning her Doctorate in Literature at Murray State University. Brenda is a lead instructor at Denver's Alchemy Writing Workshop in Dark Fiction. Her work appears in Haunted Mtl.com, the Anthology *101 Proof Horror*, *Twisted Pulp Magazine issue 3,* the Denver Horror Collective's anthology *Consumed Tales Inspired by The Wendigo,* and the forthcoming *The Jewish Book of Horror.* She also co-hosts *The Burial Plot Horror Podcast* with Joy Yehle. Currently, she writes about the haunted high San Luis Valley surrounded by the Sangre de Cristo and the San Juan Mountain ranges—known for its eerie tales of cannibals, skinwalkers, UFOs, cults, vortexes, and other strange occurrences.

You can find her on Twitter @BSTolian, Instagram bstolianwriter, and at brendatolian.com

BLOOD

MOUNTAIN

STORIES BY BRENDA S. TOLIAN

**RAW DOG
SCREAMING
PRESS**

Blood Mountain © 2022
by Brenda S. Tolian

Published by Raw Dog Screaming Press
Bowie, MD

First Edition

Cover Image:
Daniele Serra, danieleserra.com

Book Design: Jennifer Barnes

Printed in the United States of America

ISBN: 978-1-947879-41-6

Library of Congress Control Number:
2022932668

RawDogScreaming.com